SETH

SETH

ROBERT LEWERS

First published by Oceaniacom Press 2024
A division under Oceaniacom Pty Ltd.
www.oceaniacom.com

Book One: Seth

ISBN (Print): 978-1-923113-09-1
ISBN (Ebook): 978-1-923113-10-7

Edited by Sally-Anne Ward and Alethea Van Holland
Cover design by Alethea Van Holland
Cover Images: Cover and back cover images are sourced from Pixabay.com, a copyright-free and commercial-use image resource. All images have been modified for this publication.
Oceaniacom Press supports copyright. Thank you for supporting copyright and buying an authorized copy from Oceaniacom Press, a division under Oceaniacom Pty Ltd. Your commitment to respecting the intellectual property of creators contributes to the world of literature and entertainment. We appreciate your dedication to fostering a culture that values and protects the works of imagination. Together, let's continue to celebrate and uphold the importance of creative expression. Visit us online at: www.oceaniacom.com for more literary adventures.

<u>DEDICATION</u>

William O and Edna May, with gratitude and love.

Aknowledgements

In the process of producing a book and sustaining oneself through the lengthy hours required, the people matter. They need to be thanked. And so...

To my dear parents, Bill and Edna, who kept up a ready supply of comics, books, and magazines to accompany their enthusiasm for reading and learning. Their influence and love were crucial. To my much-loved extended family: my sister, Diane and Brian, and her children—Joanne, Adrian, and Amber—and their partners, Janet and Ross, and children. All encouraged and cheered me on.

I am grateful to the wonderful Sally-Anne for first publishing me; and then to Guy and Alethea and the team at Oceaniacom Press for their support, enthusiasm, and professionalism.

Some friends were instrumental in volunteering to read whatever I was producing, and so, big thanks to Richard and Val McRoberts, Stephen Baddeley, Robert Weber, and Egon Marburg.

To my daughter, Nareeda, partner Matt, and granddaughter, Ara—my thanks for both encouraging the process and just being there in a loving capacity. We have always loved and valued books.

And finally, to my partner for many years, Jennifer Anne, who has at various times typed handwritten manuscripts, posted out copies, and given me the time to lock myself away to engage in the necessary hours of writing. She was, and continues to be, a loving, supportive, and necessary piece of the creative process and of my life. Thanks, indeed!

Contents

1

Abandoned

Seth couldn't quite believe that just maybe today his luck would change. They actually wished to play with him! To have him join in! For the last time he had been noticed by the village children they had formed a circle about him and taunted him about his leg, as if his crippled leg was somehow both his fault and a mark of the devil. His uncle had seen him flinch.

"Don't you squib it every time they laugh at you—do that and you might as well give up now. Either take it or go under." And he spat as he spoke. He was unlike any other man Seth had ever met. For Seth, accustomed as he had been to people to whom kindness was as normal as talking or walking, his uncle was like some farmyard creature—tiny eyes and big snout—a snout that was far too close when advice was being given.

"And don't look at me like that."

"Like what…?" Seth defended fearing that his innermost thoughts could be read.

"You know! Uppity-like!"

He'd expected some sympathy or even support from his aunt who was kneading and pounding dough nearby, but none was forthcoming.

Her big round face flushed as she yelled over her shoulder, "Listen to him. He's your meal ticket from now on. No one else! Just him. You remember that."

I'd rather starve, he thought. As he tried to hide that thought and look away, she leant across the table and seizing his face in her hands she continued.

"Don't you look away from me, you cheeky young pup. Now you listen and you listen good. We've only taken you in because there's no one else. *No one.*"

Seth would have tried to explain his father's absence, but his aunt's hand on his face squeezed him into silence until his lips protruded and all he could do was to mouth air like a dying trout. He felt powerless and sick to his stomach.

She smelt of onions and dripping. Her eyes were glazed with an anger he didn't understand as she stared into his face.

"If you're not careful, you'll end up just as hopeless as him. If you weren't my own sister's child, bless her memory, then for two bits I'd give you away. But who'd want a bloody crippled kid, eh? Who would? Just you remember that and be grateful that you've got such good god-fearing kin as Jasper and me." And with one last self-righteous squeeze of his cheeks, she turned back to the baking.

Seth was overwhelmed as familiar unpleasant feelings seeped into his body. He was both paralysed with grief and terrified of dying. He knew what it was, for even as a small boy, he had been plagued by attacks of breathlessness which had threatened to end his short life. Attacks that had only been checked by the steadfast re-assurance of parents who could soothe and rock him until the fear went and his breath could return. He had just heard his loved family, his dead mother and absent father, insulted and cursed by people who seemed incapable of love or even kindness, and with whom he now lived.

Seth tried to stem his panic, but it had got beyond him. There seemed no escape. There was nothing to go back to. His mother was dead. His father was away at the wars and this was all he had in the whole world. The pain deepened and he could not check the irregular breaths.

"And stop that crying and wheezing or I'll give you something to carry on about."

He tried to signal his distress, but to no avail. The last he remembered hearing before he felt and saw the room begin to swim about him, was the ongoing threats of his aunt.

His aunt heard the sound of his body falling to the floor and screamed to her husband:

"Jasper!"

***

From some distant place, Seth flowed back into his body. He could hear strangely magnified and distorted voices some moments before he was fully conscious. Shapes took on solid form. Blurs assumed definition. He heard a groaning noise and realised that it was his own voice. Swimmingly, his aunt's face came into focus before him, and he couldn't check himself from starting and shuddering. He felt no joy in returning. He felt weak and nauseous, and feared he might be sick.

"There now. You're fine," she cooed. "You, young chook. You gave us such a start with your gargling and fainting and all that. We've been so worried. Me and Jasper."

"He's having some sort of fit," was what she confided to Jasper.

Jasper didn't look capable of worry, but she kicked a nodding affirmation from the indifferent looking partner and hissed at him.

"I told you he wasn't just putting it on. Why would I ask you in the first place?" Seth tried to speak, but she shushed him to rest. "You rest now. I'll tell those children that you can't go today."

Seth remembered, then tried to sit up and protest. After all, this was to be the day his luck changed.

"No. I'll be right in a little while. Please. Please let me go!" he pleaded because he saw a faint chance to escape his lonely misery by making friends with the village children. Perhaps he could find a friend and temper his misery. "I've had these before. I just need to rest."

"What do you think, Jasper?"

Jasper was thoughtful. You could tell this from his face—one eye twitched a little.

"Fresh air might do him some good." And with that measured advice, he slunk away. Seth lay back down.

She broke the silence. "I'm sorry about what I said before. Your mum was a good soul. Headstrong! When she ran off with—with your father it broke our hearts, you see? She who'd had some book learning, running off with a soldier. Our mum was never the same again. Wracked with guilt and shame she was. Couldn't hold her head up after that. No word for years—we just thought she was dead. Then you turn up. Well. It was all a bit much. Do you know what I mean? Asking on her death bed to bring you to us. We never had kids. So, it's a bit hard for us. Do you understand? And *you,* you know! You—like you are and all."

Seth nodded.

"If you want to go with the others later on, then you do. Just make sure you don't go too far away. That eldest one, that Josh, he's a bit rough, but I think he's a good lad. You hear me, now?"

Again, Seth nodded. It was Josh who had baited him when he first came.

"I'll be careful."

About a dozen of them turned up to take him with them. They were a blur of figures to him. He only really knew Josh and the small girl with a shock of red hair who talked shrilly and often.

"Come on. Come on. We've got to get going. We'll miss out!" She tugged at Seth's hand, impatient to be gone.

"Don't hurry him now. He hasn't been too well today. Now, Josh. You look after this one! Do you hear?" said Seth's aunt.

Josh nodded. Eyes not entirely friendly, smiled out from beneath the shock of tousled hair that fell over his face. He was solid for his age with an open brown face that hinted at laughter and good humour, but there was a certain stillness in the eyes that made Seth feel uneasy.

"And you, young miss," his aunt addressed the red haired one. "Don't you get up to any of your tricks, now."

By now, Seth was scared she would spoil it for him. He pushed past her and swung away towards the forest, clutching his crutches.

"Don't worry. We'll be back soon!" he called over his shoulder. And those were the last words he ever spoke to her.

They raced to catch up with him as he swung along taking the weight of his useless right leg on the rough wooden crutches that he had needed as long as he could remember.

For a moment, he was a novelty. The girl walked alongside him watching how he managed the awkward, rolling gait.

"Is it hard to do?"

"No. Not really. You get used to it. Hurts under my arms," Seth replied.

"Can I have a go?" she asked.

He'd never been asked that before. He hesitated and looked at her. "Why? Why would you want to do that?"

"Just for fun. Just to try it out. I'm Tess."

"I'm Seth. And you can have a go when we get to the woods."

"Josh wants to know how you got like that. Did you hurt yourself or something?" she probed.

"No. I got sick and then my leg wouldn't work. That's all!"

"Oh." She seemed disappointed. Seth heard Josh question her.

"So—what happened to him? Was it a horse or something?"

"No. He just got sick, and his leg stopped working." His novelty had worn off. They'd wanted him crushed by boulders or attacked by Celts.

They travelled quickly and it took all of Seth's strength to keep up with them. The largest carried sacks so as to bring back what they found while the younger ones, raced about throwing stones, fighting with sticks formed into rough swords and yelling insults at Josh and the others in the hope that they would chase them. So far, no one had taunted Seth and he was grateful. He spoke to no one. He just concentrated on swinging his weight along and keeping up. They went a long way into the forest and came to a point that obviously the older ones knew. It was just a grassy knoll in the middle of the forest with the track to the east and a stream to the west. This was their destination.

Seth was a little behind—not a lot. He'd seen to that, but it had taken some strength and energy to keep up. He clambered up to them and set himself to rest on the ground. Tess saw the chance.

"My go. You said I could." And she raced over to grab his crutches.

Seth was fearful of them being damaged, but his wish to be accepted and to *belong* was strong. He bit his lip, as all had a turn at playing at being crippled. One boy tripped when it was his turn and Seth scrambled to his knees in anxiety—a gesture that was not lost on Josh. He collected the crutches and came to wave them in Seth's face while the others crowded about him.

"Bit precious, are they? Hate to lose them?" he mocked as he held them just beyond Seth's grasp and the circle formed around him, sensing cruel fun.

Seth tried not to react as with shrinking heart he saw the game of "keepings off" that could follow and which he was powerless to prevent. He gulped but held Josh's gaze.

"What do you think? We could take these with us? We could go and throw these in the river. Then the Riders would have you."

A couple of the smaller children muffled whimpers. Others just grouped together behind Josh.

"What do you say to that? Let the Riders have you."

Seth knew that, although he was half-joking, this smirking boy was quite capable of doing just that. Fear gripped his throat and he prayed that now he wouldn't begin to gasp and wheeze. For what seemed a very long time, Josh smiled at him, holding out the crutches daring him to snatch at them while the little ones barracked from the sides.

"Go on. Leave him. Go on, Josh. See what the Riders would do to him?" said one little boy was adamant that this is what they should do. His small face flushed with excitement and crazy with anticipation as he pulled at Josh's arm, hopping from foot to foot as he poked at Seth with a stick from behind Josh's legs.

Josh wavered and then hurled the crutches at Seth's feet before turning to pick up the small enthusiast and hold him aloft.

"Matt," began Josh. "Always wanting to hurt something. Maybe we'll tie you to a stump and leave you here for them. Skinned, you'd look about the size of a rabbit. They could turn you on a spit over a slow fire."

The small boy's cheering gave way to howls of terror and misery as he was carried thrashing to the trunk of an old oak, but Josh had already grown tired of the game and dropped him on the ground to wail away his fear.

Seth breathed hard and clutched his crutches to his chest. His heartbeat and his face was flushed as the full force of it hit him—these were not safe people to be with. He should have guessed that his aunt's judge of playmates would be as poor as her choice of husband. Tess came to have another go with the crutches, but he refused her. She was not happy.

"I could get Josh over here to take them off you if I wanted to," she threatened him. Then, she teased maliciously, "He likes me. He'll do that if I ask him."

Seth wondered if they'd all drunk from a poisoned well. There seemed like no other explanation. As she reached out to take the crutches, he grasped her wrist and held it tightly.

"Don't. I need them!"

She blinked at him—hard. But she made no effort to take the crutches or yell for help.

Seth pushed on. "My dad made these."

"Where's your dad now?"

"He's a soldier or something with the army."

She stared into his eyes as if looking for signs of lies, but seeing none, she sighed and lifted his hand from her wrist.

"So's mine." She sat back on her haunches and stared out into the forest as if the shared coincidence had somehow startled and softened her.

Seth had to ask, "Who are the Riders?"

She turned to look at him with some surprise. "You come from somewhere else! Don't they have the Riders there?"

Seth shook his head slowly.

"They only come out at night, and they do really terrible, terrible things. Big horses and dressed all in black." She was no coward; he'd seen that, but she shuddered involuntarily as she spoke.

Seth insisted. "What? What do they do?"

"They just ride into villages at night, and they kill everyone and burn the cottages down. They even killed old people and children our age."

"How do you know?"

They were whispering in broad daylight.

"Promise you won't tell. Promise! Spit on your hand and touch your heart!" she demanded.

He solemnly did so.

Tess leaned over to tell him, "I heard my ma talking to my dad after I'd gone to bed. They thought I was asleep. He went to one of the villages after the Riders had been there. He said all they did was bury bodies and the bodies were all hacked and horrible. He was sick afterwards. Ma said that they're not people—that they are really demons. That's why they come out at night."

Seth shivered as he thought of being without his crutches in the forest. He heard the word "demon" and remembered an illustration he'd seen of Hell with horned creatures, pointed fangs, wings, and who came hissing and cooing.

He felt his breath gasp and pull at his chest. She heard him.

"What's wrong with you? Why's your breathing funny? Are you dying or something?"

Seth took breaths until it settled a little. "It's just this thing I've had all my life. It happens sometimes."

"So, it's not just your leg? It's your breathing as well. You got any bits that work?" And then she laughed in a way that made Seth feel icy inside.

As she got up to play with the others, he appealed to her, "Just don't let them take my crutches. I'll never get home if they do."

She shrugged indifferently and disappeared into the forest without a backward glance. It was all the reassurance he would get and he knew it meant little. He contemplated trying to escape, but felt that his best chance of survival was to simply try and do as everyone else did.

Visions of being pursued by them ran through Seth's head. He picked up kindling as best he could, and turning one crutch about, he used the armrest to sweep acorns into clusters so that they could be gathered by the others to take home as pig food.

He did this and he said nothing, hoping against hope that by drawing no attention to himself he would blend in, and make his way home with all the rest. So much for his luck changing!

*****

The shadows were beginning to stretch across the glade and at that point then the unease was apparent. The younger ones wished to return, but no one moved until Josh told them to. He'd been missing for some time and several of the younger ones had grown nervous. What if he were lost? It was not safe to be in the forest once it was dark.

A few began to snivel and talk of the Riders, but Tess scolded them into silence. At last, Josh emerged from the shrubbery. He had been experimenting with a jug of cider he had seen his father hide in a shed. He was only fourteen. There'd not been a lot in the jug but enough to make him feel bigger, stronger, and more full of himself than he had ever been. He assembled his band of little followers and began organising them by shouting and cursing.

In one hand, he held the jug and in the other a switch which he used across the legs of the youngest who gaped, but they scurried as they heard the tone and its threat of real violence. Acorns were scooped up into bags and kindling snatched up into bundles.

Josh surveyed them. He liked this. He looked at their eager fearful little faces and planned to march his little army home in ranks of three, when his eye fell on Seth. He saw difference and he remembered the unfinished game. He quickly crossed to Seth and wrenched a crutch from him.

"Right. Now we really will see if the Riders like a cripple."

Terror swept over Seth. Gone was any attempt to stay calm or detached. He begged, "No. No. I can't walk without them. It'll be dark soon. I'll die out here. Please. Please. Don't do this!" His cries fell on worse than deaf ears.

"Don't whine. Maybe you'll learn to walk again. We could have a miracle. Like those nuns are always saying we should pray for. How'd that be? A real miracle?"

Seth heard these words and knew that there was no hope of compassion—no point in trying to placate or please and as he did, he felt rage replace terror. The crutch felt quite light in his hand as he swung it at Josh's head. It hit hard and Josh flinched and staggered back as the smaller children gasped and clutched at each other. Seth braced himself for the beating he knew must follow, but saw with astonishment Josh's face change from shock and rage to a strange lopsided sort of grin—the face of an amused weasel. He stroked his face where the blow had landed.

"One! I'll leave you one. For having guts!"

And then, with that strange smirk on his face, he swept everyone else off down the track towards the distant village with the small ones wailing and crying. As they went, Seth thought he saw Tess glance back at him and wave his stolen crutch, but he wasn't sure if her actions were encouraging or taunting.

He yelled to them, but they ignored him. He tried standing on one. He had been used to the two as long as he could remember. The first attempts at walking were disastrous. His left arm hung by his side like a bird with a broken wing, and without the familiar swing of the two crutches moving in unison, he found himself pitching forward to land on his left knee. His efforts were hindered by the panic and misery that raced through his brain. He felt that he would die out here all alone miles from anyone.

Utterly and completely alone!

After his third tumble, he forced himself to lie still, to not try to leap into action and to check the thoughts that raced through his mind. He remembered his father telling him endlessly when he was in the midst of his breathing attacks, "Don't tense up. Don't panic or else the fear will tighten in your throat. You're not going to die."

And he remembered how hard it had been for him to consciously halt the dark images that flashed through his mind. But he'd learnt to do it, soothed as he had been by his father's reassuring presence. He sensed now that he needed to do the same if he was to escape from the forest and avoid the image that swept into his mind—that of caped figures on horseback plunging through the forest like demons on some dreadful and demented errand of destruction and he, standing slumped on one crutch in their path, solitary and defenceless.

2

Forest Dangers

Seth lay back in the grass of the forest. The dark was crowding in and clutching with icy fingers. He could feel the cold catch at his exposed face and hands. Already, moisture was on the grass, and he could feel the cold seeping up through the earth.

The others had gone from sight, and he was a long way from his home. He felt the gnawing of terror in his stomach and the catching of his breath in his throat. Every fibre of his body screamed to push himself to his feet and to hop, roll, or even crawl towards the village. He forced himself to lie still until he had a plan. Only then, did he roll onto his stomach and then drag himself up.

On one crutch it was hopeless. Seth tried not to think of it, but he knew there were still wolves in the forest—fewer than before, but still enough to scent and track a small boy in trouble. He knew what he must do. He'd have to find or make another makeshift crutch to get him home.

By the fading light, Seth found and experimented with branches that he had found on the floor of the forest. The first he tried was the right size, but it was rotten in the middle and as he put his weight on it, it broke and flung him face forward.

The second seemed perfect, but it was still attached by its bark to the tree and despite his frantic efforts he could not pull it free. Again, he felt the hopelessness rise in him, before he fought it down and continued his hoppity-skip search through the forest floor.

The branches were either too big and cumbersome, or too small and incapable of bearing his body weight. He began to doubt the wisdom of his plan. Seth was about to abandon it and try to find a hollow in the ground that he could pack with leaves for warmth and cover, when he noticed a small bird creating a disturbance to his right. He saw it to be a blue wren.

It brought a faint smile to his face as he remembered in another time and place, being told by his mother, "Blue wrens alone, they signal home."

In the absence of any better plan, he followed the noise.

It was good that he did. Either by chance, coincidence or fate, near where the chirping had come from, he found a broken limb. It was a bit rotten, but the core was still solid. Breaking bits back as much as he could, he finished with a "Y" shaped stick that fitted under his left arm and was about the same length as his other crutch. Gingerly, he eased his weight onto the forked branch and could have laughed aloud when it held firm. It hurt under his arm but he had his crutch back. He was not done yet.

The image of the Riders was hideous in his mind, and so, he resolved to make his way in the light brush at the side of the track. He reasoned that if he heard anything then he could hide in the denser forest, and in the meantime, follow the ease of the path before him. Having decided that, Seth put his head down. Determined in a regular rhythm, as if he were rowing a boat, he scooted along the edge of the forest. Biting his lip, ignoring the pain in his arms and where the stick crutch caught him, he made good progress.

Maybe he could make it.

He went along as far as he could until exhaustion overcame him. He couldn't be sure, but he felt he was not far from the edge of the forest; and once there, he knew he would see fires at the village and make his way back there. But at present, he could go no further. Sweat poured down his face and back as the blood pounded in his face. His arms and hands felt hot and sore, and the makeshift crutch had chaffed under his arm until it was raw and tender.

He dropped to the ground and his breath came in great gasps and gulps. He was torn between struggling up again or waiting until his breath abated. It was just as well; he chose the latter course.

Seth was lying with his back on the forest floor with his head thrown back, gasping for air. He was in the act of grasping his crutches when he first noticed it. He wasn't sure if he heard it or felt it or whether it was a combination of the two. But as he rested his hand on the ground, he felt it tremble—just flutter a little.

He'd seen his father do it, and so he placed his ear to the ground. He felt a shaking of the very earth and he knew what it foretold. A large group of horses was coming this way and with the encroaching darkness, he had no doubt who it could be.

He was surprised by his calmness. Yes. His heart was pounding, but somehow his mind stayed clear and coherent.

So, he thought, *just as I saw them. I can't run away. I can't climb very easily so I'll have to hide really, really well.*

And then, he set about his task. Seth searched until he found a shallow ditch by the track. He swept leaves and debris with his crutch head into it until the deviation in the ground had become as flat as the ground around it. When Seth was as sure as he could be about that, he burrowed into the leaves and covered himself and his crutches until all that faintly protruded was the top of his head and that was crowned with sticks and debris.

This was as safe as he could be and still see without being seen. From where he lay if he just raised his head a little, he could see down the track into the forest and where the same path led out over the cleared land to the village.

He blinked and panted as he could feel the forest floor begin to tremble and rumble with the approaching cavalcade. He wanted to flee but knew that he had made his choice. There was no point in trying to run now.

Nearer and nearer the sound came, until he had to force his head down into the leaves to stop himself screaming or trying to run. Crouched in his burrow, it felt as if the noise and tremors were directly above him, and that at any moment an iron shod hoof would strike through his meagre canopy of camouflage and maim or kill him.

Then it stopped, and there was silence.

Seth felt moisture down his legs and knew he had wet himself, he felt childlike and helpless. Slowly, ever so slowly, he raised his head and looked around. It was the thing of nightmares as he had seen it in his imaginings.

They were all about him. All he could see was the stamping legs of horses and the leather clad legs of their riders. There was the overpowering smell of sweating horses, leather, and men—men who clinked and chinked with armour and weapons. He could hear snatches of conversation—just snippets that fell between the two Riders who were closest to him.

"…Not much longer. Just 'til it's fully dark…"

"…Just the same as before. We do it and we leave nothing or no one behind."

Horses were settled. Equipment was checked. They were waiting for the last of the light to go.

Seth settled as deeply as his cover would allow. At least he knew they were men. Men. Not phantoms or ghosts or demons, but men who were following orders. As Seth settled, he felt as if he might even survive. He would make it home eventually—what to, he wasn't sure, but he could do it. All he needed to do was to be patient, to outwait them, to lie low like a rabbit until the fox had passed.

He heard some men dismount—the creaking of the leather and the footfalls on the ground. He heard the sounds of men relieving themselves and smelt the acrid smell of urine. A horse or two snorted or farted. Reins jingled.

A hoarse whisper was heard from the village side of the track, "… Someone is coming. Take care!"

And in a trice, the atmosphere of comfortable waiting was transformed into nervous expectancy as horses were mounted, reins were tightened, and war horses' hooves began dancing.

"Six to the left. Six to the trees. Easy now," Seth caught the whispered command as men and horses moved into ambush positions.

Seth tensed.

Through the gathering gloom and evening mist, a figure could be seen making its way from the village path to the forest. The light was fading fast and the mist began to eddy and twist. Seth heard the soft sound of arrows notched and swords clearing scabbards. As the figure approached, so did a sound become recognisable. It was a voice, that of a woman or a child. But what would either be doing here at this time of day in this place?

Seth heard a muttered comment, "Careful. It could be a trick."

As the figure neared them, Seth's heart sank. He recognised the hair, the walk and what was clutched in a small hand.

"Hey. Hey! Hey, you! Crippled boy! Where are you? Hey! I've got your crutch. Come and get it before it gets too dark…Where are you? Hey! Crippled boy!" Tess walked down the track, her eyes flickering from side to side. Tess with his crutch in her hands and the sight of her brought a sweep of terror to the prone Seth. It could not end well—that seemed sure.

Go home! he screamed in his head. Now he had someone else to worry about.

She got no further. A figure swept her up and she managed a short cry before a mailed hand was placed firmly over her mouth. Seth saw the terror in her eyes as she was gathered up.

"A girl!"

"Bring her here! Over here."

He saw her brought to a horse not ten feet from where he lay. The voice carried down to her.

"Listen carefully. In a moment, you'll be able to speak. If you try and scream or call out, the man holding you will knock your brains out as quick as winking. Is that clear?"

Tess nodded with terror in her eyes. The hand was removed from her face, but she was still gripped tightly.

"What are you doing here? Tell the truth and we might let you go. But lie…and you know what happens?"

Tess gathered her breath. Between terrified gasps she managed, "Please. I wasn't doing anything. There's a crippled boy who had his crutch taken from him, and I thought he might die if he didn't get it back."

"What nonsense! What are you saying?"

"It's true. Honestly. I swear. He just came to the village and he's got one leg that doesn't work. This boy, Josh, took this other boy's crutch as a joke. True! Honest!"

Seth could feel the indecision.

"No chances. Remember what we're doing," muttered a Rider.

"A likely story. Crippled boys. Crutches. You. You know what to do." And he pointed to the man who held Tess.

Seth knew this was coming. He'd known it since he had first laid eyes on her. He'd felt the growing terror in his body as he had lain there and watched the scene play itself out in the way he dreaded it would, and the part he must most reluctantly play. He couldn't let her die when she'd tried to bring his crutch back.

Yes, she had mocked him and joined the others in belittling him, but she had dared to come through the gloom to offer some help.

It was the one small ray of kindness that he had seen since his mother had died, caught in the trembling and fever that had taken her life, and in the silence afterwards, Seth had known his life would never be the same again. Now he knew, with a knowing he could not ignore, his painful duty.

It was not a heroic entrance. It lacked a certain grace and poise. Seth simply lurched out of the leaves into a sitting position while he fumbled for his crutches. It lacked grace but it created havoc. The noise he made and the direction he came from, bred pandemonium and so it ruled for a moment. The sounds of the leaves crashed through the comparative silence and in the darkness, it could have been anything. Forests still held fears for more than small boys.

A horse reared. A Rider fell off. The commander of the troop blasphemed mightily and swords already whipped from scabbards sought foes. A moment later, a sword was under his chin and tickling his throat.

In the gloom, Seth could make out the dark, armour covered figure that leant down towards him. He wore a beast mask with horns and raised metal cheek plates that obscured most of the face. The eyes were alert and dark.

"So, young, crippled boy. What are you doing lying in ditches and leaping out at people? Wanting to die early?"

"Please, sir. I'm the boy who needs the crutches."

The guffaws were cut short by the leader. Then silence.

"You present a problem. Both of you! Do you know what I normally do with problems?"

Horses paved the ground. Others snorted impatiently. Between the boy and the man was just a steady silence.

"Do you?" the man gruffed.

Seth struggled onto his crutches and stared at the man. He could see little, except those dark eyes and above them, dark eyebrows.

"You could kill us!" he whispered through his terror.

"Yes. You're right. I could. But I tell you what." He paused. "If you can give me a good reason, I might not. How's that?" The eyes laughed and mocked him.

Seth looked to Tess. He'd seen how quick she was with words. Surely, she'd have a reason, but he saw that fear had dumbed her.

"Hurry up. Either give me a reason or else…" and the Rider drew his hand slowly across his throat in a deadly implication.

Seth hushed the roaring in his head and heard his voice begin, though he had no clue where the idea came from: "Do you know the tale of the lion and the mouse?" His voice sounded weak and feeble—too feeble. He knew that he had just this one chance and it gave him gumption.

Moving forward until he was directly in front of the hooded Rider, he looked up into the eyes almost hidden by the helmet. The man was leaning forward over the horse's neck his hands crossed in front of him.

Seth steadied himself, gulped and began. "There was this lion. See! He was very fierce and strong. One day he caught a mouse and was about to kill it, but the mouse begged him not to.

"'Spare me. Spare me!' he begged.

"'Why should I? You'd make a tasty morsel.'

"'Please. If you spare me then one day, I'll save your life.' The lion thought this was really funny because the mouse was so small, and he was so big and powerful and the idea so silly that he let him go." Around him Seth could feel the amusement, some admiration and expectancy.

"So, what are you promising me—the chief lion in this jungle? What are you promising me, small crippled mouse?" The smile beneath the mask was mocking and taunting.

Seth took a deep breath. "If you let me go—both of us, then one day I'll save your life."

"...Like the mouse?"

"Like the mouse," Seth repeated.

There was just a silence. And then, there were suppressed chuckles that became laughter all about him as the Riders joined in with their leader. He lent down from his saddle and Seth tensed. But the man just smiled at him. It wasn't a pleasant smile, but it was a smile.

"Well, well. So, young storyteller, I accept your faithful promise. One day, you'll set me free. Is that our deal?" His amusement was obvious. Seth dared hardly to breath, but he nodded.

"I trust he honoured his promise? This lucky, lucky mouse."

Barely able to stand with the hope of life shaking through his body, Seth replied, "He freed the lion from hunters' nets by gnawing through the ropes."

"Keep your teeth sharp then, little mouse," he advised as he hauled on the reins of his massive horse and signalled to the soldier holding Tess.

In the gloom, Seth saw the massive ring on his left hand and the sword strapped to his right side. She was dropped to the ground and scurried over to stand behind Seth. Together, they watched the cavalcade of Riders melt into the darkness towards the town. Black forms into blackness. The last Rider paused beside them.

"Show us your tongues!" he barked at them.

They stared at each other in amazement. The Rider repeated the command. They dutifully poked out their tongues.

"Right! Good. One word, just one word *ever,* and I'll be back for them. Now, go! And don't come back to the village if you know what's good for you. Just thank your stars he's in a good mood."

Then he was gone, and they were safe. Seth sank to the ground. He felt tears of exhaustion and exhilaration swamp his eyes.

"I think they're going to raid our village and kill everyone. That's what I think. We've got to hurry back and warn them," Tess said.

"I can't. You know that," Seth protested.

"But I can."

"You won't outrun the horses. You're better off staying here."

"I have to try."

As Tess dashed from the forest red hair bouncing, he remembered to yell after her, "Thank you! Thank you for bringing my crutch!"

"Maybe one day you'll gnaw some ropes free!" she yelled back. And then she was gone, and Seth was left in the dark woods yet again.

He didn't hurry back, even though he knew the track. He couldn't. Exhaustion and terror had caught up with him. As he see-sawed his way along, he heard the sounds of the conflict up ahead of him. Born on the faint wind he could hear the yelling of voices, the whinnying of horses and the terrified screams of women and children. He was in no hurry to get there. He doubted that the Rider's mercy extended to twice in one day.

He rolled over into heavy tussock at the side of the track and waited for it to be over.

Once there, and despite his best intentions, he sat and then fell asleep.

***

He had no memory of dreaming. He awoke with a start, unsure of where he was. As he cast around for his crutches, it came back to him. He was in the middle of a field halfway between the forest and the village and he was cold, stiff, hungry and covered with dew.

Slowly, Seth made his way to the village. The first light of day was just showing and early mist mingled with clouds of smoke that eddied from the village. Nothing could have prepared him for what lay stretched before him.

The village as such had ceased to exist.

Not a cottage or a hut still stood. All that remained of them, was still smouldering stumps and blackened half walls. And lying among these ruins, were the bodies of the villagers, their dogs and their domestic animals. Some were still feathered with arrows, but most showed red, black cuts where they had been speared or hacked.

Already, flies were settling on open wounds. He had no hope of their survival, but he found his way to his aunt and uncle's cottage. She lay dead inside it, but whereas she seemed not much more than asleep. His uncle's face was drawn back in a hideous grimace as his hands were grasped around a broken spear shaft that protruded from his chest. Seth felt horror but not pity.

Under what had been his bed, he found the rolled-up ball of cloth that held his one precious possession—the ring his mother had given him just before the fever had taken her.

He forced his way through the wreckage. He called to Tess, but only had his voice come back to him. He recognised other bodies, though neither Tess's or Josh's. It was all so senseless. Pigs and chickens lay slaughtered—not even taken away. The grain store was burst open with the seed scattered and ridden through. True to their orders, not a vestige of identity remained. Even the arrows were plainly tipped and felted.

Seth found himself retching and spinning. He forced himself to sit among the carnage and try to think. He could stay, and eventually someone would come and discover it all and him. But the wolves may beat them to it drawn by the bodies. Whatever happened, Seth knew he couldn't stay. He had to leave the terrible scene.

Seth believed that his best chance was to try and hide in the forest. Working as quickly as he could, Seth gathered a bundle of things that he knew he could carry on his back: a good blanket, a knife that he forced from a rigid hand, some scraps of bread and meat, and from a small cellar—some apples and potatoes. He also found a leather wine skin that he emptied and filled with water from the well in what had been the centre of the town. There were many things scattered about—plates and mugs and household goods, but he had no use for them.

He hoped that somehow Tess had escaped. He stopped briefly by his aunt's body long enough to wrap her in a worn cloak. Skirting his uncle's body, make for the forest. He felt no grief at his uncle's death and that worried him a little. Perhaps he'd also drunk at that well that allowed you to feel nothing when drama surrounded you.

3

The State of the Nation

It was uncommonly warm. Wasps still swarmed and made life miserable with their intrusions. No sweet drink or piece of fruit was immune to their marauding.

At the foot of the castle gates, guards nodded and struggled to stay both awake and alert. Not that it was a time for danger or fear of attack. The kingdom was still in a state of comparative peace, the legacy of a strong king, Theobald, who had ruled with a shrewd mixture of diplomacy and brute force. He had been the first to hold back the invaders from across the seas and to also demand and win a degree of loyalty and co-operation from the other lords who ruled their lands as if they were kings in their own right.

Theobald had taken twenty years to do this—twenty years of skirmishes, alliances, truces, and plots.

A descendent of William the Great who had invaded years before, Theobald was a King who understood that there was nothing to be gained by rubbing the noses of the defeated Saxons in their own defeat. Still, there were pockets of rebellion as Saxons with various claims to the throne made pacts with each other, with disgruntled tribes from the north and even raiders from across the sea to endeavour to win the throne back.

Theobald was no fool. He rewarded loyal behaviour and imposed laws and taxes. He kept a strong army. He married the daughters of his wellborn to Saxon sons and daughters; and if all else failed, he marched this army to meet and destroy rebellious claims wherever they were found. At that point, there was no diplomacy or parleying; castles were taken, families put to the sword, and loyal Theobald supporters became the lords of new estates and manors—lords who knew to whom they owed trust, fealty and their newly acquired estates.

So, these wasps might linger before the cold came, but the nation had been settled until the King became old and his hold weakened a fraction. Then, the whispers became a litany—"Who would be the next King?" For Kings without obvious heirs, bred nobles who dreamed, schemed, and counted the forces that might oppose them.

Claimants counted how many armed men they could put in the field.

Alliances were made and betrayed.

So, it was with a mixture of awe and alarm that the nobles saw the weakening King pluck one last card from the deck with a gnarled hand. And what a card it was!

As he lay on his deathbed, the great Theobald called his courtiers and nobles from all over the country to one last grand council. They came grumbling but expecting perhaps one last entreaty to keep the fragile, though not expected, peace after his death. When all were seated in the grand old meeting hall, the King made a suitable entrance—carried by soldiers on an impressive bier. Helped to his throne, he waited for the silence that his presence demanded and then rising on one elbow and in a voice still surprisingly strong he addressed them.

"I have asked you here because I know that where there is uncertainty of succession, then ambition raises its various ugly heads. Heads that in younger days, I might have harvested with some delight."

There were muted chuckles from the floor of the hall.

"With this in mind, I have called you here to put at rest any doubts or ambitions." He waited as only a King who knows his audience could do. He called for a drink from a servant. He wiped his mouth and then, "I wish you all to meet my son!"

A stunned silence was followed by a pandemonium that it took the royal chamberlain some minutes of shouting and royal staff thumping to quiet. During the call for silence, the old King could visibly be seen chortling, smirking and enjoying himself. By the time silence again reigned, he had regained his breath.

"I have no doubt that all here wish for my speedy recovery and spend hours praying for my continued long life, but even with this to sustain me, my health remains a little precarious and I could in all honesty, delay no longer. He was born overseas to my first wife Isabella and has been raised there ever since." He gestured with known effect. "My son, Edward."

Through the curtains at the side of the royal stage, a young man stepped through into view and bowed to his father—a father he bore no resemblance to at all.

Theobald was a short, squat bear of a man with a broad face, thick arms and legs and no real neck to speak of. He looked his best in armour where man and purpose seemed to meet most perfectly.

This son was thin, fine-boned and dressed in a style that no one had seen before. It was all long sleeves and tight pantaloons. He looked as if he would be more at home in a stately ball than on a battlefield. Theobald had anticipated such a moment for months. He enjoyed his moment.

"Edward has been raised in gentile courts but take heed, gentlemen, he is my son. My blood flows through his veins and pity on the man who thinks otherwise. He is a King-in-waiting. Prince Edward he shall be until his twenty-first birthday, at which time he will become your king. In the event of my death, Lord Gloucester will continue to command the army.

Albany will oversee the realm. I can trust to your unfailing support in this matter, particularly while my Lord Gloucester commands such a fine and well-prepared army." His sarcasm was not wasted on them. Many smiled. Some smiled but hid their faces. This was no surprise to the King.

Theobald knew his stage, his role, and his timing. Within a fortnight, and despite the ministrations of doctors, soothsayers and priests, Theobald weakened and died, and Edward became the King in waiting while Gloucester and Albany served as royal protectors—just as he had left it.

The kingdom settled into a state of expectant waiting. The lords and nobles sat back to see what sort of son this was, and whether he could govern as his dead father had done before him. The plotters plotted and bided their time.

The day was warm—strange for this time of year, this added to the guards' concerns about wakefulness. As they leant on halberds and tried to stay alert, they could hear repetitive sounds coming from the inner castle. These brief moments of sound would be followed by bellows of laughter and merriment.

"Wonder what his lordship has discovered today?" mockingly enquired one of the drooping guards of his mate.

"Be careful. You never know whose listening."

"You needn't worry. It's every man for himself these days. You mark my words. There'll be scrabbling and scrapping for the throne before the year is out. He ain't got the bottle to be king and they can't protect him forever," the guard said.

"Hope you're wrong. For all our sakes. I don't fancy being shot at again. Does nothing for your digestion—all those arrows," snarked his mate.

"No arrow could make it through your fat guts. Take a flippen miracle."

High above the courtyard—the source of the laughter and games, two men stood with folded arms watching the young men at play beneath them.

"Look at him. He can't even hit the ball back when they sop it up to him as softly as a child. And he's to be king." Astor turned his head and spat.

His companion took him gently by the arm. "It's called a shuttlecock. Careful, my friend! Your vexation is showing and that will not serve our purpose at all. Watch! Learn!"

And with that, he lent forward to shout down to the young man who had just made marginal contact with the shuttlecock. "Well played, Sire. Fine shot! You'll be beating the great Jelbert soon."

The young man looked up and shone with the praise. "Ah, My Lord. You are far too kind. I'm just a beginner."

"From where I stand, one with great promise," replied the older man as the young Prince was further congratulated by the group of similarly dressed young men who made up his retinue—all silk sleeves and tight pantaloons.

"Simpering fools!"

The older Lord spoke softly to his companion, "We must appear to be not just loyal subjects, but *the most* loyal subjects. Gloucester must never have reason to look our way. As yet, we are not well enough prepared. The reward for failed treason is hardly pleasant. So, for the moment, we must praise and fawn before this overdressed young nincompoop and sustain ourselves with the knowledge that his days are numbered."

His companion, Lord Astor shrugged his shoulders and then beamed at his ally.

"As usual, my dear Buckingham, you are right. I just chafe at the bit to be about our loyal business. Not treason, My Lord—awful, awful word. Just the necessary pruning of dead wood! How Theobald sired that, I'll never know. Can't be just overseas courts. The boy is an imbecile!" And as he muttered the word, he waved hugely to the young Prince below who needed no distraction this time in the act of missing the shuttlecock by a considerable margin.

***

The flushed and perspiring young Prince leant on his racket and addressed one of his companions.

"They do love me. Not just Gloucester, but Astor and Buckingham, as well. By the time I am twenty-one I shall, indeed, be ready to be King. What a celebration we shall have then."

"You will certainly be a great king, My Lord, greater than even your father," replied his companion.

"Do you think so? I hadn't even thought of that. I suppose there is no reason I shouldn't be. Is there?"

"No reason at all, My Lord."

And the young Prince, reassured by that thought, called to his trainer to hit more shuttlecocks at him. As he capered and laughed, another pair of eyes watched him from the other side of the colonnade—eyes that were no less critical but were free from personal ambition and clear about duty and loyalty.

Gloucester paced and watched his young charge as Albany approached him.

"Does he show any greater propensity for games than he does for administration or statesmanship?" whispered the smiling elderly chamberlain.

"None whatsoever! He dresses extravagantly. He has a kind heart. Beyond that, it is too early to say what his skills may be. I can vouch that with a sword or lance, he will harm no one unless they were to fall from a horse from laughter. You concur?" Gloucester gruffed.

"Absolutely! I fear that in this regard his cohort of young sycophants do him no favours," agreed Albany.

"You are right. They'd tell him the sky was green if they thought it would please him. I think, though I fear more, the noble lords who wave to him from across the way with their smiles and their encouragements."

The elderly chamberlain raised a curious brow. "Buckingham and Astor? Surely you don't have reason to mistrust them?"

"Nothing beyond their extreme courtesy to the Prince and the way they look at him when they think my eyes are elsewhere," explained Gloucester.

"How is that?" Albany asked.

"Like foxes around an abandoned lamb or perhaps a hawk at a mouse caught in the open. We must watch for them. Their contempt is fuelled by ambition," growled Gloucester.

"It has not been an easy road this promise of ours to a dying king," Albany sighed.

"No. But a promise given, is one to be held to. The boy is not bad or cruel—he just has spent too long being idle and has no idea what it entails to run a kingdom. Heaven help us in the next few years after his majority." They had no chance to continue. They were interrupted by the sound of running feet and a messenger burst up the stairs to confront them.

"What is it?" grumbled Gloucester.

"My Lords. Pardon my state. I have ridden as fast as I could push my horses. Bad news! The Riders have savaged another village and similarly slain the inhabitants."

Albany showed extreme dismay while Gloucester straightened and looked grim.

"So; more of this! Who knows what their purpose is, but at worst, it destabilises the country and has every tin pot rebel and claimant using this as their justification why they should be better upon the throne? Thank you, messenger! Come. Albany, we must insist that the Prince takes this seriously this time and not shunt it off because it clashes with his luncheon or costume fitting. Come."

***

Across the way, the message had been heard by those less than trustworthy nobles who could barely hide their glee.

"Too good! Great timing. Just what we need to further convince the country that this fool couldn't run a country fair, much less a country. We have work to do, dear Buckingham as the hour approaches more quickly than we thought."

***

Back at the gate two sentries still yawned and struggled to stay alert.

"That last horseman was in a hurry."

"Just bringing your lunch. Don't you worry, sunshine! It's all under control. Food on the way."

The other smiled, waved away a wasp and shifted his weight from foot to foot. War or peace, it was all the same to him. You still had to worry about your food no matter what the nobles said.

<h1 align="center">4</h1>

Fellow Travelers

He swung along concentrating just on making his way to the forest as quickly as he could. Out on the clear ground he felt exposed and vulnerable. In the thick forest, he could hide. Even as he went, his mind kept playing tricks: he imagined he heard the sounds of hoof beats behind him and kept swinging about to confront nothing—just the normal forest sounds of wind and birds and animals.

Seth passed the scene of his encounter with the Dark Riders, the shallow ditch still half-filled with leaves.

He shuddered and kept going. He went to the knoll where just the day before he had played with the other children—*all now dead.*

Seth imagined whispers and muted calls as he made for the dense undergrowth that lay beyond that. He reasoned that in one of the tangles of gorse, blackberries, and small trees he would be safe. Eventually, he found what he was looking for—a mass of interlocking plants that had formed themselves into a dense thicket. Dragging his crutches behind him, he crawled into the middle of it, following rabbit tracks through the worst of it.

He was scratched and panting by the time he gained a bare patch in the middle. He picked thorns out of his face and hands, opened his food pouch and ate and drank in a measure of safety he had not felt for some time. He pulled the blanket from his pile and pulling it round him, slept fitfully for a few hours.

He woke and lay there as it all came flooding back to him. He knew he couldn't stay and so, painstakingly, he backed out of the clump of bushes dragging bag, blanket, and crutches with him.

The track led him deeper into the heart of the woods. In places the track was so narrow and the trees so tall and profuse that the sunlight was almost blocked out. Plunging into these places filled Seth with dread. At times, it seemed there was only darkness and his heart gave a different lurch. He had little notion of time. His spirits rose and sank according to the state of the track and he saw no one. Birds, rabbits, even a fox—those he saw, but nothing else.

As it grew dark, the terrors kept at bay by the light came hissing and cooing about him. His arms hurt dreadfully and his spirits had sunk when he heard voices. Not forest voices but human ones. His first instinct was to find cover and so he dragged himself over behind a massive beech tree and waited to see if black shapes emerged.

Presently, he heard the noises more distinctly. There was the creak of wheels and the sound of human voices. He felt caught between hope of safety and the fear of danger.

They took a long time to appear. As Seth made them out, he smiled a small smile to himself because he recognised their brightly covered caravans and the flags and pendants that hung off their roofs. It was a party of wandering gypsy minstrels—troubadours. It was quite a large group.

At the rear behind the wagons and caravans, he recognised the shuffling form of a bear being shepherded along by a man in a leather jerkin. As they came closer, he hopped out into the middle of the track and waved to them.

"Ho there!" he heard them anxiously yell to him.

Seth moved to reassure them. "I'm Seth. I'm lost and I'm trying to find my way to the next village."

They gathered about him and pressed for answers. An older man with grey hair and beard questioned him, "What are you doing out here on your own?"

It came bubbling out of Seth at a gallop.

"They're all dead! It was the Riders who did it! They let me go and then when I went back, they were all just dead! And now I've got no one."

"Whew! Slow down, laddie. You're safe with us. But what's this about the Riders and everyone being dead?"

Seth felt the fear of those around him. One of the women interrupted, "Let's stop. The boy is exhausted and so are we. It'll be dark soon, so let's rest and then we can really hear what's happening."

Seth was led away by the grey beard and a strongly built young man, the rest of the party pulled caravans into tight little groups and began unharnessing horses and collecting wood. Soon a fire was going.

They gave him a drink and an apple, then sat him down.

"Now from the start..."

And so, more slowly, Seth told them his story. Largely, they listened.

The younger man whistled through his teeth when he heard of Seth leaping out of the leaves to confront them. "Sure. Your guardian angels must be working overtime. It's a miracle they didn't kill you."

When they'd finished questioning him, Seth asked them, "Who are they? They're not robbers or else they'd have taken things."

"You're right about that. More, we don't know. They're not like other thieves that we've seen come and go—ones who don't last long once the soldiers come, but this lot is different. Like you say, lad. They're well-armed and organised." The older man picked at his teeth and pressed on. "We heard about them. Oh! It must be two or three winters back. Raids. Attacks. Just little bits and then it got to be villages just like you said. And no mercy! Just killing. Makes no sense."

"Since the Prince took over," muttered the young man.

The old man glanced about and hushed him.

Seth had settled. They'd brought a quilt for him and with the fire going, the light fading, and people beginning to cook about him, Seth could feel his fears starting to recede. He bit into his apple and as he did, he heard a roar behind him and saw the young man leap to his feet and looking beyond Seth, yell a warning.

Visions of Riders thundered into Seth's mind. Terrified and bewildered, Seth blundered up, turned and ran straight into a solid, furry wall that scared the very breath from his lungs. Seth was terrified and the bear was ravenous. For it was the bear he had collided with. There were a few seconds of startled pandemonium as the bear, the boy, and the apple were disentangled from each other.

"Easy! Easy. He won't hurt you! It's the apple. Give him the apple. Get out of it, Hugo. Go on. Back off you great lug."

A trembling Seth handed over the apple as the young man forced the bear to step back from him. The bear who was raised up on his hind legs, made a piteous wailing noise, dropped to all fours and padded away to his trainer howling like a child, still chewing the remains of the apple. Seth took deep breaths and tried to stem his panic—the world was becoming less safe each day that he lived.

"What? What was that?" panted Seth.

They sat him up and brushed him down.

"Hugo. Wouldn't hurt a fly! He's just always hungry. He'd walk through a wall to get an apple."

They got him a mass of old quilts and placed him near the fire. Over the sounds of his own tortured breathing, he could hear people laughing and joking about his encounter with Hugo.

"He thought he was going to be attacked and eaten!"

"Hugo just smelt the food. You know how he is."

To Seth, it was heaven to be lying in the middle of this group—to be surrounded by people and to feel the warmth and snugness of the quilts and fire. The light from which, made a circle of visibility and safety. He felt as if he'd like to stay there forever.

Some small children came to stare at him, but they were shushed away by elders. Eventually, when he felt well enough, he got up and went looking for the bear. He was on a chain alongside the man in leather.

The bear made a strange noise as he approached— something between a growl and a whine. The man looked up.

"You're right, then. He's harmless. Just a glutton with his food," observed Seth.

The bear snorted at him, and Seth thought he was friendly.

"Can I give him some stale bread I've got?" Seth asked.

"You'll make a lifelong friend and pest out of him," the trainer warned.

"I like bears."

The man chuckled. "Sure. And how does a boy like you know about bears?"

"There was a really old one in the village I used to live in," Seth answered.

The trainer's eyes widened. "The one the Riders attacked?!"

"No. Before that! When I lived with my parents. There was an old man who had an old bear who used to beg for food." Seth undid his bag. As he did, the bear sat up and took notice of him.

"Hand it to him. Just watch his claws," Hugo's keeper advised.

Seth fed two pieces of bread to the bear, who sat on his rump and made small snuffling noises of satisfaction and ate. Seth sat and fed Hugo who sighed and rolled his tongue about. The keeper asked no questions; like Seth, he was content to simply sit with the bear.

That night around the fire, they talked to him more of what they knew of the Riders.

"...Ever since Theobald died, there's been more trouble. Then you get something like the Riders..."

"This lot don't take anything. That's what makes it worse."

The group was sprawled about the fire. Small children were wrapped in cloaks and lay next to mothers, while the men puffed at pipes and yarned. Seth was full of good potato soup, and with his rug wrapped about him, he listened and tried not to go to sleep.

"Whoever they are, they ain't exactly adding to the young Prince's reputation—such as it is!"

The group tried to hush the man, but he wouldn't.

"You know what they say. That he just stays in the city with all his hangers-on and plays games and does nothing. Changes his clothes every time the wind does! These Riders do as they please and everyone thinks that he's spineless and useless."

Seth asked, "Please. If he's the Prince and all, why doesn't he do something? He could do something."

"They say that maybe he doesn't even know."

"He should know! He should. He's the Prince," whispered Seth to no one in particular.

A woman rocked her baby and then continued, "They say that there have been dreadful omens all over the country. Freak storms. Cattle dying. The dead muttering in their graves."

"Hush now. That's just rubbish."

"Make of it what you will. It's bad times," the woman insisted.

Choruses of agreement reached Seth's ears. The talking stopped when a tin whistle appeared and was played. Songs were sung as people drifted off to sleep. Seth tried to stay awake, but the fire and his day were too much for him. He slept and people left him wrapped and sleeping in front of the fire. The light of which held that darkness at bay.

***

A dream woke him. In the middle of the night, he sat bolt upright in alarm before he realised it was just a dream—dreams of Riders. For a moment, he thought that they were there, in the middle of the camp with him—horses, screams, and confusion until his blood stopped pounding and there was just the return to the silence of the night.

Even as he lay back, he knew that sleep would not come. Each time he closed his eyes then he was back in the middle of the mayhem. The dream would not go away. He blinked back and forth between the dream and the night, and then he deliberately closed his eyes so that he could see the dream—and notice it.

It took him awhile, but eventually, he realised something that made him ache and continue to look. The people in the dream being pursued and slaughtered by the riders were those who presently slept about him. He saw the grey-haired one struck down, he saw Hugo running for the forest snorting in fear, caravans being tipped over and burnt.

The Riders realised that Seth was also there, standing stock still. Fearfully seeing the one with the full-face helmet recognise him, and then wheel his horse and smile mockingly at him.

The dream terrified Seth, and that allowed him no sleep.

***

At first light, Seth was up and seeking out the grey-haired one. Trying not to sound as dismayed as he was, he explained the dream to him. The old man, whose name was Gemmel, listened thoughtfully and paid heed to him.

"Come on," he beckoned to the boy. "You need to meet Rose."

They weaved their way between the vans until they stood before a very old, old woman. She was toothless and what remained of her hair was caught back in a scarf.

"Rose. The boy had a dream. You should hear it."

At the word 'dream,' she stirred and came alive, her eyes suddenly becoming focused. At her bidding, Seth told them again of his dream. She remained silent and he thought she hadn't heard him. He went to coax something from her, but the old man smiled, holding a finger to his lips and motioned him to silence. Finally, she spoke.

"Prophecy. That be it. Prophecy!" She looked at Seth in a way that made him squirm in confusion.

"What does she mean, prophecy?" he whispered to Gemmel.

"It means she thinks your dream was foretelling the future. About what is to be," the old man replied.

Seth's blood ran cold. "It can't be. We have to stop it!"

Rose laughed. "Halt fate. As easily turn a river or stop foxes taking chickens." And with that, she turned her face and spat into the dirt.

Seth shook he head. "That can't happen. There must be a way."

She looked at him. Then she spoke as if he wasn't there. As if she were telling someone else in a strange crooning almost singing tone.

"What would happen if one of the pieces wasn't there to be put in place? Would it all still fit?" She stared at him until he was very uncomfortable. Then she blinked, turned away, and was suddenly an old woman again gathering her belongings with her back turned towards him.

Seth shivered. "Piece not there…?"

He travelled with them all day. Sometimes he walked and other times he rode on the front of one of the caravans, but the words were never far from his mind.

That night, no whistles were produced. It was a much-subdued group that sat around the fire. Seth wasn't certain but he thought he saw people look at him just a little differently to how they had before. It was like a touch of mistrust or even anxiety. This puzzled him and he tried to set it aside.

He was walking over to say hello to Hugo when he saw two small children shy away from him as he came near them.

"What is it?" he hissed. "What have I done?"

They put their hands over their mouths and half-fearful, half-cheeky they taunted him, "Rose says you're a jinx. That you're bad luck! That you're jinxed and have the evil eye! That's why you're a cripple."

They would have gone on further with choruses of 'jinx,' but Matt overheard then and boxed both their ears. Not hard—but hard enough. They ran howling to their mothers.

"Don't listen to them, lad. They're just repeating other folk's ignorance. I'm sorry you had to hear such twaddle," assured Matt.

But Seth had heard about it, and it did strike deep with him. He felt tears as he fed the bear.

That night, Seth lay with his hands under his head and looked up into a clear sky and tried to make sense of what he knew. Maybe he was a jinx. It seemed that bad things happened to people about him. His mother, his Aunt and Uncle, Tess, even Josh—all dead or gone. He knew he was one piece in the puzzle, and then it came to him—he didn't want it to, but it did.

If he was not there, then maybe the caravan would be safe, and no one would die. Maybe if he was not there, then the Riders would not come spilling from the darkness of the forest to terrorise and slaughter these good, kind people. It couldn't be completed. There'd be a piece missing. He tried not to think of what this would entail, because he knew that there would be sorrow. Being alone, and he wasn't sure if he could do that, but sleep wouldn't come.

Several times his mind played tricks with him, and he thought he heard noises like hooves and his fear returned as did the vision he had seen in the dream the night before.

Finally, he could stand it no more. There were tears in his eyes as he gathered his few belongings to him again.

He was quiet. He didn't want to be stopped. Then taking his bag, blanket, and crutches; as he had done just a few days before, he set off back to the forest.

At least, I should know the way, he thought grimly to himself.

Leaving the light of the fires behind, Seth made for the depth of the forest with both a sinking heart and a sense of having done one thing that was brave—one thing that might redeem some of what misfortune he may have brought with him.

5

Lost and Found

The rain eased a little, but that was the only consolation. He had seen no one. He had heard no one. It was as if the world had been cleared of people.

By now the chaffing under his arms had become red and painful, but he had to keep moving. He kept imagining warm fires glowing and bowls of steaming soup that he had left behind him.

Seth was starting to look for a space where he might safely spend the night, as it was slowly becoming clear to him that he would find no habitation that night. How he hated it—the thought that he would spend another night on his own, wet through, and with no company. He cursed himself for his own chosen stupidity.

He swung himself along, seeking a copse or hollow log or stand of suckers where he might hide and rest in. It was in this scanning of the forest, that he first caught a glimpse of something that made the skin crawl at the back of his neck and almost forced him to break rhythm. It was a flicker of movement, and it was the nature of that movement itself that caused the surge of fear.

43

It was a darting, slinking sort of motion that shook him. He turned to face it but there was nothing there—just the wide expanse of the forest, the moonlight casting shadows and a terrible, deep trembling in his bowels.

He started again, but now with his senses alert and sharpened by fear. Sure enough, despite his most fervent wishes, he saw at the edges of his vision, the same flashes of grey, silver colour and then he realised that there was more than one.

Seth knew what he had imagined was real.

Wolves.

Wolves, that were tracking alongside of him, waiting to see what he was, waiting to see if he was a weakling or stray from the mob that was vulnerable. Wolves who seldom attacked humans, but who would overcome that if they sensed a safe kill—that he knew. Seth knew enough to also know that they would sense the human smell and stay away for some time. Only if they were hungry enough and they sensed no danger, would they close on him until finally, used to his cries and no longer scared, would they encircle him and bring him down.

This time, Seth knew he had no hope. None at all! Even if he found a low hanging branch, he was too spent to hoist himself into the branches.

Scared and alone, he began to cry at the thought that he would die out here on his own and in such a hideous way—to escape the Riders, to do something brave—and now this! How utterly unfair!

No one was there for him—no mother, no father, no one who loved or cared about him. Just him! Just him and his terrible fear and pain…a small boy pulled down by a pack—all teeth and cries and terror. He knew it was futile, nevertheless, he swung his crutches and pushed along the track in the gloom as the shapes grew closer around him. And he felt hope begin to desert him.

They sensed his fear and desperation. And so, they no longer bothered to slip behind trees, but now came to lope alongside him; red tongues lolling as they kept pace trying to find the opening that would allow them to take him by the legs and drag him down.

Seth screamed at them. Stunned after an initial reaction, they came again. He could hear their panting and smell their rancid breaths. It could not last forever. Seth knew his strength was failing and wept with fear and fury as they ran closer and closer to him, just waiting for the inevitable opening.

And then disaster struck! With the gloom, his panic and the rain in the forest, Seth's left crutch struck a wet tree root and he crashed onto the ground. The crutch spilled from his grasp and Seth knew he would die. Seth turned his body to shield his face and neck from the expected attack.

None came.

Seth thought it must be a trick and opened his eyes to see the wolves surrounding him, except not attacking. They came as if to attack, but as they approached him, they suddenly shifted strangely, made odd baleful howls and as if confused, drew back a pace or two. In the midst of all this, Seth had the purpose of mind to reach into his pack and pull out the knife he carried. Perhaps he could wound one, watching as they repeated the same behaviour. The wolves would pad up to him with attack their obvious intent, and then, at the last moment veer away from him whining and staring.

What? his brain raced.

He knew he was alive. He didn't know how and for how long.

Seth was reaching for his fallen crutch and missed the initial impact. He heard a canine scream of pain and anguish and a sudden crescendo of wolf cries and chaos.

As he looked over, he saw the largest of the wolves squealing and howling under the largest hound Seth had ever seen. It was massive. It let go its grip on the wolf and then proceeded to put the rest to flight. One turned to protest, but the dog just bowled it over as if it were a rabbit or a stoat.

The pack left as quietly as they had come, and Seth was left facing this fearsome rescuer who padded towards him. Its jowls hung open and Seth stared into the largest mouth he had ever seen and waited for it to snarl and latch onto him. He was now beyond caring.

… And then he heard a voice.

"Well done. Come now. Come here, Tiny."

Seth saw the dog obediently drop its 'at alert' pose and wag its massive frame over to a woman who was walking towards him. He recalled childhood stories of witches in forests, and that brought a different fear to his being.

As she came nearer, he blurted out at her, "You're wasting your time. I'm skinny. There's nothing of me."

She did nothing to reassure him by bursting into peals of laughter, holding her sides and hooting with glee.

"Put your knife down, young one. Tiny and I haven't rescued you from the wolves to carry you away. We've got plans for you. They don't involve big iron pots and onions."

It made no sense to Seth at all, but he was alive. As she got closer, he saw that she was indeed quite small, very old and seemed to walk with a slight limp. She was dressed in an old dress, solid walking boots, and a cloak that had seen better days. As she came closer, she dropped her head, sniffed him and then smiled a smile of understanding.

"Aha!" she muttered.

"What is it? Why didn't they attack me? Am I jinxed?"

She laughed some but it was not unkindly.

"Come on. Pick up your crutches and I'll tell you it all once we get home," she said.

Seth, caught between hope and despair, hesitated.

"Well, you can come with me and Tiny to my cottage where there's a roof, a fire, some passable stew and even a bed. Or you can wait for the wolves to get over the fear of your smell and chew your bones," the old woman proclaimed.

Seth had no arguments against such logic. He followed her through the trees while the huge dog gambolled and frolicked around her as if he was a mere pup out for exercise. It wasn't hard to keep up with her, but by now he was exhausted.

He had to call to her, "Can you wait for me? I'm really tired."

She stopped and came back for him. Again, he was frightened of her until he saw how she looked at him and it was as if there was a huge smile just lurking there behind it all.

"Of course you are. Can you make it? It's not far. If you can't go further, I could leave Tiny to guard you and I'd go home to get my barrow and I could wheel you home in that."

He thought she was making fun of him and then realised she was quite serious.

"No, thank you. I probably just needed to know that it wasn't far."

"It's under your arms, isn't it? Chafes something awful when you have to go distances," she guessed.

"Yes. How do you know—"

But she cut him off. "Time for questions when we get there! Come on now." And she walked alongside him.

Sure enough, a short time later, they emerged from a tight cluster of big, old trees to be confronted by the shape of a cottage a few hundred metres away. As they approached, he could see the radiance of a fire and smell the aroma of something cooking. He forgot his fears in the promise of what lay inside.

She opened the door and ushered both the dog and Seth inside. She helped him to a pile of cushions placed in front of a quietly glowing fire—the coals red and alive.

"Grab some rugs to heap over yourself. I'll bring you some soup as soon as it's cool enough," the old woman told Seth.

She sat beside him and began to spoon it into his mouth. She fed him slowly. He couldn't believe how famished he was. He wanted more when he had finished the bowl, but she refused him.

"No. Just the one. In a moment you will be wanting to sleep and you won't do that well if your poor stomach is still trying to digest a great wallop of food. Now, what you most need is to sleep. First, we'll have you out of those wet clothes."

She threw him a big, old, man's shirt and he changed into that and then lay down in the cushions in front of the fire. He remembered back to his damp spot on the forest floor and his trial by wolves and felt suddenly warm and grateful.

He saw her pick up his wet clothes and remembered to ask her. "What was it about my clothes?"

She held them down to him so he could sniff.

"Bears!" he exclaimed, and she smiled in affirmation.

"Yes. Bear smell. Wolves are not very partial to it. Where'd you come by a bear?"

Seth could only answer 'Hugo' from a dreamy place before he fell asleep. Whatever he dreamt of it did not involve bears, wolves or Riders.

***

When Seth woke the next morning, the sun had been up for some time. The rain had cleared, and although it was chilly, the fire still glowed in the chimney-place in front of him. He was alone. There was no sign of the old lady, nor of her life-saving hound. He settled back into the rugs and snoozed. And that was how she found him when she came back to the cottage sometime later. He heard her moving about the cottage and preparing food.

He spoke to her from where he lay, "Has it stopped raining, then?"

"Yes," she responded. "Gone for now, but you've slept well. I suppose that you'll be wanting something to eat, now that you're awake?"

By the light of day, Seth could examine the small cottage. It was tiny, very neat, but full to the seams with so many things that Seth could only shake his head in wonder. One whole wall was made up of shelves and on those shelves was a vast array of bottles, beakers, jars, and bowls. In another corner, as he looked closer, he could see that there was a myriad of dried and drying plants tied in bunches and intentionally arranged in some sort of order.

To the left of these, stood an upright spinning wheel such as he had seen weavers and spinners use in their village. A mortar and pestle sat on a bench. A bed sat next to his, with dark wooden head and faded pillows. The whole atmosphere was one of order and precision, although it seemed that everything was faded and tarnished with use and age.

"So, what do you think, then? Or are you too busy looking for my broomstick or my black cat?" And she chuckled that maddening chuckle again.

He had to answer, and he thought carefully before he did. "Do you make things—like medicines?"

The old lady hung a pot from a chain that hung down inside the chimney and left it to boil. She flicked a grey curl from her face and turned to face him. She sat down on a small straight backed wooden chair that belonged to the spinning wheel.

"I'll not worry you anymore, even if it is just a joke. I'm just an old woman who mucks about with herbs and plants and prefers her own company to that of fools and simpletons."

"Why'd you start? I mean—to be a…" Seth was about to say 'witch' again, but then checked himself.

"…A witch you mean," she laughed.

He was confused by it all.

"Don't you worry about the words. It's just ignorant folk and there's plenty of them. What did you ask me? Oh! I know, about how I started. You'll like to hear this because it's about you as well."

"About me? How?" Seth asked, bewildered.

"I'll tell you as you eat your porridge. There's no hurry. That's one of the joys of living here. You remember, now. No hurry."

When Seth had a bowl in front of him and she put some pinecones on the fire to bring the heat back she settled herself. "I started with the master because no one else would have me. My parents had both died in the sickness and I was left on my own with no home or money."

"Why would no one take you in? What about your relatives?"

"They wouldn't take me because I was like you," she said gently.

He hesitated with his spoon to his lips.

"Do you mean like…" He gestured to his leg.

"Aye! Just like that. I was crippled. I couldn't walk. They thought I'd be a burden to them."

Seth could scarcely breathe as he felt the sadness, and something like hope well up inside him. She told him of her healer's journey, and he told her of the village of his parents and his mother's death. He related the past few days and saw her frown as he mentioned the Riders and their killings. He cried a little as he told her. She didn't interrupt; she just listened to him.

At the end of it, she sat alongside of him and hugged him close. "My! My! What a load! What a huge load! What a terrible, wonderful, awful world we live in."

He nodded.

"So, you'd best stay with me. The garden can be yours," she decided.

"The garden?" Seth repeated, confused once more.

"Yes. You know. Where you grow things." And she ruffled his hair.

Seth found his clothes, now dry in front of the fire and followed her behind the house and down a small path to a clearing by a creek. In it, was the largest garden Seth had ever seen.

"It's huge!" he gasped. "Why isn't it closer to the cottage?"

"Ah! It's all very bewitching, you see. I cast a spell from the door and they all grow." She laughed. Pointing, she continued, "Here is the best soil and here is where this slope faces north and gets the most sun. So, it's perfect for the garden. Closer to the river, we've got the orchard, so the trees don't rob the vegetables of the sun and water."

A sudden realization came over Seth. "I don't know what I should call you and you are much older than me."

She saw his confusion and smiled.

"I've been here for so long and hear so few human voices that I forgot my own sometimes. I was named Hestor and that's fine if you call me by that. So, if you're staying, is there anyone we need to tell? Anyone who might be worried about you?"

"There's my father. But he's in the army… somewhere." He lowered his eyes and kicked some earth.

Hestor enquired no further.

"Hestor. How did you know I was in the forest—with the wolves and all?"

"Signs, Seth. I just stay still and listen and watch and then I know. It's all in the listening. Maybe you'll learn it."

As they walked back to the hut, Hestor rested her hand lightly on Seth's shoulder for a moment and said, "I'm sure that one day your dad will come back for you. You remember that."

Seth looked up into the wrinkled face prepared to argue, but all he saw was a certainty that surprised and reassured him.

And so, Seth came to stay with Hestor and Tiny in a hut in the middle of the forest.

6

Preparation for Winter

Another autumn turned to another winter, and it found Seth still firmly at home in Hestor's cottage. At first, the older woman had feared he might be bored by the tasks required to keep them both alive, as each day water had to be drawn from the river. Wood had to be stacked to keep their fire going. The garden and orchard needed to be tended to feed them; but in this, she was wrong.

Seth loved it.

More than that, he *thrived* on it.

He couldn't draw water. Carrying the full canvass buckets was beyond him; however, he invented a way to fetch wood. He rigged a small harness that went over his shoulders, attached to a wooden sleigh, it allowed him to drag it behind him. Armed with that, a hatchet, and with Tiny for company and protection, Seth would set out to scour the surrounding woods for fallen timber.

He felt useful and loved, but even more than that; he came to know the forest and its inhabitants and lost any fear of being there. He had begun to listen as Hestor had taught him. He had few attacks of breathlessness and found his dreams slowly emptying of death, Riders, and destruction. He grew with the seasons, and while the rest of him was strong, his leg still dragged behind him and the crutches still chaffed under his arms.

They worked hard as with each winter coming Hestor impressed upon him: they must have sufficient food, fuel, and oil ready before storms and snow descended.

"There'll come a winter when the snow will come down so deep, that you'll have to tie a string to you, so you don't get lost. Then, all we can do is stay indoors and keep the fire going and use the lamps when we have to. It'll come to that."

For now, their task was to prepare for that winter, and once that was done, Hestor would go to town just the once to trade for what they needed. This she had not done before, but had traded via Lach, the silent woodman who came only twice a year.

So, they were busy, active, and mostly happy with each other. Seth grew to love and hate the huge garden. He took pride in what he produced but groaned at the amount of tedious work that it required. He weeded and transplanted and swore; nevertheless, he kept weeding and tending. He could kneel; he could be useful. All their spare summer vegetables that would keep were packed away in huge mounds of straw and dried grasses. Potatoes were dug and stored. Pumpkins and squashes were stored with stems trailing. Onions and garlic were threaded together in a strange tapestry to hang on walls. The shed was filled to overflowing.

At last, when it seemed the small stone shed was full to overflowing, Hestor announced that she would have to make the trip to town. It would take her two days to get there and two to get back.

Seth was terrified that she would say that he had to stay behind, but she had no such intention.

"No. We'll go together. I think your leg is strong enough to let us do it this time. We'll take our time and take some old rugs to sleep warm in the forest. Tiny will look after us and I know the signs of danger well enough by now."

For several days, all Seth could do was to haul more wood and pile mulch on the garden beds while Hestor busied herself with jars, bottles, and mixtures. Strange smells came from the kitchen.

"When we get back, I'm going to start on your leg. I've been waiting for a few plants to come into flower and for you to be ready," Hestor explained.

Seth found himself both excited at the prospect of their journey and daunted by it as well, as he knew long distances on his crutches were difficult. Hestor didn't make a definite date to go.

"No use walking through the rain. No fun in that. We'll have to take our chances about what day it is when we get there though."

It was a jolt to his system to realise that in his time there, he had forgotten what day it was. Days and weeks had become meaningless. Hestor did not count them, and so, they had no way of knowing which day it was.

"I'm hoping it isn't a Saturday afternoon when we get there, that's all."

"Why?" Seth asked.

"The markets will all be shut and then they'll have church on the Sunday. We'll have to wait around cooling our heels. It's just the chance we'll have to take."

The next day was cold and miserable.

Hestor shook her head. "No! Not today!"

"What happens if we leave it until it's too late and the winter sets in? What then?"

"Then we both die of slow starvation. But come and I'll show you. Set that mind of yours at rest. It's about knowing—the sort that comes from looking. You're always pestering me about wanting to know how I know. This time, we'll make it together and then without getting your hopes up too high, we'll have someone look at that leg of yours while you're still growing."

They stood on the step of the back door looking out to the garden and beyond. It was still drizzling from a grey overcast sky.

"Now, what do you notice?"

Seth didn't know what it was he was being asked and looked about frantically for something that he'd missed.

"So, Seth. How do you know that winter hasn't really set in and it's not a few rainy days?"

"There's nothing," he said. "It's just the rain and the garden. The same old trees! That's all that I see."

"Look deeper. Look beneath the surfaces. Mind you, don't get wet, but duck out under the big oaks, stay there and then tell me what you see and hear and sense. Like I told you, can you see what's being shown to you? Is it winter or not? Don't argue with me. Just go and do it. Off you go." She shushed him off the step.

He felt a little foolish, but he also knew Hestor well enough to know that if she was asking him to look for things, then they must be there.

"There's signs. They're everywhere if you just know how to look. Not where, but *how,*" she advised.

Seth wandered about the oaks and tried to find what Hestor was referring to.

"Go away. Don't look at me!" he angrily shouted to her, and she chuckled, closed the door then went inside.

Seth had only one thought in mind. He would not go back until he had some things he could tell. He didn't care how much it rained, how wet he got, or how long it took him. He'd find the signs. He'd show her.

***

Hestor was almost at the point of going to get him when the back door opened and the small, wet bedraggled boy clumped into the room, lay down his crutches and began to steam in front of the fire. She was wise enough to keep doing what she was doing.

Eventually he spoke, "Hestor. I think you know that winter's not quite here because"—Seth counted them off on his fingers—"some trees have gone red and yellow, but there's still some leaves left. There are still a lot of really little blue and white birds in the garden. And in the garden in the last week, all the fresh seedlings have actually grown a bit—their stems are thicker. So, there must be some warmth in the ground still. And… I know when you face the wind, even though it's wet and a bit cold, it's not freezing. There's still a little bit of heat in the air." Seth sat back with a smirk of satisfaction.

Hestor smiled.

"Did I do well? Did I see them?" he asked, hopeful.

She shook out another towel to go over the basket of potions. "You did really, really well. You're learning, young one. You're learning quickly! Seems you're listening!"

He sat and glowed and steamed. She took an old towel and dried his hair.

"Hestor?" he enquired in a faraway voice.

"Uh-oh? What's coming now?" she asked.

"No! I just want to know something. One day, ages ago, you told me that you could sense danger. Am I ready to know about that? Could you teach me?"

"I can try," she said. "If you think you're ready."

Seth nodded.

"Now, stand up. Just do as I say."

He rested on his crutches and half-smiled at her.

She watched him and then suddenly smacked her hands together and shrieked in his face. He leapt a little, but then broke into giggles because he knew she was just teasing and that wasn't really any danger. Even as he was laughing, she turned, grabbed a burning stick from the fire and thrust it perilously close to his face. He didn't laugh this time. He fell over in his panic to escape.

"Hestor!" he exclaimed. "What are you doing?"

"Right, then! Where was the fear? Where in your body?" She leaned towards him and demanded an answer.

"Here!" Seth pointed to his stomach as his heart still raced.

"Where, exactly? Don't just point. Be exact!"

"Here!" he said with his eyes closed and pointed to a spot deep down in his belly.

"Keep your eyes shut. I won't hurt you! Now when I say, 'Riders' where does that feel?"

His breath caught a little. "Almost the same spot, but sort of deeper."

"Like what?"

"Like it's further down in my gizzards than the others."

She smiled at him.

"Very good! What would you think if you felt that feeling for a while when there was no danger that you could see? What would you think?"

He looked puzzled. "I don't know. Do you mean if I could feel that feeling, even though I couldn't see anything to be scared of?"

"Yes, what would you think?"

He was going to say that maybe he'd eaten too many plums, but he knew that Hestor was very serious—that she wanted him to learn this. "Maybe I'd think there was danger around, even though I couldn't see it yet. Maybe I'd think that it was on the way just waiting to happen."

"Aha! Trust yourself, Seth. Trust what you sense. It can save your life. We all know things, just most of us don't use it. It's… you can use all the things you could notice so that they give you the bigger picture now that's true knowing—not just guess work. Now, change your shirt and get ready to eat, because I think we might be off tomorrow morning."

"How do you know?"

"Signs." She winked and Seth didn't know whether to believe her or not.

Next morning, Hestor gently shook him awake. "Come on snoozy-head. It's the day for it."

Seth leapt out of bed. Everything was lined up along the wall: the blankets, her basket, a small pack for him that held their food, and water—all rolled up and ready. They ate their porridge in silence. Tiny whined and snorted. He knew that something was about to happen. Hestor cleared and washed everything. She extinguished the fire and set the pegs in the wooden shutters. Then, she checked the locking pole on their storage shed.

"No joy if we came back to find badgers or stoats had got in while we were away," she muttered, chuckling.

She had repadded the tops of his crutches so that they fitted more comfortably under his arm.

They were away as the sun was rising and streaming through the branches in the trees. It all felt fresh and sparkling and magical. This was an adventure. They didn't talk much. They simply walked. Hestor did not force the pace, but he knew that she had picked out places in her mind that they needed to reach. The joy of the early morning gave way to a time when they could rest briefly and drink some water.

"Next rest, we'll have some lunch and a longer sit. Are you holding up alright there?"

He assured her that he was, but he was looking forward to the longer break. Hestor didn't travel by the normal paths, instead she followed a track which was etched firmly in her own mind.

"It's a lot quicker this way!" she explained. "Provided we don't get stuck."

At times, Seth could almost believe that they were following some old, forgotten path. A furrow over rocks at one point, the bark shriven from an old tree at another, and patches of bare earth at others. All the time, Tiny went before them. Occasionally, he'd ambush them and bound out to scare them, often not knowing that they could see him half-hidden and full of nervous energy and so the surprise was feigned. Tiny didn't care. He could play it forever and it made the time and miles go.

"Just a short way over this next hill and we should stare down out of the forest to a clear valley. We'll stop there."

Seth was grateful, for by then the crutches were chaffing under his arm. Sure enough, the valley was there, and they rested in the heart of the grassland.

"The next bit is the hardest. We come up out of the valley and back into the forest, but it's not the same one that we've been in. It's really old and not too many people go through it. Some of it will be overgrown by now, so we'll have to push through. I'll go first, so as to make it easy for you with your legs. But you'll have to remember how strong you were with bringing the wood in and how you kept going long after you were tired. Can you do that?"

He nodded. He hoped he could.

Seth hated the feel of the pack on his shoulders when they started off again. He'd got used to feeling light and burden free while they'd eaten.

They made good progress until they climbed up from the valley floor and entered the dark of the forest proper. Then, it was just as Hestor had described. In places there were the remnants of a track, then it would peter out and Hestor became anxious that she might lose the way. There were places where there was nothing else for them to do but to plunge into the wild undergrowth and try to push through. It would have been hard if they had just been walking without baggage of any sort, yet with the basket of precious balms, the packs and the blankets, it was nightmarish.

Their progress was hideously slow; despite this, Seth was determined that he wouldn't falter and hold them back.

By the time they had pushed, pulled, dragged, and crawled their way through the second substantial patch, both of them were cut, dirty, and tired. Seth felt he couldn't go on and so knew that he mustn't stop.

In a burst of bravado, he hopped onto his crutches, adjusted his pack and climbed up a clear, head high path that wove between the roots of ancient cypress trees. He heard Hestor sigh and follow him. They had no breath to spare for words as they climbed past the trees and down into an overgrown creek bed.

This time, it seemed they could go no further for wherever they pushed, the branches and blackberries took their weight and then sprang back in their faces like sentinels guarding the way. They tried in three of four places, but all they gained from their efforts were cuts and embedded thorns. They were blocked. Hestor knew that they had to get beyond it or fail in their attempt.

"Come here, Seth," she panted hoarsely. Staring into his eyes she began, "This is a calling moment, Seth."

"What's that?" he panted.

"It's where it *calls* to you. It's where you find out if what you believe is true or not. So, you tell me. Can we make it through there? What does your gut say?"

Seth gulped and closed his eyes. Eventually he opened them, pursed his lips and said: "Yes. Yes. We can."

"And how we shall do that? Shall we sprout wings and fly over?"

His voice was clear as he heard himself say, "Hestor. Just like you taught me—we have to look for the signs."

She smiled, nodded wearily and put an arm around him. They both sat with their heads in their hands. Tiny joined them.

They waited and Seth's heart began to sink when they both spied it together and cried aloud, "There! There it is!"

A small, cheeky blue-wren chirruped and fluttered around them, before diving off to the right of the long dry creek bed.

"Wait on. Wait," Seth called.

They followed as quickly as they could.

The creek had flooded at one stage and cut a course high above their heads and beneath trees and gorse. At times, they had to almost crawl to duck under tree roots and around gigantic rocks, but they followed it until they could see clear forest above them. There was a path!

One piece at a time, they stowed their precious baggage on the bank above their heads before finding an incline they could both clamber up. Seth hooked his crutch about a tree root and hauled himself up. Panting and sweating, they jigged with delight. Ahead of them, the forest floor stood clear and flat and passable. They had made it. No blackberries barred their path.

"That's the worst, isn't it?" Seth asked.

"Yes. It's easier from here on. We'll make it across to that ridge. If it's the one I think it is, then we can stay there tonight."

Hestor had remembered well.

In a gully, there were tall rocks that rested in the earth like gigantic pillars and wedged between three of them was a small, clear barren piece of ground. It was sheltered from the wind.

"Collect whatever dry kindling you can. Just really small things and they must be dry. It'll be a long night if I can't get a flame to hold."

As he watched, she took a flint and steel from a leather pouch in her pack, and then began to strike the flint against the steel until sparks flew into the nest of fibres. It didn't take at once, but at last with a sigh, Seth saw Hestor gently blow into the kindling and saw a tiny wisp of smoke spiral up from it all. They both watched with delight as the flames took and they fed it. Light, warmth, and hot food beckoned wonderfully.

They worked quickly while they still had light. Blankets were unravelled. They ate bread and cheese from Seth's pack as they waited for soup and the night to come. Seth could barely stay awake. He ached all over now that they had stopped, the chafe marks under his arm had grown raw and sore. Regardless, he was happy. He had kept up. He had not held them back. He could only focus on the promise of warm soup to keep him awake.

Hestor also said little, indicating that she was also worn out with their day of walking.

They pulled thorns from their faces and hands and then worked their way over Tiny's matted frame, pulling burrs and seeds from his coat.

"Is it far tomorrow?" asked Seth.

"No. Not far. About half a day will take us to the town. By early tomorrow morning, we'll be out of the forest and on to a track that will take us to a main road. If we can't get a ride, it's still not far on foot, but I think with my looks and your crutch, it'd be a pretty hard-hearted farmer that would pass us with his wagon."

7

To Town

In the morning, the coals were still aglow buried beneath the ashes. It simply took some sticks and a little breath to rekindle it. Tiny yawned and stretched as dogs do. Seth wished he could do the same; he felt stiff and sore.

"We've enough water for porridge?" enquired Hestor.

"I think so, or else I'll find some," Seth offered.

"You lie there and save your strength. There's a pool back a ways."

Seth pulled the rug, still damp with dew over his head. Unfortunately, it wasn't going to work. The cold had crept in and the day with its promise of travel would not go away.

As he gathered his crutch, he heard it for the first time. It was just a movement in the bushes and at first, he took no notice. It was probably Tiny. Then he heard it again, closer this time. It was as if something big was moving through the bushes towards where he lay. Seth hauled himself to the top of the biggest rock and peered over the top.

At first, there was nothing. He thought he'd been hearing things until it came again, very close to the creek-bed in which they had slept. Then as he watched, a man burst from the foliage and looked about him nervously. Seth had a bad feeling about him at once. He looked sly and furtive—like someone who had done wrong or was running from something.

Seth hoped that the man would not see the smoke or smell the fire. He needn't have worried. Whatever was of concern to this man, it was greater than his capacity to notice such things. He jerked his head about one more time and then proceeded to race away into the bush again as if pursued by wolves. He was plainly dressed, but Seth couldn't help noticing the flash of colour from the intricate beading on the belt he was wearing. Most belts were plain and unadorned, but this was multi-coloured and braided.

Odd. Very odd.

The man was there and then he was gone. Seth shivered with a sense of foreboding.

Seth was still on top of the rock when Hestor returned with a jug of water.

"What are you doing up there? What's wrong?"

"It was really odd, Hestor. This man just came charging through the forest as if he had wolves chasing him. He stopped here for a moment and then ran on. He looked like he was scared or nervous."

"Which way did he go?"

Seth pointed to the east.

"Towards the village. Strange."

"I don't think he was up to much good, Hestor. I felt it in my gut. I got a shiver for no reason."

"There'll be reason, but at the moment, we best feed it, hadn't we?" And Hestor turned to the porridge.

The rest of the journey was uneventful. The path led through the forest to join the larger track and that took them to the main thoroughfare. Seth was just starting to tire when they heard a wagon behind them. As Hestor had foretold, the wagon master quickly found room for an old woman and a small, crippled boy.

"My good looks that did it?" insisted Hestor.

Hestor was delighted to know that it was Thursday—that was market day. They would not have to wait to sell their wares. Seth and Hestor were tired, but both contentedly swung their feet over the side of the wagon and smiled at the memory of what they'd just achieved.

At the outskirts of the town, they thanked the wagon master and made their way slowly through the town, stopping at known customers, selling as they went.

By noon, they were at the town square and the market was in full swing. Seth found his head spinning from the volume of it all. Hestor found the stall of an old friend who made leather goods. He grumbled, but still cleared one end to allow Hestor to take her bottles and jars and set them on display. Then there was nothing else to do but sit and wait for customers.

"Seth, have a wander if you like. I'll just be here. If you get lost or any sort of strife, go to the blacksmith's in the centre of the market. Big Jeb is a friend."

So, he set off through the alleyways, between the stalls, eyeing off all that he saw. He watched a potter making pots. He smelt out the food stalls where potatoes roasted in their jackets and chestnuts beckoned. It reminded him of the town he had grown up in and he liked that memory. But as he wandered, he became puzzled to realise, that although he should have been happy in the midst of it all, he wasn't. He felt uneasy and the unease grew to be an anxiety that would not go away.

Seth realised with horror that it reminded him of a burning log being thrust at him a few days before. It felt as if something *really bad* was about to happen. He turned back to find Hestor when he heard a voice. He didn't know who it was or where he knew it from, but he felt the hairs on his neck bristle, his breath race and blood rush to his face. And then he remembered, and wished he hadn't.

The last time he had heard that voice was some years before, when he had been knee-deep in leaves, terrified for his life and surrounded by horses. It was the voice of the horseman who had bargained with him for his life—he who had led the Riders and who had listened to the story of the lion and the mouse told by a small, petrified boy.

He could not mistake that voice—it was a deep, confident voice that was used to command. Petrified, Seth forced himself to move away behind a vendor's stall and from that cover, to turn and look. A man mounted on a fine horse was talking to someone who stood alongside him. That someone wore a familiar finely braided belt, and they were deep in conversation.

Seth noted the sword held on the right side, the big green ring and the dark, well-groomed horse. There was no room for doubt. It was him—here in the market in broad daylight. Soldiers on horseback accompanied him. He was obviously a man of substance. Now, Seth was scared.

A stall keeper selling potatoes saw his obvious scrutiny of the horseman. "Do you know him, then?"

"No!" Seth lied. "No. I just wondered who he was."

"The Captain. That's all I've heard him called. In charge of the Duke's guard these days chatting away to Mr. Fancy Belt himself." The man spat. "Tad's his name and informing is his little game, if you'll pardon my rhyme. He's scum. The Captain is a blow in—came with a group of mercenaries some years back—came to find the Riders."

At this, Seth's mind stalled and the world spun a little. It made no sense. Seth scurried back to Hestor who was deeply immersed in selling a jar of something to an old man. He waited until the visitor had shuffled off.

"Old galoot. Talked for ages and didn't buy anything." Hestor noticed Seth's expression. "What's wrong? Your eyes are bulging out of your head."

Seth lent so that he could whisper in her ear. "I saw him."

"Who?"

"One of the Riders!"

As quickly as he could, Seth explained how he had heard the voice, remembered where he knew it from, and then had seen him talking to the man from the forest. "He's the Captain of the Duke's guard. How could he be that?"

Hestor pulled Seth close to her. "You're much grown since then, but we can't be taking chances. You're sure it's him, aren't you?"

Seth nodded.

"We'll not wait. We'll pack up and get out of here."

"What about all your potions?" He gestured to her wares.

"There's some things more important than potions." They packed their few belongings up as quickly as they could.

"Hestor, why are we in such a hurry? He didn't even see me and I'm much older now."

She stopped what she was doing, put everything down and lent towards him while catching hold of his arms.

"I'll not lie to you. Ever since you told me about seeing the running man in the forest, I've had a bad feeling that won't go away. I hope I'm wrong. But I sense danger when there's no real reason for feeling so."

Seth looked into those clear, grey eyes and saw fear for the first time.

Even as they spoke a shadow fell over them and a voice called: "You. You. Boy! Don't I know you?"

The horse's head was at the level of their own as they both looked up. The man they called the Captain stared down at them. No helmet this time—just the same intense, dark eyes. Seth was terrified. He forced himself to look up, intentionally placing his hand over his face as if the sun was in his eyes.

"Take your hand away. I can't see you!" The voice was clear and full of authority. The horse danced a little *too* close to them. "Boy! Speak to me. Do I know you?"

Seth took a deep breath. "No, sir. I just live with my gran."

"Strange. I don't forget faces. What do you want to be when you grow up, boy?"

"I'd like to be a soldier, sir. Serve the Duke," Seth babbled.

"Well. It will have to be cavalry, won't it?" He smirked and around him the men laughed at his jibe about Seth's crutches. With one final quizzical stare at Seth, he turned his horse, and they rode away.

All about him, Seth heard the comments made under breath and between clenched teeth.

"Fop!"

"Bastard!"

Hestor squeezed his shoulder. "In case he remembers. Even more reason to go."

A giant stallholder, the blacksmith, Jeb came over to them. "You don't need comments like that, lad. He'd no right to make fun of you. Ignorant pig!"

"Watch your tongue, Jeb. Remember where he goes, that weasel Tad is always about with his barn doors flapping," warned another.

"We'll settle him, too, one day. I can tell you."

By now Hestor was adamant that they both needed to flee. She bundled things together while frowning and muttering.

On impulse, Seth sought out the blacksmith. "Can I talk to you?"

The huge man laid down a tool, looked about him and came to squat near him so that he could see into the boy's eyes.

"What is it?"

"Mercenaries. That's those who soldier just for money, isn't it? Why would the Duke have such awful men working for him? Why would he have someone like that with him?" Seth asked.

"That's a good question," hummed the blacksmith. "It's one we've been asking. Things just aren't the same, lad. The old King is dead, and the Prince…well…what can I say to you..."

"That's he's a fop and no use at all?"

Seth thought Jeb might fall over backwards with surprise and laughter. "Where'd you hear that? Careful now."

Seth told him about the meeting with the minstrels some years ago and what they had said.

"There's just more soldiers and more fear and then more soldiers. Nothing has changed; except now, we've got the Captain and we haven't exactly taken to him and his ways. He's not caught the Riders for all his fancy horses and looking flash," explained Jeb.

Seth thought long and hard. It was now or never. He gulped and began. He felt he had to. "I know other things about him. I know why he'd never catch the Riders." He took a deep breath and told Jeb the lot: the forest encounter, the massacre, and now his recognition of the Captain as the leader of the Riders.

Jeb whistled through his teeth. "Well! My, oh my! Isn't that a tale? You're sure, aren't you? Yes! Of course you are."

"You believe me, don't you?"

Jeb nodded. "Oh, yes. I wish I didn't. But I do. What's afoot, I don't know, but it can't be good. You have to promise me that you'll not tell anyone else. This is a dangerous secret."

Seth nodded his assent. "What can we do? Shouldn't the Prince know?"

Jeb laughed wryly. "In the best of all worlds, he should, shouldn't he? But this ain't it. What's the chance of you and I arriving to tell Sir Foppish that the guard might be part of the mob of murdering outlaws that have been terrifying the country? How far would we get? No. You listen. If you want to stay healthy; keep mum."

"I wanted someone else to know. Just in case…"

"And that I understand, laddie. Remember, whatever happens, you've now got a friend here in Jeb. I'm not bright, but I'm big. Be on your way and Godspeed."

After that, Seth took the coin Hestor had given him and searched out the best potato he could find. They were almost packed when a strange and violent incident occurred. Children were playing with a baby rabbit. They'd taken it from the cage in which its mother had been offered for sale and they took it in turns to carry it and pat it.

As they grew more confident, they then placed it on the ground to watch it sit and shiver and then run behind shelves and boxes with the children in pursuit. It was a game with much chasing, shouting and laughter. And then like a bad dream, a skinny mongrel dog appeared from nowhere; without warning—seized the tiny rabbit and in two or three vicious snaps of its jaws, killed it and raced away with its prize.

In a moment the scene of fun, joy, and merriment became one of confusion, shock, and tears. The children, who an instant before had been delighting in the game fled to parents, their cries cutting through the other noises. The effect on Hestor was profound.

She swung about, grabbed Seth, and in a barely controlled voice insisted, "That's it. Come on. We won't get more of a warning than that."

Seth didn't argue. Before they could flee, the giant figure of Jeb appeared before them.

"Hestor. I'll take the boy," Jeb offered. "On your own you'll make the forest, but not with this young 'un in tow. Don't argue. I'll look after him until it dies down."

Hestor tried to protest but she knew he was right.

She spoke gently to Seth. "I'm not abandoning you, but what he says is true. Together if they come looking, we'd stand no chance. Jeb is good. You take care until you can safely get away."

***

The troop was just riding over the drawbridge and into the castle itself when the Captain remembered. It was the sight of a small girl walking with a group of women that sparked his memory. She had bright red hair. He hauled on his reins and his horse reared back causing others to shy and rear about him.

"Got it!" he cried.

"What is it?" said a soldier as he strove to calm his horse.

"I remember now where I saw him." And he lowered his voice. "I think that was the small, crippled boy that I spared in the forest those years back. He seemed very scared. I wonder if he recognised me. Come on. Back to the market." At a gallop, he led them back to the market square.

Few were left and no one wished to be helpful, but fear can be a powerful persuader. The blacksmith had closed down his furnace and was packing things into his small shop as they thundered in. In his cottage nearby, a small boy crouched.

"You. Hey, you! Blacksmith!"

Jeb tried to look disinterested as the Captain enquired after Seth. "The boy with the crutch? Is that the one?"

"Yes. Who else would I mean?" pressed the Captain.

"I'm not sure. I've not seen him before, but I think I saw them head off northwards to the river sometime back. I think they were looking for a barge to take them across before nightfall. But I might have got it wrong."

"You better not have. Here!" The Captain flung a coin at the blacksmith's feet and then wheeled his horse and the troop towards the river.

"They'll have a long search of the riverbank, I'd reckon," hazarded a neighbouring stallholder. "Doubt if they'll find anything. Could have sworn I saw the boy going south."

"Light can be very tricky at this time of day," replied Jeb, as he picked up the offensive coin, spat on it, shined it and took it to one of the children whose rabbit had been gutted by the mongrel. He pressed it into the small hand.

"Buy yourself another rabbit. Keep this one close."

"Thank you!" said the father of the child.

8

Surprises

A day later saw Seth sitting on a pile of timber alongside Jeb being drawn by a horse that, although willing, was old and tired. They had been collecting wood for the forge. It was just coming on nightfall as they neared the town. Even though it was dark, Seth could still feel his fears of discovery rising within him. What if the soldiers saw him? He found himself shrinking against the load of wood. Jeb noticed.

"Trying to become invisible? Nah! Just hide your crutches and sit up straight and no one will know you."

"Don't you ever get frightened, Jeb?" Seth asked in amazement.

"Fear is a dreadful thing, Seth. It can stop you living. It did me for a long time and then I got over it."

Seth sensed a story and pestered Jeb to tell. At first, he was reluctant. With a faraway look in his eyes, Jeb told Seth of his younger days as a brash young man who hung about with other such lads, drinking, fighting, and stayed just inside the law—*only just*—in front of the bailiff and the recruiting officers. He smiled a sad sort of smile as he told him how much fun they had, until it turned sour.

"Just a stupid fight over a sneer in a tavern! In the middle of it, this drunk pulled a knife and stabbed this young lad who hung about with us. Just a kid. Not much older that you. I was holding him. 'Don't let me die, Jeb. I'm too young. I haven't done anything yet!' And then the spark went out of his eyes. And that was that!"

The wheels of the wagon turned. Seth was both horrified and enthralled.

"Then what happened?" he asked very quietly in case Jeb didn't wish to answer.

But the big man recovered from his reverie and answered that it had changed his whole life. He'd stopped hanging about making trouble but couldn't seem to get on with anything except drinking. He kept seeing the dying face of the young follower.

"Then one day, I just heard his voice in my head as clear as day. He looked at me and said, 'Mine is gone, so don't waste yours.'" He nodded at Seth. "I know I was drunk. I knew I hadn't eaten for days, but I swear that's how it was. Clear as a bell: 'Don't waste yours!'"

This time, he waited for Jeb to start again.

"I got a job helping a blacksmith that no one else would go near because of his temper and his language. Every time he swore at me or cursed me for some mistake, I'd just remember that young boy and I'd bite my tongue and keep going. He died. Left me his forge and his tools. Funny isn't it, how it works out."

"So that's why you're not scared then!"

"In an around about way, I just learnt that each day alive is a bonus. So, enjoy as much of it as I can and don't be frightened of things that won't even happen!" Jeb concluded.

They travelled on.

"So, you do believe all what people tell you, then?" he asked with a twinkling eye that made Seth stare open-mouthed.

He stammered, "It's true. You couldn't make up anything like that could you?"

Jeb laughed as he lifted him off the wagon. "Yes. It's true. I couldn't have made that one up."

In the dark, Seth waited while Jeb struggled with the mechanism of a huge lock that was chained to the front of his home, a room that sat adjacent to the forge at which he worked.

As he jingled it and quietly complained, a door opened, and a chink of light escaped across the square.

A figure emerged and spoke. "Jeb. If that's you, I'd be careful. Them soldiers were back here again looking for you. I'd have a good reason made up if I were you."

"Thanks, Sirus. Sick relatives is the one I tend to use." With that, he won the battle with the lock and helped Seth inside the room, then lit a lamp. Seth could make out faintly familiar outlines of a neat, but sparsely furnished room, one end of which was taken up with the tools with which Jeb worked.

"Take a seat on the bed until I get the fire going, then we'll cook up a batch of something," Jeb instructed. "There's only the one bed, so we'll sleep top to toe. You know who'll get the top, don't you?"

Seth pulled a rug about him as the room was cold from disuse and watched as Jeb methodically worked at getting the fire alight.

"Amazing what a fire does to your spirits, eh?"

Seth thought for a while. "Jeb, do you think it's safe for me to be here? I mean…What if they come back to ask you and I'm here? They'd take us both away?"

"Don't fret. Golly, you're a fretter. If they come, we'll be told in plenty of time and then it'll be up to you to stay very hidden. You can do that, can't you?"

Seth nodded, but he was not convinced. He slept fitfully—while Jeb complained at the other end of the bed—tossing and turning, trying to banish his torture chamber visions from his mind.

At some stage in the night, Jeb asked him, "What's got into you? You got a weasel down there?"

Seth thought for a long time before he answered, "You can run away. I can't run away from anything."

There was a long silence and Seth thought his audience had gone back to sleep when Jeb answered, "Some would say that that's a good thing. But I take your point and we'll see what we can do."

"What do you mean, Jeb?"

"I mean—I'll tell you in the morning. Now, go back to sleep." Which was a highly unsatisfactory answer for Seth, but a snoring Jeb was not likely to enlighten him further.

***

For once, Jeb was wrong. Seth was still asleep when they came in the morning. There was no warning. Seth woke to the sound of commotion and voices. Carefully, he tiptoed to the door and glanced through the gap. He couldn't see much, but he could see Jeb in the midst of lighting the forge surrounded by men on horses. The rest he could hear.

"We've been looking for you. Blacksmith, where have you been?"

He saw Jeb straighten, resting his huge hand on one of the hammers he used to beat hot metal into shape with.

"I thought that it was still lawful to visit sick relatives and cut wood to get them through the winter," he challenged.

Horses snorted and were brought under rein. Seth couldn't see the speaker, but he knew the voice well.

"Don't be impertinent or I'll lock you up. We were after a boy. A crippled boy! It was said that you were seen talking to him before he disappeared. We need to find him!"

"I spoke to the boy here some time ago. I told you all I knew."

"Sent us on a wild goose chase," cut in the voice of another rider and there was a chorus of agreement.

"That's not my doing," Jeb responded. "They told me they were heading for the river to see someone about a boat!"

"…Someone about a boat!" echoed the leader. Seth held his breath as he saw him considering. Eventually, the leader smiled and relaxed. "Very well then, blacksmith. We'll take your word for it this time. You might be telling the truth, and in truth I need all my men in shape, not knocked out of it by well-placed hammer blows. Although, no doubt you're handling the hammer to get the feel of it before the day's work, I take it?" He smiled and laughed at Jeb.

"No doubt you'll rush to tell us if you see him again. We'll leave you to your trade, but do tread carefully, blacksmith. Swords are generally quicker than hammers." The Captain spurred his horse away and the rest followed as chickens and dogs went in all directions.

As quickly as they came, they left leaving a remarkably silent square and a barely moving blacksmith. Slowly and suspiciously, doors opened onto the square and faces appeared around them.

"Welcome back, Jeb. Perhaps you'd better go and cut some more firewood for this sick aunt of yours," ventured a wise-cracking neighbour. A chorus of laughter greeted that suggestion.

Seth stayed where he was. Jeb pretended to be simply going about his tasks, not looking in Seth's direction. When it was right and proper time for him to do so, Jeb whistled his way to the room as if going to collect his working tools from within. He hummed and whistled his way to the door and began clanging and banging his tools together while at the same time talking to Seth.

"Right, then. It's a bit warmer than we thought. You'll have to amuse yourself indoors and be cook for the day while I figure out how we're going to get you halfway across the town." He turned and gripped Seth with both hands. "You'll be best off with friends for a few days. We'll just have to take care of Mr. Fancy Belt before you do."

"What'll you do to him?"

"No. Nothing like that! He's more use to us alive if we can just persuade him to help."

"How will you do that?" enquired Seth.

Jeb tapped his nose with his forefinger and smiled. "You just leave it to me."

The day was a long one for Seth. Jeb worked as he needed to, only returning for a bite to eat and saying little of their plans. The morning went quickly enough, except the afternoon dragged. He could hear it all, but not join in.

Finally, as the day began to darken and stallholders closed, Jeb started to cover his forge fire and prepare to bring his tools in. Seth was used to the procession of tools being brought in. When he heard footsteps again, he barely glanced up and when he did, he almost cried in alarm. In front of him were a boy not much older than himself and a huge man, almost as tall as Jeb. He was about to yell to Jeb, fearing harm when Seth saw the boy place his finger to his lips. As he did, footsteps were heard outside, and Jeb appeared with the last of his paraphernalia.

He acted as if no one else was there until the door was firmly shut, then crossed to Seth, whispering in his ear, "We're hatching a little plan here. Just don't talk too loudly and don't let on that we've got visitors."

Seth was still totally confused until he saw what the man had hidden in a bundle he carried—it was a set of crutches. Then, he understood. Jeb made noises as if they were making dinner but really, he was waiting until it was darker. When he thought it was right, he signalled to their two guests. Calling to Seth in a stage whisper, he turned out the lamp and opened the door.

The man and the boy, now mounted on the crutches, closed the door and set off down the street. Quietly, Jeb inched the door open and together they watched in the shadows behind their forge.

Sure enough, a minute after they had left, a shadow detached itself from the buildings, whisking its way in pursuit. If they had not been looking for it, they would never have seen it.

"Mr. Fancy Belt—Tad!" whispered Jeb.

Jeb waited a minute more before turning to Seth with a huge smile on his face, he signalled to the boy to follow him out. Seth's few belongings were already borne on Jeb's ample back. They turned at the forge and set off in the opposite direction.

"That was brilliant!" panted Seth.

"It was that. Let's hope he follows them for miles. We'll be going the other way."

"Where are we going?" whispered Seth.

"To meet a man with a boat, and then a lady who has the healing touch," Jeb answered cryptically.

All Seth could do was to follow the huge figure who knew his way even in the dark. He followed until they came to a small jetty on the river. Seth watched a figure rise from a tiny boat, nodded to Jeb, and then settled them both in the bottom of the frail looking craft. Jeb motioned to Seth to be quiet and just to do as he was told.

Soon, they were moving quite swiftly through the dark waters. Seth could only marvel at the reflections of fires and lamps in the water, noticing the half-moon that shone for a moment before it disappeared beneath the cover of the clouds. There was little breeze. The silence and the dark encouraged Seth just to sit and wait. The trip was not long. Soon, they were slowing, and Seth could see a jetty poking into the water, distinguishing a figure standing there, gently rocking a lamp for them to see.

"Right, then. Out you hop."

"Aren't you coming?" Seth anxiously asked.

"No. I'll be about, but this one is for you. You can trust these lot. They'll keep you out of harm's way. Good luck, young'un."

Seth was scrabbling with his crutches, following the figure with the lamp who now moved in front of him, showing him the way from the jetty to the shape of a small cottage.

Seth heard the boat turn in the water, and then he was on his own.

9

Healings

The house was not unlike Hestor's and Seth liked that. The boy had guided him over the threshold into a large room that was overflowing, but orderly. There were many objects, and each seemed to have a place.

Some of those 'things' were animals, so that as Seth entered the room, there was a flurry of movement that gave the impression that the room itself was not stationary yet somehow in a state of continuous motion. Seth's eyes tried to follow it all, catching glimpses of dogs, cats, and more dogs and even an owl that barely moved except to realign its neck to see him better.

He was not frightened, but it was unlike anything he'd ever seen before. His eyes flickered over it all and came to rest on the figure of a woman who sat by a fire at the point furthest from the door. She beckoned him over with a smiling face.

Seth sat, and without preliminaries, she directed him to take off his shoe and stockings to show her his leg. When he had done this, she bent forward eagerly and took his leg between both hands, rubbing and squeezing it in a way that Seth found quite alarming. She poked it. She put pressure on his knee joint and she twisted his ankle both ways. He felt nothing. Eventually, she gave a slight smile and turned to the boy and conveyed something to him.

When he spoke, Seth realised it was the first words he had heard since he had entered the house.

"She says that there might be some chance." Then, as she made the same strange and rapid movements with her hands, Seth realised that she couldn't speak and that she was speaking through the boy.

Seth looked at the boy. Before he could think, he said, "Ask her what does she *really* think? Is it a good chance?"

The boy looked at him dumbfounded. Slowly, a grin spread across his face so that when the words came, there was no mockery in them. "She can hear. She just can't talk."

Seth blushed crimson and wished that he could shrink to pea size and roll under a door, but eventually, he forced himself to look up and face her. He went to apologise. However, he was delighted to see her miming an action for him in which she placed her hands over her mouth and shook her head from side to side, and then raised her hands on either side of her head like giant ears; she flapped them and smiled at him as if it was a huge joke. She was not insulted, and Seth was glad of that.

When he tried again to apologise, she reached over and gently held his lips together and shook her head.

"No need. A waste of words! That's what she's saying!" prompted the boy.

She mimed eating from a bowl. Seth replied to her while looking her full in the face, "Thank you. Yes. I'd like something."

Still smiling, she raised herself from her seat and went to a cupboard that sat to the side of the fireplace. He looked at the boy, but by now was too unsure to know if he should talk, question, or just sit still. He couldn't recall feeling so uncomfortable. He looked about the room and pairs of eyes followed him.

"You'll get used to it. The eyes. It's good!" the boy said.

"Have you? I mean, do you live here?" Seth asked.

"Aeron took me in when I was a baby. I've lived here ever since. Just us and the rest of our family!" He swung his arm about to include the many animals that watched. "She—that's Aeron—takes in strays; dogs and boys."

"Oh," ventured Seth.

"You've come about your leg and because they're after you as well. That's what the messenger said? What are they chasing you for?"

Aeron reacted by placing a hand on the boy's shoulder as if to silence him; however, Seth was happy to find his tongue. "No. It's fine. I saw some things that they didn't want me to."

"What did you see?"

"I saw the Riders one night."

The room became very quiet.

"What were they like?"

"They were just men. They killed people that they didn't even know."

By now, the boy was bursting to ask him everything, but the restraining hand on his shoulder held him in check.

"They captured us, me and this girl, and they were going to kill us," Seth continued, "but I told them the story of the lion and the mouse, then their leader made me promise that like the mouse I'd set him free one day. One day, he recognised me in the square."

He could see Aeron's face brighten as he talked. She had long brown hair that was greying and he guessed that she must have been very beautiful when she was young. She was firm, and sure in a way that made her seem strong and handsome. He wondered about her inability to speak.

"I don't want to get you in danger," Seth said, cautiously.

Aeron made a rush of gestures and the boy looked up to see.

"Soldiers don't come here," the boy explained. "You're very safe here with us. The animals would warn us if anyone came close. You must stay with us and see if we can mend your leg. Oh… and Aeron says that I am to tell you that my name is Caleb."

And then somewhat awkwardly—like small men— they shook hands.

"I'm Seth."

"I know. We were told."

At this point, Aeron took Caleb's hand and pointed to both of them, and then the animals.

"Don't try to pat the owl or creep up on the old mastiff because he's deaf and gets a shock when you appear. He might bite you," advised Caleb. "All the rest are quite safe. If you want a seat or a stool, you have to pick the animal up and just move it. Oh, and you sleep in the bed closest to the fire—the one that's got about four terriers on. You can kick them off or they'll stay snug with you for the night."

They got Seth some soup and bread, then left him to eat by the fire while Caleb and Aeron fussed over some small animals in a cage.

By the time he had finished, the effects of the day had closed in on him as he remembered that just that morning he had been in the town, under the strong protective umbrella of Jeb. Again, Seth felt alone and small. It was a familiar feeling—he knew it from before, as if he'd known it most of his life.

Seth didn't move the terriers. He simply made room for himself in the middle of them and went to sleep. Perhaps they kept him warm, perhaps he was just too tired, but nothing woke him until the following morning and that was to the unfamiliar sound of small piteous whining's and yelping's.

With a single eye open, Seth could see a tight semi-circle of the largest and oddest collection of dogs he had ever seen; big dogs with small heads, small dogs with odd markings and huge heads, big-bodied dogs with small terrier like legs—mongrels all.

Aeron was bent over a large pot that hung from the fireplace that contained their breakfast. The dogs could barely contain themselves. Some of the smaller ones, their haunches quivering with excitement, would stand up only to be warned by a soundless look or a spoon pointing, to wait and be patient. Then, and only then, did Aeron lift the large pot and carry it outside escorted by a small army of dogs in various stages of hunger, distress and excitement.

Seth looked for Caleb, but he was nowhere to be seen.

Hearing noises from outside, he swung onto his crutches and made his way to the front step. In front of him, there stretched a small zoo of animals. The noises and movements that he'd heard on his way in that night belonged to an array of animals such as Seth had never seen before. There were normal domestic animals that he knew well, such as sheep, cows, horses, and goats; but it was the profusion of wild animals that made him gasp and wonder. There were stoats and weasels, as well as foxes, badgers, and small possums that Seth had only heard of.

Between the rows and hutches, Caleb moved, checking and tending to the needs of the animals.

"Hey!" Seth called to him.

Caleb looked up from his work and waved him over.

"Do you like this? Doing this?" Seth almost shouted over the sounds of the animals.

The honking and the shrieking of a litter of pigs didn't distract the other boy as he poured a bucket load of grain and fruit pieces into the trough.

"It's how we live," explained Caleb. "Without them we'd have very little. This way we look after them and they look after us. Some days I don't like it when it's wet and cold and there's duck shit everywhere. Mostly, it's good!"

Seth watched him feed lot after lot, and for once, he remembered not to ask all his questions in the first ten minutes. There was a small shed, not big enough to be called a barn, but large enough to safely protect the bags of feed, the wooden boxes full of grain, and the stooks of straw and hay. It was on top of these that the two boys paused from the feeding.

They both eyed one another. Both almost began—stopped, and then Seth waved Caleb to go first.

"So where are yours? What happened to you?"

"My mum died. She got sick and my dad is off somewhere with the army," answered Seth. "And yours?"

"I don't know. Aeron found me left on her step with a dirty shawl wrapped about me. And that's all I know."

Seth's mind raced. "Oh! Then how did you learn to speak, if Aeron can't?"

"For a long time, an old lady lived with us. She was really, really old. She was like Aeron's mother but she wasn't. She used to talk with me all the time. She died—Oh! Some Christmases ago!"

"Was she the healer lady? The one who taught Aeron?"

"I think so."

"Don't you get lonely with no one to talk to? I mean, with Aeron not able to talk back and all?"

"It's not that bad. Mostly I understand what she's saying with the signing. But if it gets too bad, she can write. Read as well. The old lady, Minerva, she taught her."

"Can you read and write?"

"A bit of both. Aeron keeps me trying, but I didn't see the need, to be truthful."

After, lunch, Aeron signalled to Seth that she wished to start on his leg. She had Caleb explain to Seth what she was going to do.

"She says that some of it will hurt because she's going to rub this oil—this special oil mixed with herbs into your leg. She's going to try and waken the bits of your leg that have gone to sleep. She says not to worry about it. She also says that not much will happen for a while and not to be disappointed."

Afterwards, Aeron pulled back the tunic he wore to expose the thin, withered leg with its useless, flopping foot that he could hardly bear to look at.

It was as Aeron had said. Although Seth wanted to say that he could feel what was happening; he couldn't. It was as if Aeron was working on a half-full sack of grain that was attached to his frame, from which all life had gone. He watched her.

Sometimes she worked his leg like he had seen his mother making bread—kneading and turning it with great vigour and energy and then she would stop, almost as if she was listening and just rest her hands on his leg with her eyes closed. He wished he could feel something, but he couldn't. When it was all over and Seth was deep in doubt and despair, then something did happen. As he tried to get up, he felt faint, then was overcome with nausea and before he could do or say anything, he threw up his breakfast all over the hearth.

That was all he needed. In a fit of misery and self-loathing he dragged himself to kneeling and began to apologise to Aeron. But he was amazed to see her glowing at him with a smile that was huge and full of joy. She hugged him and clapped him on the back. Seth was dumbfounded.

Caleb told him, "Aeron says that your vomiting is a good sign. It means that what she did has had an effect on your body and that's a good sign. Also, not to worry about the mess. Dogs love it."

And so, it went. Every day Aeron would spend time working on the leg. Except, now she was careful not to feed Seth before she began. He no longer vomited at the end of the session, but each time he felt nauseous and one day, he could barely move from the ache in his head. Seth had to lie there for the whole afternoon, because to do anything different sent pain like rods through his brain. Caleb continued to reassure him, but Seth was certain that it was all just a painful waste of time.

"It was better when I didn't even think about it," Seth told him.

***

For several weeks, all that they did revolve around a pattern of caring for animals, preparing food and massaging Seth's leg.

Jeb did not come back, but he sent a message via a barge carrying wool down river. A small skiff came from the huge unwieldy craft and a message was given to Caleb. He raced back to tell them.

"He can't come yet. They're watching him like hawks. The plan worked a treat and Fancy Belt is no longer as popular at the castle. He said that he's thinking of you and he's coming down to race you."

It was in the second week on a cold and drizzly day that they all knew that Seth's leg was healing. It was not spectacular. Aeron had almost finished with his leg for the day when he felt it like a pulse in his calf. He looked at Aeron for confirmation and saw the look of wonder on her face. She went over the same spot and again he could feel it—like a tiny spasm, and then nothing. Caleb heard Seth's cry and came running.

"It moved. I tell you. It really did. It wasn't much, but it was like hearing a voice down the end of a tunnel or throwing a rock down a well and hearing it splash way, way down. It was there. I swear it," Seth exclaimed.

That night, they had rabbit stew, potatoes, carrots, and parsnips.

Seth was scared the following day that he'd imagined it. He almost couldn't bear Aeron to start on the leg again. But she did, and again there was a faint twinge of sensation as if from a very dark, deep place. She warned him again that if the work was to continue, then he would begin to get great pain from the waking leg. And she was right. On the fourth day after he had first felt the twinge, Seth could barely allow Aeron to touch his leg, so great was the pain.

Caleb told him quite sharply, "She says you must let her work on it because this is the only way it will get better. She says I'm to give you this rolled up towel and as she works on you, then you must scream into it with all your might. She says that the scream will let the pain out and it will help heal you. She says you must if you're to get better."

"So, she wants me to shout into the pillow?"

Caleb nodded.

Seth lay on his stomach and began. At first it seemed futile, and then he understood. He learnt that if he yelled with all his might while Aeron massaged, then the pain was somehow bearable. When he didn't, then he found himself swatting at her hands in primitive self-preservation. He stopped being embarrassed at the noise and tried to give it his all. He yelled as loudly as he could as long as she touched his leg and rested in between. Eventually, he got into the rhythm and focused his being into each scream, knowing that this was the only way he could bear it.

"Just be right in the scream is what she says, and I don't understand that any better than you," Caleb assured him.

At the end of the session, Seth was exhausted, crimson in the face and soaked in sweat. Aeron hugged and wept with him.

"She says you're very brave. And—and I think you are too," said Caleb.

That night, as if to confirm what had happened, Seth was woken by an unfamiliar sensation; his withered leg was very painful—as if it was *burning* with the pain. Aeron sensed that he was awake almost immediately and came across to him.

"My leg. It's like it's on fire." He could feel himself trying to draw away from his own leg as if it didn't belong to him.

Caleb joined them, still drowsy with sleep. He watched Aeron and then spoke to Seth, "Is the pain the same as before?

Like when she was massaging it and you were yelling? Is it the same? Aeron says it is very important."

Before this, Seth would have said pain was pain and all of it was bad. But he'd lived with Hestor and been taught to look for signs and differences, so he was able to know that it was different. He took his time before answering. Again, she repeated the gestures, which he had come to know—the crossed arms over her breast to signify bad or harmful, the right hand on the heart to signal joyful or good. Seth closed his eyes and felt the pain. It was intense and throbbing, but with his eyes closed he felt it as a white light that beat fiercely.

It hurt. It hurt a lot, but it felt warm.

Slowly, he opened his eyes fearing to reply in case he was faking it; he smiled at Aeron and laid his hand on his heart. He saw her sigh of relief and then place her hand also on his heart. Suddenly, as if angry for forgetting, she clutched Caleb to her and had him place his hand, also on Seth's heart. For a moment, all three of them stayed very still and very quiet. Abruptly, Jack the ageing mastiff farted mightily in his sleep and the moment became one of hilarity.

In the morning, Aeron changed her methods. The leg was red and swollen, so she brewed a mess of pungent herbs in a pot. After soaking a bandage in it, she wrapped it about his limb. In the afternoon, she didn't massage it but simply spent a long time with the leg cradled in her palms and her eyes closed. When she came to unwrap it, Seth's anxiety returned. The flesh was now all mottled like an old man's and it seemed that liquid was seeping from it. He felt his breath quicken; however, Aeron touched her hand to her heart and nodded before bathing the leg and wrapping it afresh.

That night, he slept badly. The pain took hold and convinced him that he might die. He was glad when he saw the grey light of day and the animals begin to stir and speak around him. He felt awful and could see from the look in Caleb's face that he also looked it.

After the morning ritual of animal feeding was complete, Aeron summoned Caleb. Together, they unwrapped the bandages and washed his leg. When Aeron was satisfied, she sat back, whisked a slither of hair from her face, and she placed her foot in front of him. Holding it clearly so Seth could see, she wiggled the toes of the right foot. Then squatting on her haunches, she gestured with her hand for Seth to try the same.

Now, he was terrified. He took a deep breath, focused, and sent all the strength he had down his leg to his foot. Nothing happened. It sat there as it had for most of his life like a dead fish on a line and Seth could feel the lump swell in his throat as he thought, *All this. All this—for nothing!*

Aeron nudged him. She entreated him to place his hand on his heart and to try again. He breathed deeply. He placed his hand on his heart and as he did, his mother's face came unbidden to his mind. With tears in his eyes, he was not the first to see. Caleb was. Seth heard him holler and the dogs bark, which brought Jack suddenly awake and snapping in confusion at imaginary foes.

He brushed the tears away and saw with utter amazement and delight that his big toe was, ever so slightly, moving up and down in a rhythmic, systemic way. For a moment, Seth knew it was connected to the rest of him. He found himself to be a howling, blubbering mess being held in the shaking and comforting arms of Aeron while around him dogs howled and yelped in total chaos.

He cried until he thought he would be ill, and then he began again, spasms of weeping taking hold of him in a manner that was beyond his control. Eventually, he stopped. He felt hollow. He disentangled himself from Aeron and looked about him. Even the animals were now silent. Caleb squatted near him with huge smiles in his eyes. Aeron, with eyes full of tears, smiled at him.

There was only one thing he could do—Seth placed his leg out in front of him, and with much greater certainty, he concentrated. His toe responded and felt his joy alongside the others. He managed to say, "Thank you," to Aeron through tears that threatened to choke him again.

"I'd like to tell Jeb," Seth managed.

Seth would never know what risks the blacksmith took to come, but that night as they were settling to sleep, there was a commotion outside followed by a knock at the door. Caleb was there in an instant, lifting the latch board and Jeb's huge, smiling presence filled the room.

"Couldn't miss a miracle, now, could I?"

Seth was overjoyed to see him. A display of toe movement was carried out with great ceremony and aplomb.

Jeb was suitably and humbly impressed. "If I hadn't seen it, I would never have believed it. Aeron you're a wonder, you are!"

She explained through Caleb that there was still a long way to go, and that Seth would have to endure even more of the same if he was to have any useful movement and take any weight on the leg. But they had a start, and it was a good one.

Jeb told how there had been another massacre of a village by the Riders. Among the aftermath of fear and terror, people were calling for a council of nobles to take control of the country until order was restored.

"The Prince won't be ruler anymore?" Seth wondered.

"Oh, he'd be there, but even more of a figurehead!"

Jeb explained, while trying to make light of it, that the night they had brought Seth to Aeron's he had only barely returned to his hut and got into his bed when his door had been beaten in by soldiers. Jeb had been frog marched before the Captain to explain his movements.

"I just looked innocent and asked the sergeant to repeat where they had found me. Of course, all he could say was that I'd been in bed asleep. The sergeant wanted to do me some harm and throw me in the dungeons, but the Captain just sat there smiling at me as if he actually knew that I'd outsmarted them, and he quite liked the whole game."

"Does he have his sword on the right?" asked Seth.

"Aye! How'd you know?"

"He's the one!" confirmed Seth.

"You mean the one from the forest. The Riders? He just looked at me with this smile on his face like he thought it was a great joke. He told the rest that I wasn't to be harmed, and in the absence of any proof then, I was to be escorted back to my home and the door would be repaired. He just smiled at me all the way, as if he knew I was lying and he knew that I *knew* he knew, and that was what made it all so great—made me shudder. All of it—just pretending!

"They took me back. Eventually, the castle carpenter came and repaired the door, but by this time, the whole story had come out. How'd they'd followed Fancy Belt to the house, kicked in the door and found only a family of tall men and small children having an evening supper. It was a fine how-to-do of who trusted who, and who didn't, and who was playing games with each other. I lay very low and just ran the forge until it got very exciting. I was pounding plough shares when I heard this noise. I turned about, here was this mob with Fancy Belt in the middle of them!

"The castle had decided he wasn't any more use and so they set him loose—dumped him in the square after ruffling him about, and then making it clear that they wouldn't be protecting him anymore. So, they were just hurrying him down to the river when I saw them. I knew he'd been a low life and all, but I still felt sorry for him. Him, that was always so neat and stylish, and there he was covered in tar with chook feathers from head to toe.

He looked terrified. I think he thought they were going to drown him," recalled Jeb.

"What'll happen to him?" enquired Caleb.

"Oh, he'll probably go on to another town. Change his clothes, rub the tar off, and do the same somewhere else. I don't think he knows how to be honest," the blacksmith speculated.

Jeb couldn't risk being away too long. He said his good-byes, wished Seth a swift healing, and disappeared back onto the river, leaving the household in a state of anxiety and excitement.

10

Recuperation

Winter brought rain and hail that made Caleb's outside tasks miserable. Puddles became small lakes, dirt paths turned into muddy expanses, and over the whole animal enclosure there lingered the smell of mud, dung, and rotting hay. Caleb complained a little to Seth, but never to Aeron.

Inside the home, the fire needed to go all day to feed and heat its residents. Aeron continued to divide her time between the care of her animals and the care of those who came to her for healing, of which Seth was one. Increasingly, but slowly, his leg recovered. It was all too slow for him, and one day he saw her almost grow impatient with him when she discovered him propped up, ready to try putting weight on his crippled leg. She snatched his crutch up and looked as if she might do something violent with it, then shake her head, and place the crutch down very gently before coming over to Seth to take his head in her hands and chastise him. He knew that; come what may, he had to be patient and trust the healing process. She knew better than he.

Much of Seth's time was spent lying on his bed by the fire with his poulticed leg out in front of him. Aeron took that time to teach him to read and write. Caleb joined in with him each day

96

before lunch. Aeron would gather down the slates she had from her childhood, then she would show them the signs and symbols which gradually made sense to Seth.

They became a good team.

First, Aeron would write the symbol, then Caleb would sound it out for Seth to follow suit and learn to recreate on his own slate.

The first time he wrote his own name was doubly sweet. On that day, Seth managed to move all the toes on his foot. He found himself being able to dream of walking unaided and one night he woke from a dream in which he was running alongside a stream for mile after mile.

Many people came to Aeron's door. No one was turned away. Over the course of the winter, Seth watched a file of people, mostly poor, knock on her door and stepping past animals, bring their ill and troubled to Aeron. He watched with horror as she washed maggots from a horribly diseased wound on a young man's thigh, bathed away the stench and then wrapped it in a herb saturated cloth requiring him to return daily. It was clearly a sword wound, but no questions were asked, and no answers were required. Seth saw the red inflammation die and the wound's edges begin to dry and heal.

He also saw small babies brought, their small stomachs distended and their faces purple with screaming. Aeron would unwrap them and make up a concoction of yellow flowered plants and when it was cooled, she would dip a cloth end into it and drop the liquid into their tiny mouths and watch as their convulsions ceased, their limbs relax and sleep settle over them. She would bottle the remainder of the liquid and send it away with the mother—normally a young one, Seth observed.

Seth watched as a hunter was carried in by red-faced and anxious men to see him lain down and have them uncover a long and cruel gash on his stomach where a wild boar had slashed with its tusks into the kneeling man.

"He won't be doing that again," Seth heard them laugh.

He witnessed Aeron guide the men to strip the wounded man's shirt away and then hold their companion as she produced a needle and thread. Washing the wound thoroughly, she would darn a tear in a garment, and then she stitched up the gaping wound. Only once it was complete, would she allow the men to feed the hunter the skin of rough spirits that they had brought with them. It was clear that Aeron wished him to stay and rest; but, now that the man was stitched, it was like they wished to be gone as quickly as they could.

Seth noticed and said to her, "They think you're a witch." Aeron smiled and imitated an old, wizened hag.

Often Aeron was offered money or jewellery in return, but she never accepted, even when the sick and their relatives were insistent. Seth was surprised until he realised that an exchange was made, which was as vital for Aeron and her extended family.

One day, Seth saw a cart pull up by the shed and watched as grain and hay were unloaded. A party of men, one of whom now carried a pattern of needle-prints over his stomach, unloaded their cargo. Then, they were gone. A debt was repaid.

In late winter, Seth put his first weight on the leg. Gingerly and carefully, with Aeron on one side and Caleb on the other, he lowered his weight from his left to his right. For a moment it held, shortly collapsing in shock as Seth plunged forward before either could stop him. Both were horrified as they bent down aghast at their failure, expecting to find Seth miserable and defeated. Instead, they found him giggling and silly beyond words.

As he recovered, he could only mutter, "It held. I just got such a shock!" And then he was away again, back into laughter.

Jeb brought him an oak walking stick that he had trimmed to size, and then Seth began in earnest.

It began with the stick taking the weight of the right side of his body, his toes barely touching the ground. It improved until the stick and his foot shared the load. His progress ended when the stick merely supported his leg.

Seth overdid it despite Aeron's warning. He wanted *so much* to get better—to never have to return to his crutches.

So, he tried too hard. He walked too far. He didn't rest as he was told. That first night, Seth awoke drenched in sweat with his leg aching as it had in the early sessions, the pain driving him to squirm and shift in his bed. Aeron shook her head at him, but continued to prepare the sleeping draught that would deaden the pain and help him to rest. Belatedly, he learned to do it slowly, while appropriately using the walking stick as to avoid exerting his recovering leg.

As he walked and limped regularly—sometimes still quite painfully—the muscles in his leg strengthened, and gradually began to fill out. Soon, Seth was able to help Caleb with many of the outdoor tasks.

As he recuperated, Seth felt that there was a restlessness growing within him. It showed sometimes in a lack of patience with one of the older or slower animals.

Aeron noticed and drew his attention to it. As they were writing together, she leaned over him to write on his slate, *Time to be going?*

Seth reddened and tried to deny it. "Why would I want to go? Why would I want to leave you two after what you've done for me?" And as if to silence his own misgivings, he rubbed it out and wrote, *I stay here. This is my home!*

But Aeron rubbed it out. She spoke through Caleb, "She says you are always welcome here, but she understands that you have to go and complete what you started?"

"What did I start?" he asked.

This time she took his slate and wrote on it, so her words were hidden until she turned it to face him.

On it she had written just four words: *The Riders. The Prince.*

Instantly, Seth realised she understood his impatience. It also occurred to him that in the spring he could go back into town with Jeb and his crutches would no longer betray his identity.

Sheep were lambing and the cows were just beginning to get to full term when Jeb came for him. Seth took his things down to the boat and then returned with a tight throat and chest to say his goodbyes. As he had formally 'met' Caleb, so he farewelled him with a handshake and a mutual avoidance of eyes.

He simply hugged Aeron and then said, "Thank you for my leg back. I'll always come back to see you."

It was only out on the water that he could let himself feel the tears. Seth sniffled a little.

The boat skipper asked, "What's the blubbering about?" Only to be told in no uncertain terms by Jeb that it was manly to shed tears at the parting of good friends and—in a more hushed tone—how would he like to swim to the bank. Seth left with a pair of crutches and returned with just a stick.

"First thing we'll do when we get back is to find out about Hestor. Then, we'll get you some new clothes. Nothing wrong with the ones you've got, but we want to give you a new start to go with your new leg. Besides, it'll throw the soldiers off if they haven't run out of curiosity."

11

The Past Returns to Haunt

To Seth, the following few months were the best of his life. Jeb looked after him, but due to his workload, had to trust to Seth to make his own fun.

And he did. He explored the town. He met friends and became theirs as well. He visited Hestor briefly, reassured to see her well and full of cheek and threats. He lived in the market and came to know it. He grew to like and trust those who had first hidden him when he had to flee Jeb's house on that first morning. He kept a keen eye out for horsemen and spies and his leg grew stronger.

And…he almost forgot what he had come there for.

It was only in summer that events conspired to remind Seth of the promise he had made and the reasons he had first come to the town.

The longest day of the year approached, leading to a festival that was being held and people came to share in it. Peasant families would stop work for a day or two to join in. Meanwhile, wealthier families would make the journey across the land to stay at the castle to join the Duke in the annual council and watch the celebrations take place. As these noble families came through the town, the people would stop to watch parties travel through with their own servants, horses, litters of women and children, and accompanying soldiers.

Old men would identify them based on the standards that were carried or the insignia on the soldiers who accompanied them.

"Them be the Roses. I know them by the white rose they wear on their livery," one said.

"The bear with muzzle. I served with his father when I was a boy," another muttered.

They would gape at the wealth. The women would stare with envy at the brightly clad ladies carried in the litters swung between horses. The children all looked clean and well-fed. People cheered and applauded as they passed, but some faces that saw them were too hungry to see the nobles without cursing and wishing that places could be traded.

Nearby, Seth stood and watched.

The flow of the procession was halted. In the confusion of horses and shouts and counter-orders, Seth pushed through to see. A horse carrying a litter had lost its footing on wet cobblestones in the square and was having trouble rising to its feet again. Wisely, the horse was unbuckled from its harness to allow it to do just that. A soldier held the horse's head while others helped the travellers from the litter. A woman and a child stepped down from it, an older girl who Seth only really noticed when she turned her back to him to observe the horse.

Then he saw the flow of red hair down her back. All sorts of alarm bells went through his mind, and he felt his heart race.

"Don't be silly," he told himself. "She's dead."

But he was drawn to look as she tossed her head and turned back to the litter. As she did so, he saw her face clearly. It was Tess. There was no doubt. She was clean and well-dressed without a smear of dirt or a smudge of wood smoke; but it was undoubtedly her—*Tess*—taller and living as one who was highborn.

Seth's confusion and dilemma were solved by a village lady just next to him. She called in a familiar way:

"Your blessings upon us, young lady!"

With well-practiced ease, Tess turned to the speaker and lightly touch her on the arm. It was at that moment, she locked eyes with Seth; and despite the years, recognition flickered in her eyes.

He watched the chain of emotions sweep over Tess's face as she said, "You! I thought you were dead!"

"Who is it?" called the stately lady. "Bella, do you know someone?"

Tess gulped and with a quick blink, all confusion left her face.

"Lady Eloise, it's just a boy whose family used to mind our horses for us when I was young." And with that grand lie, she held out a gloved hand to poor Seth who overcame his shock, fear, and embarrassment long enough to bow his head and mutter: "Milady!"

As he raised his eyes, Tess held his firmly as if to silently order him to listen and follow her lead.

"So, boy! How is your family? Do you still tend horses? Cat got your tongue!"

It took Seth a moment before he could even make a sound, garbling, "I'm learning about blacksmithing from my uncle. That's why I'm here."

"Good." Tess moved away as the horse was buckled back into the traces and then she asked, "Lady Eloise, may I have the boy brought to the castle? I would like to ask him more about the friends of my childhood."

The Lady looked Seth up and down as if he were a lizard or perhaps a centipede. Then, she half-smiled.

"Of course, Bella. We'll send a horse for him tomorrow morning with a groom. What's your name, boy? Where do you live?"

"Seth, ma'am!" He dipped his head. "I live with the black-smith—the forge in the centre of the square."

"Very well then, young man. You'll dress in your best clothes, and we will see you tomorrow. Is that clear?"

He nodded. Tess, also known as Bella, nodded, and they departed in their litter, leaving Seth gawking and gaping.

"Close your mouth, lad. You'll catch a fly!" joked a passerby.

Seth hurried to Jeb, who was involved in the intricacies of removing dents from a piece of armour. He tried to get his breath and hastily tell Jeb at the same time. It was clear that Jeb had no idea of the enormity of the changes that had occurred.

"No. You don't understand. It's all different! Even her name! They call her Bella and she's living with a noble family!"

Jeb could see that there was no future to be had in trying to work while Seth was in the state that he was in. He lent the breast plate against the forge and put down his tools. Seth explained how when he knew Tess last, she was a fierce, grubby child full of spit and cheek. Now, she was a lady-in-training.

"Jeb. What am I going to do?"

"Well, you either hide or else we'll have to borrow a cloak for you, wash your face, and pack you off to hob-nob with the gentry."

"What about the Riders? What if they see me? You know—with the girl. What if they remember?"

"Then you'll just have to be very, very careful, won't you! But remember, you are no longer the boy on crutches. Remember that."

The following morning brought disarray. Jeb had no bath. Decidedly, Seth was taken to a neighbour's where a communal copper was used to wash clothes and wash bodies. A complaining Seth was soaped, flannelled, and dried. Then, his own clothes were replaced and a borrowed cloak was thrown over his back. Through all this, Seth could see Jeb was barely able to contain his amusement. When Seth was finished, he could see the mirth in the big man's eyes threatening to boil over into outright laughter.

Sullenly, Seth asked, "What do I look like?"

"If you could wear a cap and do a flourish, you'd pass for one of them page boys." And with that, Jeb doffed his own cap, lent back on his back leg with the other outstretched before him and solemnly intoned: "Lord and Lady Muck. Assembled notables and other assorted thieves and knaves. We present to you, Sir Seth, the marquis of Forge Blacksmithing."

The household exploded into boisterous laughter as Jeb picked up tucked Seth under his arm, who all the while complained, "The shoes have to go back!"

Later, Seth sat in a state of nervous expectancy outside the forge while he harassed poor Jeb about: the passing of time, the likelihood of being forgotten, and the social niceties that might be required of him particularly if he was asked to eat with them.

"Well, I guess you say, polite like—'thanks for the grub, your worthiness,' and then you scoff everything in sight while asking for seconds." As Jeb burst into laughter, Seth realised he was no help.

Finally, a rider appeared dressed in groom's livery. He made his way to the forge.

"Are you the boy who has been summoned by Lady Eloise?"

Seth said that he was. Jeb came over, picked him up and placed him on the front of the horse with his stick.

"Look after yourself. Remember you're as good as anyone," Jeb told him in a low tone. Then, he turned to the groom. "Would you like me to come and get him?"

"Thank you, but we'll bring him back when the young lady has finished with him," the man promptly answered before hurrying the horse through the square.

"You're a lucky young man to be called for. I was called into service at about your age," the groom said.

"Is it good being 'in service'?" Seth wondered aloud.

"It's a lot better than living in a village in the mud, caring for pigs, and waiting to be called away to get killed in some battle of your lord's making."

Seth was about to say that he quite liked pigs but thought better of it.

They rode out of the town and up the hill where the castle sat like the sentinel that it was. They passed rows of soldiers and rows of beggars, then up over a guarded drawbridge and into the body of the building. They were in a walled courtyard where soldiers trained, animals were cared for, and the Duke's family lived, safe from harm. The groom dismounted, then swung about to reach up and lift Seth from the saddle.

"I'll walk you to the main doors. There'll be some-one waiting to escort you from there," the man explained.

Seth thanked him. Shortly after, they arrived before the large wooden doors that allowed entrance to the main chambers. There, sure enough, waited a lady who was formally dressed in a blue gown that fell to the floor. Without speaking, she motioned him to follow her. She led Seth to another door down an unlit hallway, knocked on it, opened it, and ushered him through. Seth didn't know what to expect, but it was worse than he could have imagined. It was a lady's room where half a dozen women, richly dressed, sat at tables, talking and working with fabrics. Around them rustled their ladies-in-waiting and their older daughters who did most of the weaving, embroidery, and tapestry that went on. He made his way almost unnoticed to where he could see a mass of bright red hair.

"Ah! The young horse boy. Bella, please present him."

Seth would have almost preferred to have been captured by the Riders again, but he rested on his stick and holding his head high, met the eyes around the room as Tess began, "Lady Eloise.

Lady Exeter. This is Seth. His family were the grooms for our family when I was young."

"When Bella lived up north before she came to live with us, before your poor family became so ill," explained the stern lady that Seth identified as Lady Eloise. "I suggest that the two of you run along to the courtyard—you know where that is, Bella. I doubt you need a chaperone. We'll let you talk, and then Bella, you'll bring Seth here to say his goodbyes. Don't be too long. You have French lessons in an hour."

Seth did a funny little bow, which brought titters from the ladies. Thankfully, Tess escorted him out a side door, down some stairs towards an area of garden.

"What are you doing here? Last time I saw you, you were in a paddock," Tess hissed at him.

"Last time I saw you didn't wear dresses; you weren't clean, and your name wasn't Bella," retorted Seth as he negotiated the last of the steps.

They sat at opposite ends of a bench that had been placed in a garden that was surrounded by walls. At one edge sat the turret and battlements that even now held soldiers on duty, on watch. As well as he could, Seth explained what had happened since they last had seen each other on a dark night in a dark forest. He didn't tell her his thoughts about the identity of the Riders or the Captain. In truth, he was more interested to find out what had happened to her.

Tess told how after avoiding the Riders she had left the village in flames and been taken in by relatives who lived a few miles away; however, they had been poor and had not liked her or the burden she represented. They had heard of a noble lady who had wanted children, but tragically, had only produced two stillborn red-headed little girls. They had seized the opportunity to pass 'Bella' on to Lady Eloise, believing they were aiding Tess and ridding themselves of another mouth to feed. They had invented a story about 'Bella' coming from a noble, yet poor family who had been devastated by the plague and then changed her name. No longer Tess, the village girl, but now Bella, a young lady-in-training.

"Lady Eloise has been very patient with me. You won't tell them, will you?" Tess implored.

Seth smiled to himself.

"I wouldn't betray someone who brought me my crutch. I don't want to scare you, but there is something you need to know."

She stared at him and at once he could see the terrified young girl being held by a rider in her wide eyes.

"What is it? Is there someone else that knows where I come from someone to betray me to Lady Eloise?"

"No. It's not like…well, it sort of is. You have to promise to tell no one. You have to *promise!*" urged Seth.

She looked around, ensuring there was no one else to see, before she spat on her hand and touched her heart as she might have done before.

Seth leant forward and checking around he whispered to her, "I think the Riders are from this castle! The Captain of the guard here is the leader of those we saw that night."

He waited to see what effect his words had upon her, and was amazed to see her flush not with excitement, but with confusion and rage.

"The one you promised to free? The one you told the lion story to? I don't believe you. You're making this up."

"I'm not. I promise!" he pleaded.

"Yes, you are! These are our friends. They're not the Riders. You're jealous that I've escaped from the village and the mud and the turnips. You're jealous that I've made a life that is good, and now you want to ruin it for me by making up some stupid story. How could a soldier of the Duke's be the leader of the Riders? It makes no sense. And to think I took your crutches to the forest for you. And this is what you do! You take your fears about the Riders and make up this story. You're no friend of mine!"

Angrily, she leapt up and fled back up the stairs, leaving Seth flabbergasted and wondering where it all went wrong.

Even as he stood open-mouthed, Tess swung back to hiss at him, "Don't even think about telling Lady Eloise about me or else…" However, she could think of nothing terrible enough and instead, screwed up her face before flouncing back up the stairs.

Seth blinked but was unable to even mumble a reply.

<h1 style="text-align:center">12</h1>

Truces and Plans

Seth sat for a moment, not knowing what to do. He had never felt so misunderstood in his whole life—and he had simply been trying to help to warn her of the probable danger. He doubted he could get her to listen to reason even if he could find her. She might just shout some more.

Fear set in when she did not return. He got to his feet and made his way out of the building, across the courtyard and out, across the drawbridge. No one challenged him.

He got halfway down the hill before the billowing, half-formed thoughts in his mind gave way to one clear one. She was still in danger of being recognised. The Captain lived here. The Riders lived here. She, too, might be recognised simply by the colour of her hair; he would not have her caught.

Daunted, but not defeated, Seth turned around and made his way back up the hill, formulating in his mind what he would say to the guards on the gate.

It was not a problem.

One said to him, "You're the boy from this morning?"

"Yes. I've left my cap in the building. My dad will kill me if I go home without it."

The guards laughed, commiserated and let him through.

Once in the courtyard, Seth waited until he saw two servants admitted. While the door was closing, he slipped in to be confronted by an older man in long flowing robes.

"And who are you?" he enquired.

"I'm Seth from the town. I came to see Lady Eloise this morning and I left my cap here."

Seth was hoping that the old man would direct him and be on his way, but instead escorted him up the stairs to the same room with the same lady's present. There was no escape. The ladies looked up at him.

Lady Eloise stared before recognising him. "Ah! Bella's friend. Seth? Bella has already gone to her lesson."

He fought for which story to tell and settled on the one that seemed most harmless.

"I know. I just remembered that…I hadn't said goodbye and thank Lady Bella."

"Well, we must reward such gestures of nobility. Therese. Please. A small coin for the young man."

He was both overwhelmed, overjoyed, and hoping that he could escape the kindness and attention as quickly as possible. He still had Tess and her French lesson to find. He did a strange, little cross between a bow and a courtesy, gathered some more chuckles, and left the room wondering how he could find her in the great mass of rooms within the castle. Seth knew he needed a story ready. He walked back, away from the hallway that led to the big doors and made his way down a maze of corridors until he heard voices up ahead. He prayed it would not be soldiers.

Relief flooded Seth when he saw that it was stewards carrying eiderdowns to a room.

"Excuse me," Seth began, "I've got a message for Lady Bella. She's new to the castle."

"Well, I could take the message to her for you," offered one of the stewards.

It was what he dreaded, but he was prepared.

He feigned a bashful smile. "It's sort of private."

The two stewards almost fell over themselves in laughter. Seth knew that laughter was a good sign.

"So young!"

"At that age I was still chasing rabbits." Again, the two of them broke into gales of mirth and fell about.

"Come, young Romeo. We'll show you the way." And with much gaiety, they showed Seth along a stairway to a small door. He was ushered in. It was a small, but empty room. There were only desks and slates. Luckily for him, they had names assigned on each one.

On Bella's he wrote, *I spoke the truth. Be careful!* and left it face down.

This time, Seth didn't stop walking until he got home to Jeb and the forge.

They ate and Seth wondered aloud if Tess would have got the message, and if so, what she would make of it.

"Law unto themselves," muttered Jeb. "Who can know what a woman will think. Do that and the gates of paradise are looking very shonky!"

Seth nodded as if he knew and understood.

Several days went by, Seth was beginning to believe that it had all been for nothing; that Tess had either not turned the slate over or had not believed him. The latter thought irked him. He hadn't lied, and he had tried to warn her. He was bad company for a few days.

On the Thursday, which was the big market day where farmers brought animals and produce from all over the country, Seth was sitting at a friend's house when he was surprised to see Jeb poke his head about the door with a smug smile.

"You've got a visitor!"

He noticed the red hair almost immediately.

"Right!" she said, her mouth set quite tight and hard. "I'm meant to be having an outing with two of the maids who are buying produce for the kitchen. Walk alongside me and pretend to be helping. You can do that, can't you?" She spoke to him as if he was an imbecile.

Seth was about to react when a look from Jeb reminded him to bite his tongue. Jeb mimed her in the background looking faintly regal and haughty, Seth had to mind not to laugh. He fell in alongside Tess and began picking up fruit, smelling it, before passing it to her.

He waited until she began, "So, why do you think it's them? How can you be sure? You could be wrong!"

Seth explained how he had recognised the Captain, and then in turn, had been forced to flee.

"These cabbages are really good, when you squeeze the head its firm and solid and the outer leaves must have some deep green in them," Tess observed thoughtfully.

They went from stall to stall. He could see that she was thinking. As they moved to pomegranates and quinces, which Seth knew little about, Tess sent the owner for fresher produce so that she could have a minute with Seth.

"Where'd you learn to write?" she asked.

"My mother, and then a lady who healed my leg."

There was a pause before she said, "I believe you. You saved my life once, and you're too stupid to make up such a huge lie."

Seth smiled. He couldn't believe how good it was to be insulted and believed at the same time.

"Can you get me into the castle?" he asked her.

With a smile, Tess told how she had already prevailed upon Lady Eloise to have Seth invited to her classics lessons, so he could help her to keep an eye on who came and went from the castle.

"Even if this is all true, what are you going to do? Who can you tell?" Tess probed.

"I don't know," shrugged Seth. "I think I have to find a way to tell the Prince."

"Tell the Prince!" She looked at him as if he had suddenly lost his wits. "You think that you're going to get to the Prince—that you'll get a message past the stewards, the guards and the advisors—that the Prince will listen to you."

Her look of disdain and dismay was striking. He felt himself fold over in the face of such derision. She stood bouncing an apple in one hand, briefly he thought she might hurl it at him.

"That's your plan, then! Is that right? To find out who they are and then to clump in with your stick and demand an audience with the Prince! That's it?"

Seth felt humiliated and embarrassed, but there was also a tiny part of him delighted to know that she was still as rude and fierce as he remembered. She hadn't become a lady quite yet; there was still some Tess left.

"I got a message to you," he sullenly defended himself.

"Oh yes! And what a brilliant way! You blunder into my French class without a clue in the world and write on a slate that anyone could have seen."

"You still got it." He was still downcast, but dogged.

She carefully placed the apple back in the stall and he noticed that her face matched her hair. He saw her clench and unclenched her hands.

"Tell me if this is true? You expect me to secret you into the castle, so that you can spy on men who you think are killers. Then, when you've gathered some sort of evidence, you plan to prove this in private audience with the Prince. This is the total of your planning. True?" Tess glared at him.

"Yes." He nodded.

"And because this is just such a wonderful well worked plan, tell me, how do you plan to get to see the Prince? Going to interrupt his French lesson? Perhaps write on his slate?"

Seth cleared his throat. "I thought that *you* could do that!"

The look of stupefaction on her face was wonderful to behold, even if a little frightening.

"Me! You thought I could do what?"

"Well, not *all* of it." Seth rolled his eyes. "But it's obvious that you know noble people, and I don't, so I thought you'd find a way. You know. Find out where the Prince was and where he goes—all that."

Tess stared at him. Seth thought it best to continue talking, as running from her didn't seem a very graceful option.

"And what? What else were you going to say?" she challenged.

"Just that I know that you're all dressed up in fancy clothes and you learn French and all that. But I also know who you are—you're Tess. And you're not really polite and hoity–toity. You're rude and fierce. And I also remember...."

Except, she had already registered what he was saying. Swiftly, she reached over, and as an aunt had once done to him, she grabbed his lips and squeezed them tight.

"Shut up!" she hissed into his face. "Just shut up!"

He did. He wanted his lips back.

A voice called. "Bella. Bella? What are you doing with the boy?"

One of the kitchen maids, open mouthed, produce in hand, stared at the scene from behind a fruit stall.

Tess could still lie with absolute confidence. "I was showing him how some women paint their lips these days. Wasn't I, Seth?"

He nodded vigorously. The blood had flowed back into his lips. He had a feeling he might escape with his life.

"Well, we'll be getting back in a moment unless you wish to stay and play with your friend. I'm not sure if Lady Eloise would like that, but..."

Tess—now acting as Bella—flung her head in a gesture of annoyance. "Play with him? It seems I'll have to put up with him in my class. You know how kindly Lady Eloise is to those who are less fortunate." And she flounced her way over to the maid. Together, they walked away.

Seth hollered after her, "Monday, then!" But if she heard, she showed no sign of it.

He went to find Jeb, more confused and exhilarated than he had felt for a long time. Jeb took one look at him.

"Trouble with your lady friend!" he announced while leaning on the arms of the huge bellows that pointed into the heart of the forge.

Seth looked at him in amazement.

"It's not magic. It's just a look us men get regularly over the years."

"What does that mean?" Seth enquired.

"It means"—Jeb looked around him—"just don't pretend that you're smarter, because even if you were, it wouldn't count. You know nothing. Do you understand? You're just a dunderhead. Don't pretend otherwise. There's an old saying that goes: every woman knows her husband is an idiot, it's just that he doesn't."

Seth didn't understand the specifics, but the general tone was sympathetic.

***

The days in between went slowly. They spent some of Seth's money to kit him out, so that he would look respectable. Sure enough, on Monday, the same groom came to collect him on horseback.

"You obviously took notice of what I said. I will advise you some more," the groom began. "Remember to be bright, but not too bright. Never, ever look as if you know more."

"Why?" enquired Seth. "I thought you'd want me to try really hard and get to be really clever."

"I do. But, remember that they're nobles! You are not. You must not look as if you're cleverer or brighter or more able than they are."

Seth asked, "Is that what you've had to do?" He twisted to look up at the man and saw a smile momentarily come across his face.

"Yes, in answer to your impertinent question, that is *exactly* what I have had to do. The family I serve are kind, generous, and dim-witted. Dividing their time between banqueting, gossip, tournaments, gossip, hunting, and then idle plotting. Beyond that, they have no imagination and no plans beyond coveting their neighbour's lands or titles. Behind the scenes, I flatter their plots and make sure that none of them gets beyond the drinking stage or are heard outside the castle."

"I thought you were a groom," ventured Seth.

Again, there was just a touch of a smile before the answer.

"Perhaps some nobleman with brains, might one day recognise my skills, and I could become a steward to a great house and be able to leave horses in stables."

Seth thought on this, "When the Prince thanks me for saving the kingdom by making me a knight, I'll need a steward."

The man laughed. "Should I wait in my present position or resign at once and wait for your word?"

Seth knew it was a joke and even if he half-understood it.

"It might take a while. Perhaps best to stay."

They both laughed. Seth felt pleased.

They rode the rest of the way in silence.

Once more inside the keep of the castle, he helped Seth down from the horse.

"You're a fine young man. Do listen to what I've said, and if you ever need a friend, my name is Hewitt," the groom introduced himself. "If I see you about the castle, I will treat you as any other boy from the village. Is that clear?"

Seth understood. He smiled. Hewitt smiled back. Afterward, they both adopted faces more akin to a groom presenting a small village boy to be received by exceedingly gracious noble folk.

As he guessed, Seth's path wasn't exactly easy. First, he was taken to Lady Eloise so that he might understand the extent of his opportunity.

"Bella has told me that you are a boy of some promise. That already, despite your humble beginnings, you have made efforts to learn to read and write. This is admirable and must be supported. Your teacher, Sharrock, is content to give you this time each week with Bella and the others. I hope you will take full advantage of this opportunity."

He'd prepared a pretty speech, but Lady Eloise waved it away.

"The greatest gratitude you can show us, is by being an attentive and willing student."

Suddenly, he was whisked away by 'Bella' to join the class, who was seemingly unaware of the tone of their last conversation.

"Just listen. Don't ask too many questions, and most of all—"

"I know. Don't look like I'm smarter than the others!" interjected Seth.

Bella stopped in mid-stride as if the thought was too preposterous for contemplation.

"I meant, don't go trying to leave class to look for clues. Right?"

He nodded.

As they got to the door, she hung back a moment. "There is a troop of horseman preparing to go out soon."

Seth's interest picked up at once. "How do you know?"

But as if knowing what her words would do, she just smiled inscrutably at him before opening the door and leading him in.

This was a real class as Seth had always imagined, described by his mother when she was a privileged young lady from humble beginnings, who had been given learning opportunities by a very benevolent employer.

It was a large, airy room with open windows that allowed the light and the wind in. There were rows of tables and benches neatly arranged. Seth analysed there might have been a dozen children there, sitting at the tables with slates. At the front of the room, there sat a very old man, dressed in flowing robes whose grey hair almost covered his back and his beard down his chest. It was the same man who had showed Seth into the castle on that first day.

"Ah! Young man, we've been expecting you! Please. Take a seat. No. No! Not with the young ladies, but with the other young men. We can't have you fraternizing when you're meant to be studying. There. Yes. Sit there. There is a slate in front of you."

Seth sat and tried not to notice that the other children were obviously staring at him.

"Staring is rude," he heard Bella hiss and heads turned back to slates.

"We are following the path of the great wars between Troy and Greece," instructed the old teacher. "I do not expect you to read in Greek—*yet*. I was reading to you the extract that comes after Hector, the great Trojan warrior is killed in battles by Achilles. His father, Priam, comes to Achilles to plead for the return of his son's body."

Seth's heart skipped a beat. He knew these stories. His mother had told them to him on the long days when he was recovering from another of his wheezing attacks. He had learnt of the great war between Greece and Troy.

"'…And overpowered by memory both men gave way to grief. Priam wept freely for man-killing Hector, throbbing, crouching before Achilles' feet,'" recited the older man. "Why do they weep together? They are enemies, remember!"

No one spoke. Seth knew to hold his tongue. His heart gave a small flutter, he knew this bit. They had played it out—he and his mother. It was tempting to volunteer, but he remembered Hewitt's advice.

"Come. Why would enemies sit with each other and weep? It was after all, Achilles who had just slain Hector. Why would he weep with Hector's father? Why would Achilles weep with Hector's body still in his tent?"

Still, there was silence, Seth felt the teacher's gaze sweep the room. Seth knew what must follow.

"Young man. The boy from the village! Do you have a name?"

"Seth."

"Seth, a good name. Well, Seth. Enlighten us. Why would Achilles weep with Priam?"

Seth's mind was racing. Hewitt's advice rang clear in his mind, but his natural wish was to answer so as not to seem dim and, besides, he knew the answer.

"Sir. Because Achilles knew that Hector had been a great warrior, even if he had killed his friend."

The moment Seth added the final sentence; he realised that he had blundered.

Now here was a very different silence in the room.

Eventually, that startled look left the old teacher's face and he enquired almost casually, "Well, well. Young Seth, is it? Please tell us, where have you come across the works of Homer before? But no, I am putting the cart before the horse. Who was Achilles' friend that Hector killed?"

Through tight clenched teeth, Seth answered, "Patrocles."

"And what was the manner of his death? Come, tell us! Don't be shy."

"He dressed up in Achilles' armour to try and frighten the Trojans back from their ships."

The old man raised his forehead and smiled.

By now, Seth was petrified, yet also swelling with the joy of being able to answer and not appear dumb. Not only might he be asked more questions, but now he had done just what Hewitt had told him *not* to do. He had drawn attention to himself, he had begun by looking brighter than the other students.

"Right on both accounts. And your manner of coming across Homer's tale is no business of ours. But it is pleasing. To return to Hector in his tent with Priam, who had come to ask for his son's body back. The Greeks loved drama. Let us now pretend that we are all going to be Priam and ask for Hector's body. What would we say? I need a volunteer or else I shall choose you all, one by one. Who will be Priam, King of Troy? A father pleading for the body of his son!"

One of the older boys raised his hand.

"Ah! Please. Stand in your seat and exhort the great Achilles."

The young man cleared his throat. "Oh, great and noble Achilles. I have come to beg for the body of my son so that his mother and sisters might bathe the body and prepare it for proper burial. I hope you will grant this!" Then he sat.

"Quite good. Well tried. Don't you think?"

The class agreed.

"I liked, 'Oh, great and noble...' And you remembered about the preparation of the body. A good start. Suitably respectful! But it was a little short." The old teacher smoothed his beard, continuing, "Let us ask ourselves if we were Achilles, all of us—would we have granted Hector's body back to Priam? Would you? Bella. Tell us!"

The class knew it was a well-weighted teacher trap, but there was no way around it.

"I wouldn't have given the body back," Bella stated.

"Ah! Not moved by your classmate's appeal. Well obviously, *you* could do better."

"Well. I would have offered—"

But he cut across her. "No. No. You must be Priam. Come, Miss Bella. You are Priam, begging for your son's body. You are not asking for a loan of a potato or for a comb to be returned. Use the language. We are all given this gift. Even master Reece on his eloquent days."

Bella stood, breathed deeply, coloured red and began.

"Achilles. I know you are a great warrior. You had to be to kill my own son. As a great warrior, then I know that above all else you love your honour. In the name of honour, I ask you as Hector's father to release his body to my care, so that he may be buried with honour, and Achilles' name will be remembered not just as a warrior, but as someone who loved honour above all else!"

The teacher applauded alongside the whole class.

"Well. My! My! What a speech! That would turn Achilles' head if ever it was going to be. The appeal to his vanity! The appeal to how he would be remembered for posterity. Well done. Well done, indeed! You may sit, Bella."

Seth beamed at his friend's cleverness.

"Master Sharrock, I was wondering how our village boy would ask for the body. If he had any other ideas?"

The boy who asked, Reece, was smarting a little from the jibe. He was the Duke's son and was not happy about the prospect of seemingly clever servant children.

The teacher was no fool, nor did he allow bullying in his class.

He turned to Seth and quite gently enquired, "Seth. You have been challenged to come up with an answer, but you do not need to answer if you don't wish to. Normally, I oversee any challenges that are issued in this class. Is that clear, Mister Reece, Duke's son or not Duke's son. Respect and manners are essential. Paramount. Do I make myself clear? It is not an honourable task in life to make the lives of others, miserable. One day you will rule, and your task will be to take care of your subjects."

"My father says that my task is to rule strongly so that my subjects will respect and fear me. That is what he says matters!" retorted Reece.

"Does he, then? Well, he is a Duke. And Dukes should know. Seth? Do you wish to answer?"

Seth felt caught between two rocks. He didn't want to anger this boy now that it was declared he was the Duke's son, but he also did not wish to let it go.

Perhaps if he did in a quiet way... "I could only think that he might call on the gods."

Again, there was that buzz, then silence that Seth despaired he had blundered again. He saw that eyes flashed, and not with admiration.

Sharrock considered. Finally, he spoke, "This is a good answer, Seth. However, as with Bella, I ask you not to describe Priam, but to *be* him. To be fair to all of us, then I must ask you to stand and evoke the gods."

Seth saw the look of dismay and fear on Bella's face, and he considered saying that he couldn't when he noticed the smirk on Reece's face. That was it. Consequences would be as they would. He would startle that smirk.

He rested his hand on the bench and addressed him, "Achilles. You are a great warrior. You have slain my son and put Troy to siege. The gods have smiled on your courage and skills, but the gods dislike vanity and pride. Great leaders must be more than warriors and do more than just inspire fear. They must show brains and understanding. Then the gods would truly love you, as they loved Hector."

Seth's voice rose and gathered strength as he spoke. He wasn't sure where the words came from. He barely recognised them as his own. He had a flash of standing in a forest glade years before, standing before a horse and rider and feeling the strange power of words come to him.

The mocking went from Reece's eyes as Seth warned him about pride. He even coloured and dropped his gaze. In that moment, Seth discerned although he had won, he had also made an enemy who would not easily forget this form of defeat.

"Well done, Seth," Sharrock said quietly. "We have heard some excellent examples this morning, from all of you. Hector's body has been returned. Now, I will read on. Your task is to listen."

The rest of the class went quickly, but Seth was aware of the anger he had stirred in the heart of the Duke's son. His sense of triumph evaporated as he realised that by his actions, he had probably made it harder to do what he wished, which was to seek out answers and clues in as secretive a way as he could muster.

At the end of the class, he was anxious to be away, but the teacher waylaid him.

"Seth. If I could have a word! Everyone else, goodbye. Yes. Even you, Bella. Goodbye."

Sharrock motioned for Seth to come and sit by him.

"I have a boy who helps me with my tasks. He stays with me for several years before he moves on to his own position. My present one is due to do just that in a month or so. Perhaps, you might like to take over his vacant job?"

Seth didn't know what to think. He was dumbfounded.

"What would I have to do? It's just that I live with Jeb, who is a blacksmith and he's been very good to me."

"And you'd be sad to leave him?" he enquired. "This is good. It means you're loyal. I have many things I have to do, some of it is slow and painstaking; copying documents to make copies for records, copies of legal documents. This I do, as well as my teaching. My assistant helps me to do this, and in return I give him free tuition, clothes, and board. Sometimes my work is in one location, and at other times, I must travel from place to place. I spend another two months here, and then I go to court."

Seth couldn't contain himself. "Do you mean to the Royal Court? Do you mean to the Prince?"

"Well, we have hit a rich vein, haven't we? Unsure whether to assist a learned teacher, but suddenly excited about being in the company of royalty. Perhaps I have underestimated you, Seth?"

The boy looked confused and unhappy. "No. No. It's not like that. It's just that, that I always wanted to see the Prince because my mother met the King when she worked as a lady-in-waiting as a young girl."

Seth toyed with the idea of telling what he knew but decided against it.

"Thank you for the offer."

"Seth, we'll keep it as a secret between us. You consider it and I'll see how you take to my classes and to this way of life. It's very different to living with a blacksmith in a village. You understand that?" Sharrock raised a brow.

Seth nodded.

"Be off now. I've no doubt young Bella will be not too far away. If you have trouble with Reece, then you will tell me. I may be just a teacher, but I am not without influence."

The teacher had been correct. Seth had only made it to the main corridor when Bella darted out from an adjoining passage.

He was expecting for her to be angry with him, but she took his arm and led him down the stairs to the garden courtyard where they had talked just a week before.

She remained patient. She waited until he had sat down before she began, "Well. What was that about? Are you in trouble? You always seem in trouble. You're so stupid."

Seth sighed. *Why was she always so mean to him?*

"I need to know about the horsemen first!" Seth exclaimed.

13

Plans

S eth took a deep breath. "I'm not in trouble. Where are the horsemen?"

"I saw them last night. I saw the man they called the Captain. It was him. There was lots of movement about the stables."

"They must be going out on another raid," Seth suspected. "Now we just need to catch them coming back."

Bella looked at him intently. "Is this like getting an audience with the Prince?"

Seth ignored her jibe, instead sharing how Sharrock had offered him a role and that he saw that as a way to the Prince.

"I don't want to leave Jeb and Hestor. They're my friends. They've all that I've got. Except you, of course. But…well, I *think* you're my friend." As Seth thought aloud, he found that he'd wandered into yet another ambush, this one of his own making. He turned crimson as Bella examined him with a look of deep puzzlement.

"Seth. What is wrong with you? Why wouldn't I be your friend? You saved my life. You burst out of that hiding place, all covered in leaves like a crazy forest goblin. How could I forget that?"

Seth was feeling better and better about this up until his comparison to a goblin.

"You'd brought my crutches back to me. That was brave!"

"I just wanted to see how far you'd got." Bella grinned, cheekily.

As she made light of it, Seth was about to argue with her, when around the corner of the colonnade, came Reece.

"The orphan and the village cripple," he sneered.

Perhaps it was not well-thought out. Perhaps they could have tried talking first, but it didn't smack of careful fore-thought. They went to attack him, Bella with stones from the ground and Seth with his stick.

Who knows what would have happened next if there hadn't been an unlikely intervention.

Seth found his arm stilled by the man he least wished to be physically close to in the whole world.

"Steady there!" smiled the Captain, who in checking Seth, also stationed himself between Reece and Bella's arm.

Seth gasped as he waited for recognition, torture and eventual decapitation. Luckily, he was mistaken.

"Lord Reece, do take yourself out of range before I have to worry about your safety. You can leave me to deal with these," commanded the Captain.

Reluctantly, Reece withdrew with his two flunkies in tow while still mouthing insults.

"Well, what is this about?" came the Captain's low timbre.

Seth could feel his breathing begin to wheeze for the first time in ages. He prayed that Bella could carry it off.

"He's just a pest. Because we're brighter than him, he thought he'd be rude. That's all!" Bella explained.

Seth was amazed to see that this much feared and in-domitable soldier was actually amused by what she said.

"But he's the Duke's son. He's an important person. Surely you don't want to make an enemy of one so powerful?" The Captain raised a dark brow.

Seth drew breath.

Bella simply said, "Friends are people you like."

He thought the Captain would burst into laughter, but the soldier checked himself. "Well, such fine sentiments." He gave the pair a strange look. "Do I know you? You both seem familiar."

Seth took a breath, whereas Bella was in full stride, saying with ease, "I am Lady Eloise's handmaiden. I am staying here at the Duke's pleasure. This—this boy is from the village. He is being allowed to study with us."

"Ah! I thought I knew you both. Well, that's that. Do try not to attack Lord Reece. I serve his father, you see. You will both promise me."

The Captain looked at both of them in turn. Reluctantly, they both nodded. This time, he really did smile. After ruffling Seth's hair, he gestured a serious mock bow to Bella. Still chuckling, he withdrew to the castle. By some miracle, they had not been recognised.

Seth and Bella were dumbfounded.

"How is it that he's so nice?"

They got no further. Bella was called for by Lady Eloise.

"I have to go. I'll try to keep an eye out. There are still lots of horses being shod in the stables. I still don't understand if he's the leader. He seems so—lovely! Not cruel at all."

"Maybe he's cruel and lovely. I don't know!" Helplessly, Seth shrugged.

Bella made faces at him as she skipped up the stairs.

Seth was careful on his way out. He had no wish to run into Reece again. Hewitt was not around.

He walked back to the square and to the sound of the forge. He had lots to tell.

That night as Jeb snored, Seth lay awake worrying about what had been discussed. He knew Jeb was right. He just didn't want to give up on something he had begun, but the thought of losing more people in his life made him shudder.

The following morning, Seth asked Jeb, "If the horsemen were out at the moment, then how would they come back? They couldn't just ride in through the gates still covered in grime and battle and wearing their capes. How would that be?"

Seth stayed close to the forge for the next day. He watched as Jeb cautiously put it about that he had heard there were horses moving about at night. He did it in the style of a man who makes his living working with horses and had a right to know about the movements of large numbers of horses, and their hooves that might need shoeing.

Seth thought as he went about his normal tasks. He washed clothes. He went to the market and bought fresh food for their meals. He prepared and made simple soups or stews that Hestor and Jeb had taught him to cook.

He walked to lumber merchants to get prices on the wood that was necessary for their heating, cooking, and to keep the forge going as Jeb worked. Seth knew lots of people now and he felt easy among them, not like he had felt at the castle. He did not want to exchange his life at all. This felt good. He felt safe and not alone.

It was late in the afternoon. Jeb was closing down the fire for the day, ensuring that he placed hardwood blocks in the centre of it, so that it would hold its heat in the night, when the first information came back to them. A villager on the outskirts of the town came to tell Jeb that he'd heard it told, by no one in particular, that single horsemen or small groups had been see entering the castle by the narrow path at the back of the castle and mostly at night.

"Can't say for sure and I can't say who told me, but it's happened half a dozen times in the last year. Just a rumour. Mind you. Might be nothing to it!" Then, the villager was gone.

"Folks are mighty cautious these days," observed Jeb. "Good right to be, I reckon. So…Seth. It might be that we know which road they use, but how is that going to help us? You're not going to get people opening their doors to look out at night. Not with this going on."

"Jeb, how would you organise it if you were the Riders? What would you do to make sure that you weren't caught?"

The older man pondered for a moment. "Well, I reckon that they couldn't risk coming into the castle, even the back way dressed as the Riders. Too risky. Also, they couldn't be seen to be arriving back from anywhere just as soon as there'd been another raid. So, I think they must store their gear and wait for a few days, and then maybe just ride back through the forest gate as if they've been out searching. How's that sound?"

Seth grinned. "That's what I thought, too. If that's right, then we have to find where it is. Then we'd have real proof to take to someone. Not just our word."

"When are you planning to find it? We can't go traipsing across the countryside. We don't have horses."

"Jeb, maybe I can talk Hewitt into it."

The following day, Seth returned to the castle for his next class. Hewitt was punctual as usual. Seth dreaded what he knew must come. They were halfway to the castle before the groom spoke to him.

"I have heard that you may not be taking my advice all that seriously, Master Seth."

Seth knew what was coming. He tried to deflect it.

"I couldn't help it. He's just such a…" He was searching for a word that he could use in front of the groom.

"…A dolt, or perhaps…buffoon. They may be words you would think, though not say, but that is the whole *point* of what

I've been telling you! There will always be noble idiots who think that they are better than others. Better than you, Seth. You must not respond. That is the trick that you must learn. What would happen to me if I took offence every time His Lordship is angry with me because his favourite horse is lame on account he rode it when he shouldn't? Or when no one has told him some piece of gossip that is common knowledge to all but the deaf or the stupid? What would happen?"

"You'd have no job!"

"Exactly! You must not make an enemy of Reece. As you quite rightly point out, the boy is a dolt and a bully— heaven help us, he will be our next Duke. So, do not antagonise him further," advised Hewitt. "I've heard that you did a wonderful job of insulting and threatening him while pretending to study Homer."

Seth gaped, impressed. "You really do hear everything, don't you?"

"It's my job. As well as horses."

"You don't like horses, do you?"

"Not much. Never did. Big stupid creatures who mess wherever they go," Hewitt replied.

"So, I'd better hurry up and become a knight, yes?"

"The sooner the better!"

Seth saw the tiny touch of the smile at the corner of his mouth.

They were crossing the drawbridge before Seth dared ask what had been on his mind. "Hewitt. You really do know what goes on in the castle, don't you? I mean, you really do!"

"I boast. But yes, I do. It's my job. It's how I am of use to my noble Lord and Master. Why? What terrible secret do you want to know?"

Without hesitating, Seth told him of his fears concerning the identity of the Riders. As he did, he felt Hewitt react in a way that made icy shudders begin up his backbone.

It was as if Seth had slapped the groom on the face or cursed. The blood drained from his face and his lips tightened into a thin, taut line. "What? What did you ask?"

Seth, now scared that he had put lives at risk, asked again, "Hewitt. I have to trust you. Could the Captain lead the Riders?"

Hewitt glanced about him. Then, he called to a boy fetching wood.

"Boy! Tell Sharrock that Seth will be late for class as I have something I need to show him." Before Seth could protest or even be fully afraid, Hewitt galloped his mount back through the drawbridge. Turning sharply, he raced the horse down the hill and into the forest that bordered the castle. By now, Seth was terrified.

He's going to kill me, he thought. *I'm so stupid! Jeb tried to warn me.*

Hewitt rode to a clearing where the remains of a stone wall cut across the land. He leapt off and hauled Seth after him.

"Now!" The man had never looked so enraged as he grasped Seth. "What do you know about the castle's horseman? Why do you ask me a question like that? Tell me, boy!"

Seth trembled but knew there was no point in lying. He had gone beyond the point.

"I know that they're the Riders," he said simply.

Hewitt had dropped all pretence. He walked over to the wall. He waved his arms in the air. He picked up a rock and hurled it with an oath into the decaying wall where it smashed with a dull thud into tiny fragments.

Then he came back and squatted alongside Seth.

"How do you know that? You can't know that!"

Seth had no choice but to tell him the whole story from forest terror to village recognition. As he did, Hewitt stroked his chin, staring at him.

"Do you know how dangerous it is to know that? Do you know how risky it is to do what you just did? How do you know that *I'm* not a Rider myself? How do you know that I'm not the one who looks after their horses? Eh? How do you know? *I* could be your *death."*

Seth trembled but managed to speak, "I think because you're a good man. You wouldn't do that!"

Hewitt shook his head.

"Sometimes we only see what we want to…" he said it quietly and sadly with his head in his hands.

Seth was unnerved by it. He had expected anger, possibly violence, but not this. It was as if he no longer existed and that Hewitt was in some strange, private, pained world of his own. He was scared because he didn't know what would happen next.

Eventually, Hewitt stood up and without looking at Seth, he gestured him to follow him. He walked him to the wall, half-fallen as it was.

"Seth. Do you know what this is?"

"It's an ancient wall. It's where they tried to hold back the tribes. That's what you told me!"

"It's the spot on which your forebears finally agreed that no one else would occupy this land again," explained Hewitt.

"But it did happen. I mean, when they came from across the sea."

"Yes. They came and ever since they have been the Lords and Barons of this land. Do you know who the Prince is?"

"He's the son of the great King—Theobald!"

"The Great Theobald! Oh yes! And do you know who the Duke is a descendent of?"

Seth shook his head.

"He's a Saxon." Hewitt pressed on, "His wife is a direct descendent of he who was High King before the invasion. He is the last descendent of the great Saxon Kings. Do you understand?"

Again, Seth shook his head. "Do you mean that the Duke should be the King?"

As he looked at Hewitt, he suddenly saw a man who seemed not to know anything.

In response to Seth's question, he shrugged and then murmured, "Who knows? He'd certainly like to be. Who knows what is right? At one time, to put a Saxon back on the throne seemed a just and noble aim." Then he was back into his reverie.

"I have to go to my class, please."

It was as if nothing had been said. Hewitt helped Seth mount and then climbed up himself.

As they re-entered the castle, he spoke to Seth, "You must promise me that you will tell no one of this. *No one*. There are terrible things happening. It does not help for you and I to be killed with it. Don't breathe a word. We will talk more when we are sure it is safe. Trust no one."

Seth floated to his class, still unsure what he had done. The clever, always amusing groom with his sly humour and worldly advice had become a stricken, terrified man.

He knocked on the classroom door and admitted himself on the command!

"Enter!"

Seth noticed no one, lost in a daze, made his way to his place where he tried to settle so that he could pay attention. He listened to more Homer. At the end of it, Sharrock stopped and turning to Seth asked him where he had been that required his absence.

"The groom knew we were studying the Greek wars and he wished to show me a wall nearby that people say was built to hold the tribes at bay. He thought it might be a good spot to take the class to see," Seth excused easily.

"Perhaps if the weather permits, we could take our lunch and investigate this place. No. Not today. Today we must see Troy destroyed by the Greeks—by a famous subterfuge—a Greek gift."

The class passed with Seth in a private daze. He waited for Bella after the class. He went to talk. He had so much to tell her, but she cut him off.

"Listen. I've only got a moment. I overheard them talking. A troop of horseman, led by the Captain left today. I'll try to watch for them coming home."

Seth insisted that she listen to him. "I can't tell you now. Just don't do anything that might get you caught. Don't try unless you're absolutely safe. It's really dangerous. Can you come with the maid's tomorrow morning? I'll tell you all I know then. Just trust me! There's been lots happening. All I can tell you is to be really, really careful."

"Can't you tell me more?" Bella pressed.

"No. No. I'm not being mean. It's just not very safe at all. I'll see you tomorrow!"

As he left, he looked for Hewitt but there was no sign of the troubled groom.

Again, Seth had but one aim, and that was to escape the castle and find safety by Jeb's forge.

14

Plans and Plots and
Dangers

Jeb sat and ate by the light of the fire. He chewed at a rate that normally infuriated Seth.

"Does you good to chew your food. And there's no joy in eating if you don't taste it." That's what he normally said as he slowly, laconically chewed his way through his meal. This time, Seth didn't mind at all, as he knew Jeb was thinking.

"It was like you told him something he really didn't want to know. He might have his reasons. Who knows? But the main worry is; will he betray you or will he trust that you'll stay quiet? That's the real worry."

They talked and argued, but got no further than speculation when a strange thing happened. Someone knocked at their door. Strange, because people didn't call on each other after sunset unless it was very important, and strange because mostly their friends didn't knock—they just arrived. At once, both of them were wary and apprehensive.

Jeb raised himself to his full height and laid a hand on his forge hammer. He spoke quietly to Seth, "If this is trouble and they come through the door, I'll make a path with this, and you make it away into the night. Right? Do as I say!"

Seth tried to argue. Even without crutches he doubted that he'd get far. But it was no time to argue. Jeb swung the door back and tensed his hand on the hammer.

For a moment the doorway was empty, the darkness flooded in and then Hewitt stood before them.

"I'm not here to harm anyone. Is it safe to talk here?"

Jeb drew him inside the door, peered into the darkness and then left to check the surroundings. "I didn't reckon you've been followed. Better to be safe than sorry, though. Jeb!" He offered his hand.

Hewitt took it. "No doubt young Seth has told you about me."

"He's mentioned a thing or two, but I'd reckon your being here means there's more to say. Please. Take a seat. I'm sorry there's nothing I can offer you to drink!"

Hewitt dismissed it easily. "I've come because after what Seth told me, I need to find out what you know and what I have found out. Maybe in that we can find some way to move forward. I only know what the lad has told me, and once I was convinced, then it all seemed to make sense."

"How? In what way?" Jeb asked.

"That there's treason afoot. Treason of the worst sort," the other man stated.

Hewitt stretched his long legs out in their small hut and began his story. It was one of noble wishes and sentiments that had been derailed and changed by greed and ambition. There had always been a group of Saxons who had wished to take back their country from the invaders, but they had wished to do so without plunging their country into further grievous civil wars.

They had waited and plotted for the time, when an unpopular king was on the throne, therefore they would move swiftly to unseat him. An alliance of Saxons and some northern knights waited in readiness until the time would be right. But plans had begun to change and unravel.

"After talking with your young Seth here, this is what I think has happened. The Duke must have grown impatient. He wished to destabilise the country and make the Prince more unpopular. His impatience must have grown more so and has created this scourge to create havoc and prepare for the Prince to be dethroned. The Captain was handpicked. He's a mercenary who has fought all over the world. He fights for who pays him. No loyalty, except to who pays him. They brought him in because they were probably worried that under another commander, they might be squeamish about killing innocent people."

"So, you're stuck," Jeb concluded. "Wanted a Saxon King and you've got a monster."

Hewitt picked slivers of bark from a twig and hurled them into the fire. He seemed totally absorbed in the task he was involved with, before replying, "It seems so."

Seth was nothing if not persistent. "What would happen if the Prince really knew what was happening? Like, if he believed you that the Riders were being organised by the Duke, what would he do? I think you should tell the Prince!"

"And what about the chance to put a Saxon King back on the throne? What about the hope of that?" Hewitt countered.

"You can't make him King. You just can't. You can't have a bad king," reasoned Seth.

Jeb hesitated and then muttered, "…From the mouths of babes…" which Seth didn't quite understand.

Hewitt looked about as grey as Seth had seen him. He watched the man rise, striding towards the exit. Hewitt growled, "You think that's the answer, don't you? To me, it's not that simple! We've planned this for years. Believed in it for years. Just one strike, and finally—freedom."

Suddenly, he hesitated at the door and turned to them. "One thing you can be sure of, neither of you will come to any harm as a result of what I do or say. Whatever happens, we need proof, not theories."

And then he was gone.

For a long while, Jeb sat and stared into the fire.

"I suppose he thought it would be doing us a favour by dropping in and telling us all that…some favour!" he snorted.

Seth remained quiet and waited. He knew Jeb hadn't finished.

"All very well for him with his fancy ideas about Kings and all that. As if that mattered. Poor folk don't have it any better under whoever is King. It's all the same…"

Seth sighed. "I understand that the Prince isn't much of a ruler, but at least he doesn't go about killing innocent people that he's meant to be looking after."

Jeb nodded. "Aye! I'm with you on that. It's just that…I want to be a blacksmith and not get involved in things that don't concern me. I'm not a coward, Seth. I just want to live my life, simple-like. Do you know what I mean?"

Seth moved in closer to the fire, until his knees almost touched those of the older man. "At one time, all I wanted was to get my leg better. I used to dream about one day that I wouldn't have any crutches. And now, it seems like I have to keep following the Riders because…"

"…Because it's your fate," Jeb finished it for him. The big man put an arm about Seth's head and enclosed him in a gentle bear hug. "You're a one! Sounds like you're getting to track 'em down? Find out where they hide and take it to the Prince. Am I right? Tell me if I'm close?"

Seth didn't even try to disengage. He felt snug and warm where he was. He murmured from Jeb's armpit, "How do you think I can get to follow them?"

Jeb did another huge sigh.

"I think you're right, that your groom might be offering you a ride sooner than you think. He's no fool."

***

Next day saw Seth up and waiting expectantly for Bella. He was impatient, and fortunately, he didn't have to wait long. Stalls were still being set up, wares were being put on display as Seth saw the party from the castle appear. Two kitchen maids carrying large baskets were accompanied by a soldier, alongside them was a familiar blaze of red hair.

Seth began moving towards them, when to his horror, he saw that the tall, stately figure of Lady Eloise accompanied her. His heart sank.

At once, he knew that something was wrong. He could see it in the way each member of the party walked and spoke. Normally, the girls were relaxed and pleased to be outside the confines of the castle, they would joke and laugh with the small stall owners and soldiers. Now, they walked with straight backs, their heads held demurely down.

Bella held a basket and said nothing as she walked, while alongside her, Lady Eloise strode grimly. Seth looked for and caught her eye. In her look, he read that he should not talk to her, but move to the north end of the market. He didn't need further prompting. He turned and made his way.

From the stiff posturing of the party, it was obvious that Lady Eloise didn't intend to buy vegetables; she was there to chaperone her young charge and keep an eye on her. This could only mean that something had changed, Seth guessed that it was not for the better.

Bella was anticipating that, despite Lady Eloise's good intentions, the novelty of the market would distract her. It did. As Seth watched nearby, he saw Lady Eloise stop and pick up small handcrafts made by farm craftsman. She raised small carved dolls to better examine them, and in that pause, Bella moved past the two kitchen maids toward another booth where Seth stood.

The small group stopped by the gate, Seth could make out several horses and the shapes of men moving alongside them. He heard a voice say, "Ease on. You've done well, lad. We're here now, we're home."

There was no need to knock or signal. They were obviously expected. Seth heard the stays on the gate removed and a figure with a light appeared.

By this faint light, Seth could count the half dozen horses; four of which, had been ridden by upright soldiers who now swung from their saddles to the ground. The two others were occupied by figures who slumped over their horse's necks like large inert sacks. From one of these, the moans erupted again.

"How are they?" asked the figure carrying a lantern.

"Not good. This lad will live. An arrow through the leg. But the other one—no! A stomach wound."

"It's a disaster. They're not meant to fight back."

"Soldiers back from wars," replied the first voice. "They were staying in the village and still had their weapons with them. It was a bloody mess; I can tell you. The rest have stayed behind to patch up."

"Let's get' em inside. Both of them," the figure urged. "We'll have to make up some story about the dead one."

Two bodies passed through the gateway. Seth watched the gate barred and the small procession led by the lantern bearer make its way to the inner gate. Meanwhile, tired horses were turned to take another path that led to eventual rest.

Silence returned to the night. Seth waited as long as he could before he looked over to Jeb.

Jeb whispered across to him, "Stretch your muscles first. Don't try to climb down yet. Do the little exercises like I told you. Then, follow me down."

Seth did as he'd been taught. He exercised his hands and legs, and then massaged his limbs until he felt they might work.

Slowly, and quite painfully, he made his way to the final bole and there, Jeb waited on the ground to lift him down, gesturing them to be quiet. Carrying their nets and cages, they made their way slowly and carefully back home. Once there, they both added wood to the fire and then began to talk about what they'd discovered.

"Well, then. That's put the cat amongst the pigeons and no mistake. They didn't count on them fighting back. Now they got a dead one, and one who will take some explaining."

"Jeb, do you think they're more likely to try and hurry their plans and kill the Prince?"

"Could be, lad. No doubt we'll know more when your Hewitt pays a visit."

Seth straightened. "Do you think he will?"

"Oh. Aye. He'll be more anxious than ever before." Nodding, Jeb continued, "Mark my words, he'll be here before too long. I've a feeling that if your Mister Hewitt is what you say he is, then he'll be making some hard decisions about now. And now, it's time you and I turned in. I know you spent most of your time up the tree snoring, so you'd better add to it."

They were almost asleep before Seth thought to ask Jeb, "Was I really snoring?"

"Something chronic. Thought it would bring the guards. Like a wild pig—that's what it reminded me of. Snort! Snort!"

Seth smiled to himself. "Not too many pigs climb trees, do they?"

"Not that I know of. And very few boys live long when they keep asking questions late at night!"

Early the next morning, Seth was ready for his class. But this day, Hewitt was there almost as soon as he had eaten breakfast. He didn't wait.

"I've got permission to take you to follow the ruins. I'm actually not going to do that. I have thought on what you said, and with or without you, I intend to try and find where the Riders are using as a halfway house."

Jeb and Seth exchanged glances.

"Seth, I think your phrase, 'you can't make a bad man king,' has stuck in my gullet ever since. It may do no good, but we need to try and alert the Prince. Who knows, it might wake him up. I'm happy to look on my own, it may be less dangerous for you both, but my excuse at the castle is that I'm helping your class to find ruins."

Jeb turned to the boy. "Do you want to go, Seth?"

Seth nodded vigorously.

"I've no intention of trying to fight anyone. My task is to try and gain some proof that we can take to the Prince. If he believed us at the moment and searched the castle, he'd find nothing beyond the ordinary. He has to be shown evidence he can't ignore."

"What do you have in mind?" asked Seth.

"I don't know. Perhaps to find the place and have the Riders caught red-handed."

"Do they know that I'm with you?"

"And not in class, yes. Jeb, I will look after your young friend to the very best of my abilities!"

"Good luck to both of you, then."

So, mounted on Hewitt's horse, they made their way from the square to follow the road that Seth had seen a party of wounded men creeping back along the previous night.

15

The Search

They took the road into the forest and past the village, in which, there lived a most reluctant informer who had dared tell Jeb of the passing Riders. Seth had never travelled on a horse for any distance before, and he found that like sitting in trees, there were some activities that were tedious and body numbing. They rode for three hours, and by now, had travelled beyond the small villages or occasional farmlet to be in the heart of the forest.

Seth wanted to stop for a rest, but he knew that they had precious little time to look.

Eventually, they came to a fork that was not at all clear which path had been most used.

"We'll stop. The horse needs it and so do I," Hewitt stated. "Which path? I haven't got time to take the wrong one."

As they stretched and the horse cropped grass, they both bent to examine each pathway for signs of heavy use. There had been only light rain, and the soil gave little away.

"I don't know. There's no way of knowing."

Seth was reminded of something, but he wasn't quite sure what it was. It was just like the brush of wind on your face after a long time of being indoors.

Finally, it was the movement of a small bird, an ordinary little sparrow that sparked his memory. It reminded him of a blue wren on a different day and a different way of knowing.

He was hesitant to suggest it, but eventually he plucked up the courage to speak, "Hewitt. This might seem silly, but…"

"But what? If you have an idea, then let's have it."

"Hestor. She was the lady I lived with in the forest. She used to tell me to look and listen. That if you wanted to know which direction to go in the forest, then you had to ask the forest."

Hewitt looked at him as if he were crazed. "Ask the forest?"

"I know it sounds odd. But it used to work."

Hewitt shrugged. "Well, we can try. What do we do?"

"Just ask for the way to be shown!"

"Out loud? Do you want me to face a tree or something?"

"No. Just ask in your head. And see what happens."

"Shame to ask. What am I looking for?"

"Shh! You have to trust. You have to wait. Sometimes it's just a little thing. There! There! Do you see it?" Seth asked in a hushed voice, full of excitement.

He pointed and Hewitt could see it.

A few hundred yards down the track to the right, a large fox had padded out onto the path and was warily watching from a distance. As they watched, it took scent of them and began ambling its way along the track!

"See. Did you see? I told you it worked!"

"So, let me understand this. You're saying that on the basis of seeing a fox on the right road that we should say that this was a sign and follow it?" Hewitt asked, bewildered.

"Yes. That's how it works!"

"And will the fox lead us to the spot where the Riders dismount or will we have to find that ourselves?"

For a moment Seth didn't realise he was joking with him, and then realised.

"You only get pointed in the direction. The rest, we have to do," he replied.

Hewitt shook his head. "Well, it makes us much sense as spitting into the wind. Let's try it."

They walked the horse a little way and then remounted. Then it became a case of Seth wishing and wishing that round the next bend or over the hill there would be a sign or something. However, the deeper they went into the forest the less likely it seemed. After they had gone a ways, Seth could feel Hewitt's impatience and his concern for the horse.

"If we don't come across something soon, we'll have to turn back!"

Seth felt his heart sink. What if he was wrong? What if he'd led him down the wrong path? Perhaps he'd missed the signs.

"We'll go to the next turn. If there's nothing, we'll have to stop," Hewitt declared.

Seth wanted to call out not to stop, that they'd find it, that the forest never lied; but all he could do was hope. It was to no avail. At the next bend, the road stretched out a mile or more, and there was nothing in sight except the road and the bush.

"I'm not blaming you, Seth. We had to choose one way. We must be wrong or else they travel a very long way from the castle."

Reluctantly he turned the horse, and they began to make their way home—no nearer to answers, no nearer to proof.

They were halfway home when Seth was feeling angry with himself, with Hestor, with the forest for having let him down.

Stupid forest. Stupid signs. How could I do that? It must only have ever worked for Hestor. Stupid. That's what I am. Stupid and useless!

He almost missed it. Or perhaps the forest never intended to let him. Sulking and sullen, he saw the blue wren and almost ignored it.

"Stop!" he shouted. For a moment, Hewitt had to restrain the tired, but startled horse.

They stopped.

"What is it?"

"Let me off. Just let me off." Seth tried to wriggle out of the saddle.

He wasn't going to risk saying anything before he knew. With his weight taken on his stick, he followed the lead to the spot where he had seen the wren disappear.

Hewitt watched in amazement as Seth seemingly disappeared into a dense piece of undergrowth, then he heard him yell with excitement.

"Come on. Over here. I've found it!"

Hewitt drew his sword and followed Seth in.

The bushes that had seemed so dense and secure, pushed away before him. Hewitt realised that they were merely faced with bushes that had been piled up to disguise a track that led down around a bend and out of sight.

"Well, well. I won't ask how!"

Hewitt moved some of the piled brush to one side so that he could move the horse through and found that the track was quite wide and had been recently used. Together, they walked down the trail, around the bend and there—sitting alongside the bank of what had once been a broad river sat the squat, solid frame of a stone water mill and a series of outhouses. It looked old and deserted with the track leading to it.

"There's probably no one about, but we'll be careful. Stay with the horse and I'll look inside," Hewitt warned.

He threw the reins to Seth before dodging from tree to tree, sprinting towards the building. Seth saw him, sword in hand, duck through the broken doorway of the mill. Seth waited impatiently, until he saw Hewitt reappear and signal to him to come.

He tied the horse to a broken rail, joining Hewitt inside.

"What is it?" whispered Seth, unable to conceal his excitement.

The inside of the mill, long deserted, had been cleared and cleaned to indicate recent use. It was all there—the spare equipment for the horses, plain armour and weapons, grain for horses, a renovated fireplace which had been in use. In large trunks in the upstairs room next to the mill store itself, lay the ultimate proof that they sought, chest after chest of plain black cloaks.

Seth watched as Hewitt held them up. On his face, Seth could see both dismay and delight.

"You were right, Seth. This is what we came for."

"What will we do? Now that we've found them?" Seth asked.

Hewitt replied, "We'll take one with us. We'll have to use it to get to the Prince. Maybe we can make him listen." He rolled one of the cloaks up in a ball. "They won't miss one. Try to find us a bag that we can hide it in. Try not to touch too much. I doubt if they'd notice, but we don't want them to know that we've been here. So…this is where they change from Duke's soldiers to Black Riders."

They drank spring water. They packed up the cloak in a hessian bag that had once held animal feed and after lightly feeding the horse, they walked back to the fork in the track which had been so well concealed. They worked to return it to its original state. Finally, the pair set off back to the castle.

The sound of the hooves faded.

The forest returned to its natural sounds when a man stepped from a thicket of trees. Having ensured that they were indeed gone, he led a tall black horse from the natural hiding place and set off towards the mill. He smiled to himself as he did. It was not a particularly pleasant smile—it was one forged from the hope of success and memories; of tar painstakingly removed and the thought of rewards.

Tad adjusted his belt and smiled.

***

Hewitt rode past the castle and through the square to the forge. Seth could see by the expression on Jeb's face that he had been worried. While trying to appear as if his forge work was still what occupied him, he enquired of them:

"You took your time. How'd it go?"

Hewitt pretended to warm himself by the dying forge fire while Seth took the bundled cloak inside.

"We found it. We've got a cloak," Seth cheerfully answered.

"Well done! That's good!" praised Jeb.

"I won't stay. I don't want people to think that I'm doing anything beyond dropping off the boy. We're leaving the cloak here. It'll be safer here than in the castle," Hewitt explained.

"Thanks for taking Seth with you!" Jeb said it aloud in the manner of a man grateful for a favour bestowed on a village boy.

Seth couldn't wait for Jeb to finish and come inside, but he knew that there was no use hurrying him. He'd simply have to wait for the big man to finish and complete his tasks as if it was just another day.

Finally, the door closed, and Seth could tell him of the day.

"Whoa! There! Steady! If you tell me too fast, I'll never hear it all. Now get your plate. You can try to eat and talk at the same time."

Seth told him of the day, of the doubts they'd had, and how he'd used what Hestor had taught him to show them the way. Finally, the delight of finding the secret location just as they had hoped they might. They talked about the mill, how well it had been hidden and forgotten.

"What a great place to choose. Nothing but rats and mice. Hasn't been used for years. Ever since the river changed its course. They're cunning, those ones. That's for sure. With a bit of luck, they'll be too clever for their own good!"

Neither of them wanted to go to, bed but knew they must. Seth had stopped talking and sat while Jeb made occasional comments.

"You tired, then?"

"Yes. On the horse—it's hard!"

Jeb cocked his head and looked at him. "Are you alright? You sound sort of strange?"

Seth protested that he was fine, it was probably just the events of the last hours catching up on him. But, as he said it, he knew that he was lying. His voice broke off halfway.

"You're not, are you?" insisted Jeb.

"It's nothing I can tell you, Jeb. It's just like I feel that something is about to happen. That's all I know!"

Jeb tried to understand. He sat alongside him, placing a hand on Seth's shoulder.

"It might be nothing, but it might be something. If Hestor said you should take notice, then you should. What's it about?"

"Honest, Jeb. I don't know. It's just like a really sick feeling in my stomach. In the pit of my stomach! Hestor used to say that it meant to be wary."

"What should we do? Is there anything?"

"I don't know. It might be just me being silly."

"Well, I can only do what I can. We'll hide this cloak behind the box of tools. Then, we'll see about sleep!"

Eventually, Seth dropped off into a troubled sleep.

They needn't have bothered to hide the cloak. The soldiers found it as soon as they kicked the door in. Seth woke to the terrifying sound of the door exploding off its hinges into the room, followed by the sight of soldiers filling the small space. Jeb had time for nothing. He was reaching for his hammer, when a sword rested under his chin and against the bottom of his throat.

"Stay. Don't move blacksmith, and no harm will come to you. Don't blink. Just stay. Move, and we'll kill you. We haven't come for you. We've come for the boy."

He was a soldier—one of the Duke's. He commanded tension in the space. He'd once threatened Seth's tongue.

"Get the boy up and ready to go. The rest of you look through the hut," the lead soldier ordered.

The bag with the cloak was turned up very quickly, indeed. It was not a large hut.

"Don't struggle, boy. We'll let you walk if you will, and if not, we'll carry you. Now get going!"

Jeb attempted again to intervene, but there was nothing he could do.

"Jeb! Don't move," pleaded Seth. "They'll hurt you! I'll go. I'll go." Hastily, he hopped into his clothes, ready in an instant.

The last thing Seth heard from the hut was Jeb threatening, "Touch him—hurt the lad, and I don't care who you are, I'll break every bone in your body. You mark that now!"

"Don't worry, blacksmith. We'll take very good care of him," the lead soldier responded.

Seth was bunked up in front of a large soldier who took the reins with one hand, while keeping a firm grip on Seth with the other.

"Where am I going?" Seth asked.

The soldier gruffly replied, "Ask no questions; be told no lies."

They galloped through the deserted town, to the castle where there were still guards on duty at the gate.

Seth was swung down and half-escorted, half-pushed into a doorway that was guarded by fully armed soldiers.

Seth's first view of the interior was of the floorboards where he was hurled by one of the guards. He heard a voice as he looked up:

"My, my. The young lad again. Not content with attacking the Duke's son. Now he really wants to make himself famous."

He knew *that* voice.

Seth looked up into the amused eyes of the Captain. That was terrifying, but what was even more so, were the two figures who sat alongside him. One was Hewitt, arms tied to his sides, his face battered and bruised; looking more ill and desperate than Seth could have believed. The other was Tad, who appeared as smug as smug could be.

The Captain wasted no time.

"We'll have answers from you both in the morning." He flung the black cloak at Seth's feet.

Hewitt had to be helped out of the room. Seth was escorted down rugged steps to a small room alongside the barracks. It had a solid door with a window at head height, which was just a hole in the wall. Small metal bars were welded over the space to make escape impossible, even for a small boy.

A moment after Seth was placed in it, the door was flung open again and a blanket was thrown through at him.

Another moment later, he was alone again with the surge of terrified energy still coursing through his body. He knew that he had done well, that if nothing else, he had sowed doubt in the minds of those who were holding him and Hewitt. He just hoped that those around him would be safe.

Sleep came fitfully.

16

Jails and Bears

Seth woke to the sound of the men and horses moving just outside his window. It was early light. Seth realised that his cell was half-dug into the dirt. His window with its bars were set in the ground, showing him the feet of men and the hooves of horses. It reminded him of forest floor some years and a lifetime ago.

A troop of horsemen were on their way out. Dirt was thrown through the cell window by the restless hooves. Seth watched the horsemen ready themselves, and then depart. After that, the silence was overwhelming. He dozed and was woken some time later by the sound of the lock at his door being opened.

Two guards came in, one carrying a tray with food on it.

"Wakey, wakey! Here's your breakfast. Make the most of it. Could be your last!" He sniggered to his partner.

"Not sure if they can make nooses to fit small necks," said the mate.

Seth couldn't be bothered wasting time on them. He thanked them courteously for the food, which seemed to upset them more than if he had cussed them. He ate his breakfast of cold porridge and hard bread but kept the solitary apple in case his lunch was not forthcoming.

Seth waited for something to happen, but nothing did. There was nothing for him to do, other than doze or watch the legs of passersby.

He thought it was early afternoon; however, he wasn't sure, when he saw the dresses of women swish past his bars. He heard noises, then suddenly, there was Bella leaning down to look for him.

"Psst! Psst!" she began.

Seth was by the window in a moment. "Bella. What's happening?"

"Shut up! Just listen. They're going to hang Hewitt tomorrow. They say that he was involved with the Riders—that he had one of their cloaks. I don't know about you. I'm going to ask My Lady to ask for mercy."

"Tell Jeb," implored Seth.

"I can't leave the castle and they won't let Jeb in. He's already tried today. You have to find a way out. I'll try to help. Here. It's not much, but I brought you some food."

She dropped a bundle through the bars and then hurried off. The food was good. There was bread, cheese, cold sausage, and pickles. There was also another apple. Seth ate as much as he could and saved the apple with his other.

Nothing happened that afternoon. No one came for his tray. No one came to talk with him further. His only conversation was with a barking dog.

By now, his spirits had fallen as low as they could. It seemed that after all this, after getting *so* close; that he was about to fail and die—that the Captain would leave no possible hints to his involvement. Mostly, he just felt numb from the day's events. It was just starting to get cold in the late afternoon when he first heard the music.

At first, Seth thought it was the noise of people practising in the village when, as it grew louder and louder, Seth could make out the tin whistles and the drums, he realised that a circus was in town. The troupe had come to the castle in the hope that the Duke might pay them to perform before his court.

Seth heard them come up the hill and circle the courtyard in a mixture of tin whistles, drums, and fifes. It was a distraction, and nothing more; until he heard the snuffling and groaning of an animal. He looked up to see the bear pawing at his window. There was no doubt it was Hugo.

Something akin to hope shot through Seth's body. He tried to think, then remembered the apples. Biting into one, he moved so the bear could see him before he proceeded to eat it noisily, with much lip-smacking and obvious relish. The bear almost went crazy as he did so. It howled and shook the bars. It bounced its body off the window and tried to get at the apple by reaching through.

If only...thought Seth.

He had only just begun when, unfortunately, guards arrived to shoo the bear and its trainer from the window. Even as Hugo was dragged away, Seth continued to eat as if the apple was the greatest food he'd ever had. Seth prayed that the bear might remember in the recess of its tiny brain.

All too soon, the caravan was turned out of the courtyard, the cold came down and the light went. The door was unlocked by another set of Guards who brought him some dinner in a bowl, took away his other, and left him a bucket for his bowels.

"What's happening?" Seth enquired, but all he got from them was a stare and a grunt. Then, the door was locked.

There was a sort of soup in the bowl with some coarse-grained bread that was as hard as rocks. He broke it as well as he could into the soup and ate it slowly. It wasn't as good as he could make but it was lukewarm with barley, and some type of lank meat. Despite his situation, and despite the growing cold, Seth lapsed into sleep remarkably quickly.

He was woken by the sound he wanted most to hear in the whole world. Something was grunting and shaking the bars of the cage. Seth recognised the tiny snout of the bear as it burrowed into the ground holding the bars.

If Seth had teased the bear before, now he taunted and goaded it with a will that could almost have made him feel guilty, if his escape hadn't hinged on its success.

"Come on. Come on, you silly old bear. Here's the apple. See Hugo. There's the apple. Come and get it." He held the fruit directly in front of the bear's nose. When the animal smelt and saw it, it went berserk.

Seth could only hope that it could break the bars, preferably before a guard heard the commotion.

"Come on. Come on, bear. Come on, Hugo!"

The bear sent a veritable dust storm of dirt behind it as it dug up the ground into which the bars were deeply set. Then with its tongue out it, gripped the bars to its huge, hairy chest; groaning deeply, it pulled on the bars.

The bars were old, but strong. The bear was old but driven by a famished wish for food. The bars gave way. With a rush and a scraping noise, the bottom of the bars lifted clear from their setting and a narrow pathway presented itself.

Seth paused long enough to press the apple into the huge paws of his rescuer and then crawled from his cell, dragging his stick behind him. His first instinct was to make for the gateway, until he heard the shouts from there and realised that the guards were on their way. He realised his only way to escape was to do what he didn't wish to, which was to go further back into the castle itself. He struggled to the main doorway, counting on the noise to rouse those inside. If not, he would be left stranded outside for the guards to find him.

He heard the welcome sound of the latches turned inside, the stewards and guards raced out of the doorway to investigate the noise. Taking advantage of the chaos and the darkness, Seth slipped inside the open door and made for the classrooms where he believed he might hide.

He raced about a corner of the corridor and ran smack bang into Bella coming the other way.

They both stared at each other in horror and relief.

She always thought quickly. This, Seth was grateful for.

"Quick! Into the classroom." She pushed him and followed him in.

They looked at each other. Neither had a clue what they would do from there.

"How'd you—" she began.

"A bear!" Seth responded but realised it would take too long. "Don't ask. Just, what am I going to do from here? How do I manage to help Hewitt escape?"

"First things first. You have to hide somewhere safe. In a moment, they'll search the castle room by room, even if they think you've gone out the gate. Where's the safest place?" She thought for a moment when her face brightened. "I know! Quick, come with me."

They made their way back down the maze of corridors. Bella scouting ahead as they went. The castle was in an uproar. People ran everywhere. Guards at double pace clanked down hallways. Seth had no idea where she was taking him. Perhaps it was to the garden, except at the last moment, she turned from the tower exit and moved further into the castle. When she stopped at a door, Seth realised and groaned.

"Yes. You'll be safe here. I'll make some noises. You crawl in and get under my bed. They'll not bother to search there, because Lady Eloise will assure them that they don't need to. Stay there. I'll pass a pillow to you and a rug. Don't argue! You'll be safe."

He had no wish to be confined, but he had no time to argue. He knew she was right, that soon the hallways would be full of soldiers searching every nook. He could never outrun them.

Bella opened the door and motioned him to crawl in. Then, she closed the door and shuffled towards her bed across the room with Seth trying to keep pace with her on all fours.

Lady Eloise was not asleep. She called aloud, "Bella! Bella! Is that you? What are you doing?"

Bella crossed to the bedside, and in doing so, opened a path for Seth to crawl towards the bed. As fast as he could manage, while trying to be as silent as possible, he reached the bed. Quickly, Seth pushed his stick in front of him before he crawled under the bed and waited. It was not as bad as he feared.

There was a space several feet high which he encountered. He heard Bella talk to Lady Eloise, "One of the prisoners has escaped. It's not to be worried about, because it's only a boy and they think he's fled across the bridge and out into the village."

"Even so. You shouldn't be out there. What if he attacked you? I thought after that episode of sneaking off into the garden you'd have been more careful."

"I just checked the hallway. That's all?"

"Well. Lock the door just in case, then go to bed. We have a busy day tomorrow."

"Very well. Goodnight, Lady Eloise!" He heard Bella kiss her on the forehead and cross to her own bed. In the noise of getting into bed and fluffing pillows, Bella slipped a pillow and a rug beneath her bedframe to Seth. He was grateful. The wooden floor was icy.

Carefully and quietly, Seth eased the rug beneath him and folded it across his body. The pillow he placed under his head; he was almost comfortable. He dozed. He was scared to sleep but was too tired to stay awake. The night passed until knocking at the door brought him fully alert, with his heart pounding.

"What is it?" trumpeted Lady Eloise.

"Excuse us, Your Ladyship. We have orders to search every room in the castle. There's a prisoner escaped, and we need to check your room," came a guard's voice behind the door.

There was a pause. Then, Lady Eloise did precisely what the two younger people hoped she might do. She sent them away in a voice that brooked no argument.

"Go away. I will not have my room searched in the middle of the night when I and my ward have been safely locked in our room for the evening. Unless he is very thin and has crawled under the door, then we have nothing to fear."

"Your Ladyship, we've got orders to search—"

"I know your orders. I am not deaf or senile. I am just giving you another set, and they are to *go away.* If you insist, I will show you over my quarters in the morning once I am dressed and receiving guests. Is that clear?"

"Yes, Your Ladyship!"

They heard them tramp away to the next room, perhaps a little louder than they needed to.

Seth sighed. There was morning to worry about, but at least for now, he was safe.

***

Seth must have slept, for at some time later he heard birds and saw the light was beginning to make its way into the room. Now he needed to have a plan. None came easily to mind. Yes, he might escape over the back walls, but he couldn't go near Jeb without risking his life. Where would he go?

And then there was the idea of leaving Hewitt to be hanged. How could he do that? Yet, what could he, a single small boy, do to help a prisoner escape from a dungeon in front of a garrison of fully armed troops? There seemed no way he might succeed and his escape could only be seen as an admission of guilt. How clever of the Captain to turn it about like that; make it seem as if Hewitt and he were the ones with the links to the Riders. Who would help him? The thought of the bear came to mind along with a sense of an idea.

He felt movement above him and heard the two women begin to move around. He waited with a bursting bladder.

Finally, a head was thrust under the bed and Bella began, "She's gone to breakfast. What do you want me to do?"

"Can you smuggle me out of the castle through the back gates?" Seth replied.

"No. They're locked since last week. I can't get keys."

"How can I get out the front? I'm not leaving Hewitt; I just have to get to some people."

"Who?" Bella asked.

"The players in the travelling troupe."

"Why!" she gasped.

"They're my friends. I travelled with them before. I think they might be able to help," he answered simply.

"I've got an idea," said Bella. She smiled wickedly as she did.

Ten minutes later, two young girls made their way down the stairs to leave via the front doors. One with red hair, had a market basket with her. Behind her, head slightly bowed, came another girl who wore a very large bonnet with a shawl wrapped around her, almost covering the lower part of her face.

"I feel really stupid. They're bound to know!" Seth muttered.

"Just shut up and try not to limp. Remember, you're a girl."

Bella went over to meet the two girls who went to the market.

"Do you mind if I bring my friend?" she enquired.

The two girls stared at them.

Bella waved a hand. "Don't mind her. She's really shy and she has a twisted knee."

"Oh!"

Together, they set off through the gates while the guards made lewd suggestions to the kitchen girls.

"Lady Bella," one of the market girls said." I thought you were meant to be going out with Lady Eloise?"

"I'm just helping my friend, and then I'll go straight back. I won't even come to the market. She just wanted to see the troupe of travelling troubadours, and I said I'd come with her."

They walked as far as the caravans, with Seth terrified that at any moment his leg would give way on him. Fortunately, he managed until they reached the tents that had been set up at the base of the castle walls. There, Seth—still mortified by his disguise—ducked out of sight and Bella began a rapid retreat to the castle after returning Seth's stick to him.

Seth didn't know where to begin, so he went looking for the bear. Alongside Hugo, he found who he was looking for.

"I have to talk with you."

"How do you know me, girl?" questioned Hugo's handler.

"I'm not a girl. I'm Seth; Seth who travelled with you for a day or two."

"Well, Seth. It has to be you that the bear set free the other night. Either that, or you're taken to impersonating girls since last we met." The man laughed.

As quickly as he could, Seth told him the story.

When he had finished, the bear handler whistled and shook his head. "That's some story! What do you want us to do? I'm not sure what a few jugglers, singers, and storytellers might do?"

"I don't exactly know how," replied Seth. "But I have to get Hewitt out before he's hanged."

"Oh. And do you have a plan?"

"Yes. This is what I'd like you to do. I want a message to get to Jeb and then I was wondering how you'd like to do a performance just inside the castle…"

The following morning, the castle was woken by the sound of the minstrels playing their music as they marched back up into the castle. Wisely, in the name of diplomacy the bear had been left behind.

Then as many times before, the old man dressed as a sage and a town crier exhorted the crowd of soldiers, maids, and stewards to take a moment from their busy days and the needs of their nobles to observe and join in some amusing scenes from their lives.

They were skits, short plays involving figures and characters they already knew. There was the fat grocer who ate so much that his stomach exploded. As it did, a dwarf bounded from the massive stuffing about his middle. There was the evil noble who seduced young village girls and then left them, always in front of an angry mob until finally he was captured, castrated and made to become a monk.

Each small scenario was played out with much exaggerated beating of people and yells of dismay and joy. Soon, most of the unoccupied members of the castle retinue were gathered, watching the troupe perform and using the steps to the main castle as their stage.

The gateway to the dungeon lay behind the barracks. A figure in a chook suit, slid his way behind the two guards, who were watching the plays and slipped into the stairway behind them. There were not many cells with only two occupied. One, with a wounded soldier whom Seth had seen before, and the other was simply a locked door with a small grille that Seth was too short to look in.

All he could do was to shout through the bars in a stage whisper: "Hewitt! Hewitt! Are you there?"

There was no answer. Seth's heart sank.

He tried again, this time hammering on the door. "Hewitt! Hewitt! Are you in there?"

He was about to give up when there was a commotion from inside the cell. Something or someone lewas moving.

Two hands appeared on the grille. A voice called, "Who is it? What do you want? Is it time already?"

"Hewitt. It's me. It's Seth."

"Seth. Is that you? What are you doing here? Go quickly before they find you."

"Hewitt! Be quiet and listen. In a moment we'll be down here to free you. Just be ready!" Seth pushed a suit of clothes through the bars.

A moment later, a small, faintly limping chook burst past the two guards as if it had been part of the play and did a round of the players while flapping and calling.

The play changed to a mock drama; two thieves were discovered stealing from a blind man who walked around falling over steps, barrels, and dwarves who deliberately got in the way. The captured thieves needed to be punished and guarded. Two of the prettiest players in the troupe enticed the watching guards to come and play a small part and, how could they refuse such lovely girls. They left their posts to guard the thieves. That was the given chance.

A huge man dressed as a giant with false hair, beard, massive shoes ducked into the corridor led by a small chicken. In his hand there was a large heavy hammer that had lately seen work on a forge.

"Step back from the door, Hewitt," Seth whispered, and then they waited.

In the play, they were executing the two criminals. With each fanfare there was a series of drum rolls created by the players for effect.

With each series of blasts, Jeb battered the lock on the cell door with all the force he could muster. Three series of rolls rang out above, causing alarm and merriment in the watching crowd and a cover for lock smashing below. It took all three rounds of Jeb's blows to separate the lock from the oaken door, but finally, it was done.

The play had almost finished. The guards were tired of being extras, and so luckily, before they walked back to their places, three figures burst from the doorway and did a lap of the crowd: A giant roared at them and threatened them with a hammer. The chook screeched and flapped. A clown in a harlequin suit capered and shook his rattles in the faces of the most serious.

Perhaps to a seasoned watcher of such plays, it may have appeared that the giant seemed to be sweating rather a lot. The chook seemed a little lame in one leg. And the clown, in particular, seemed gaunt, tired, and barely able to shake his doll-faced rattles.

"Laugh at them! Shake the rattles. Dance about because your life depends on it!" whispered Jeb between movements.

"Not long now. Just follow Jeb's lead," Seth murmured, hastily.

The thieves were about to be re-sentenced in heaven, when the three blundered into a mock court and fell about. At once, the judge bellowed at them. The dwarves tipped the blind man over again and the soldiers, guided by the comely wenches, used their pikes to evict the three from the courtyard. The three would pretend to flee and then try to come back, but each time they'd be driven off until, howling, screeching, and cock-a-doodle-do doing they fled across the bridge and down the ramp to the tents.

When they came to the tents, they took huge breaths and hugged each other.

"I never thought it would work."

"I didn't think the door would give!"

"I was worried that someone would recognise me in the clown suit! What now?"

"How long before they'd notice the cell door?" Seth wondered.

"It depends," gulped Hewitt, whose face still showed the scars and bruises of his ordeal. "If they think I'll have lunch, then they'll change the guard and feed me at noon."

"Noon!" chorused Seth and Jeb. "That's not long!"

Hewitt looked between them. "Do we have a plan? Or do we just try to wait 'til dark?"

"No! We've got a plan—out of your joker's costume. We have two horses waiting. One for you, and one for Seth. I'll get rid of this and get back to my forge. I'll come tonight, unless it's too hard."

"Where are we going?" asked Hewitt.

Seth smirked. "To the place we hope they'll never think of looking."

"And where's that?"

"Hestor's."

Back at the castle, a red-headed girl sat and could hardly contain her relief and excitement. She had not been a part of it. She had wished she could have, but did not get too close in case her presence in any way threatened the success of what she saw. She knew who the figures dressed in their costumes were, and because she knew, she had watched them closely and had seen the plan unfold behind the disguises. She had held her breath as the three of them had been chased from the castle, then had to pretend to want to return, while she knew that every instinct in them was telling them to run and keep running.

After the troupe had left, the crowd had dispersed to begin its lives again, Bella remained. She suspected what would happen eventually. She saw food carried towards the cells, guards leave places to accompany those stewards and new guards. She waited. Sure enough, in a moment, pandemonium began.

Guards and stewards streamed from the underground cells, shouting, and calling for help. The guard in the barracks turned out in force. Bella saw both the Captain and his lieutenant stalk from the castle proper and begin issuing orders and supervising the despatch of mounted soldiers through the gates.

"Two prisoners in two days!" she laughed to herself as she tripped up the stairs to her room.

She skipped into the room and stopped. Sitting on the bed with a look of horror and concern on her face, sat Lady Eloise. Alongside her sat her classics teacher, Sharrock.

In front of them, on the floor lay the blanket and pillow that Bella knew had been under her bed. The very same that had been slept in by Seth.

Lady Eloise, to her credit, looked more concerned than horrified. "Bella. I need to hear from you a good reason why I should not summon the Duke or his Captain to this room and show them what I have found; or should I say, what the maid found when she was making your bed. I need to hear a *very* good reason. I want no lies!"

For once Bella—Tess was lost for words.

17

The Mill

Seth and Hewitt tried to ride to the forest, in a way that favoured speed, also considered the possibility of horsemen at high-speed attracting attention. Through small outlying villages they walked their horses as if they were in no hurry, while in the safety and seclusion of the forest, they raced their horses as fast as they dared. They didn't stop until they came to the camouflaged path that led to Hestor's.

It was a nightmarish journey. They were tired, they were conscious of the danger involved, and so they had to force themselves to be alert and vigilant. At the start of the journey, that wasn't hard. But, by the time they had avoided the town by barely passable tracks and walked their horses through dangerous places, then fatigue had set in with them all. Nervous energy had given way to an abject yearning for rest.

They took it in turns to try and rally the other.

"Come on. Once we're over the road then it's all forest and we're safer there. Just stay awake!"

Seth tried to be strong and brave. By the time they reached the trail to Hestor's hut, he was happy to slide off the horse, grasp his stick, and begin on the way with Hewitt alongside him. Probably, they weren't very careful. Probably, they would have easily been seen or heard as they trekked through the forest. They tried to be watchful, but all their remaining energy was focused on keep continuing to move forward. It was the certainty of the destination that kept Seth going.

As they neared the place that Seth had remembered, the hairs on the back of Seth's neck began to stand up and his heart began to race. Something was very odd. He felt his spirits drag. To come this far and find that something was wrong—it was beyond imagining. He checked with Hewitt.

"Stop. There's something very wrong!" he hissed.

He heard Hewitt draw his sword. "What is it? What's wrong?"

"I don't know. It just feels wrong."

"Like what? What do you mean?"

"It's just a feeling, but Hestor taught me to trust them."

They hesitated at a distance from the hut.

Hewitt noticed it first. "There's smoke coming from the chimney. Look."

Seth looked and he was right. Against the pale night sky, you could see the soft smudges of smoke puffing.

"It's maybe okay," was all he could mutter.

Who knows how long they might have circled and plotted had not the back door suddenly swung open, a light appeared and a very small familiar voice call, "If I were you Seth, I'd bring my friend in before he gets frozen or before Tiny forgets you and chews you up!"

Seth's spirits soared. Despite hours of care and silence, he yelled and plunged forward.

"Hestor!" he cried.

Hestor it was. A little gaunter and greyer then when he'd seen her last, but undoubtedly her.

Hewitt watched in amazement and humility as he saw the two—the small boy and old woman—reconnect. Hestor hugged him and kissed the top of his head with tears running down her face. Seth was beside himself and could only hold on to her and hop about. All this, while a huge dog capered and danced about them, with his deep barks filling the space.

"Dear boy," she said at length. "Let's look at you. My golly. How you've grown, and look—will the Lord have mercy—look at you. You've thrown away your crutches!"

"What about you, Hestor? Where have you been? We came to see you just lately."

"Pardon us," Hestor invited Hewitt. "It's just that we haven't seen each other for such a long time. And you, young man; surely, I am allowed to leave here without your permission. Please! Come in. You must be weary!"

Hewitt cleared his throat and entered the small, tidy hut.

The next hour was chaotic as Hestor served soup up for both of them, attempted to be polite to Hewitt while maintaining a non-stop to-and-fro question and answer conversation with Seth. All this interspersed with moments where she would leave off what she was doing, cross to Seth and bury his head in her arms.

Hewitt sat silently and thankfully with his soup, realising that he was witnessing something that was unusual, which filled him with delight and wonder. He sat and heard of Hestor's slow travels to fellow healers and potion makers. From Seth, he heard with awe of the boy's time with the mute healer and shared with Hestor the delight in his story of miraculous cure.

"She was always good. Always! It was her nan—Minerva that cured me. Ah! But you already know all that."

More soup was had. Beds were made up. They'd barely got to speak of their present dilemma, but despite their weariness there was no way they were going to sleep before the stories unfolded.

Seth watched Hestor as she busied herself about the hut. He watched her for signs of illness or weakness yet could see none.

"You're sure you're well?" he asked for the fourth time, which drew Hestor over to pinch his cheeks and wobble his head from side to side.

"I'm well enough to get you to dig in the garden tomorrow and beat you with a big stick if you're too slow!" she joked with him.

Tiny settled with his head in Seth's lap. Finally, the saga of the Riders and their respective parts in it emerged. There was laughter and delight in the story of their chicken and bear inspired escape. Then, eventually they had to settle to the enormity of where they presently were—two fugitives with important information pursued by ruthless and ambitious people who would kill them without a thought. At best, they had a vague plan for getting Hewitt to see a Duke; who might or might not take him seriously; and might or might not act upon that information.

"Can't leave you for a moment," chuckled Hestor. "Go to visit a few friends and you're in the middle of creating a civil war. It's not neighbourly, Seth."

"Stop joking. Hestor. It's serious!"

"Aye. It is. Serious enough to get you killed, you great prawn. I don't know what you're thinking of..."

"But you taught me to do what was right. To do what you really felt you had to. You used to send me out to the garden 'til I knew what I had to do. You did!"

Hestor and Hewitt laughed at his insistence.

"I did. I can't deny it."

"What should I do then, Hestor? And no, I don't want to go and dig the garden 'til I know."

"Not much of it left, really. Still, it'd come back really quick if we did, but seeing you've grown past digging the garden, you'll have to tell me—how do you know what you're going to do? Hey, Mr. Big-for-your-britches?"

"I think Hewitt should go to try and see Gloucester. I think I'm worried about Tess and that's why I want to go back to the castle. I don't know, Hestor. I really don't..." Seth trailed off shaking his head.

"I think you're too tired to know. We can all do with some shut-eye, and who knows, you might dream an angel dream during the night."

"What's that?" enquired Seth.

"It's where an angel comes and brings you a message in a dream so that you're clear what you have to do."

Hestor could see Hewitt cock his head on an angle as if he was unfamiliar with such an idea—unfamiliar and probably not very convinced.

"Mr. Hewitt, I'm not telling young Seth big whoppers. I'm just telling him what I know, and that is that when we truly don't know what to do; but refuse to believe that there isn't a way, then things happen. Sometimes it's not the clouds opening, but just a little thing that occurs to help us know what we need to. Isn't that true Seth!"

Seth nodded. "It was the fox and the blue wren that showed us the mill road. Don't you remember, Hewitt?"

Hewitt threw up his hands in mock surrender. "I don't judge what I don't know. I might say it's all chance or coincidence, while you seem certain that it's a sign or an omen. I have no idea about it. I know that as a boy, we were warned not to meddle in things we didn't know. To be careful."

"Fat lot of notice you took," chuckled Hestor.

"It's different, but I take your point," agreed Hewitt with a smile. "If I'd stayed happily being a groom to a great family, then this would not have happened."

"So maybe that's your path, Hewitt? If there isn't much chance luck involved, then maybe you have a task that you need to carry out!"

"I thought it was to place a Saxon back on the throne."

"Maybe it's to help place a good king right there. Maybe that's more important."

They were silent for a moment.

Then, Hewitt spoke, "Maybe you're right. Perhaps not all is lost. I'll just have to take some convincing before I start following blue wrens."

"Belief tends to follow proof!" offered Hestor.

Loathe as they were to move; as they were warm, fed, and comfortable, they got up to enfold themselves in blankets, eiderdowns and pillows to rest for the following day.

18

Explaining

"What do you have to say for yourself?"

Bella looked at Lady Eloise and Sharrock, then at the bed clothes lying on the carpet and found that the only lies she could think of were too large and too fanciful to be believed. She knew that she had trusted her guardian as much as anyone she had ever met. It seemed that the truth was the only way. She came and sat alongside Lady Eloise.

"I hid the young boy they were looking for," she began. "It is Seth, the boy from the village whom you have already met. We share a great and dreadful secret. I need to know, Lady Eloise, that you will listen to me all the way through, for it is a story that begs credence."

Lady Eloise stared intently at the girl she had grown more than fond of, and for whom she had great plans and dreams.

"Bella. When we first met, you would lie about anything or anyone to avoid punishment, of late this has not been your manner. I pray that this will not be another error of your past."

Bella grasped her hands.

"I swear on all the goodness and patience that you have shown me that I am not lying." She turned to her teacher, Sharrock. "This is the truth, but I am fearful that you will not believe me; or that if you do, then your lives will also be in great danger."

Lady Eloise rose from where she sat and walked to the door. She secured the latch from the inside.

"The maid who found the bedding has no idea of its significance. Sharrock here is an old and valued friend. We are here to listen to this story through to the end. Just don't lie child, even if it is to spare someone else."

Bella gathered herself and began. She began as a small ruffian child in a small village and seeing for the first time a very thin crippled boy come to her village on crutches.

True to their word, they listened to the story to its end until at last, Sharrock said, "This is a dreadful and disturbing story, Bella. But why does it endanger you now? The Riders, no doubt, come from far north. They are raiders who serve old and false gods."

Bella hesitated and then plunged on.

"This is the piece I beg you to listen to with patience and fairness. The Riders don't come from northern chimes. They live and breathe here in this castle."

They both were deeply shocked and moved to interrupt.

"I know this is hard to believe. Just hear me out," insisted Bella.

And so, she told of Seth's recognition of the Captain and of their efforts to identify the Riders, then carry proof to the Prince.

"Bella. I don't understand why the Duke would challenge the Prince when his life is good. Why would he?"

"I don't know exactly," she replied. "Hewitt told us that it was something to do with him being a Saxon descendant of the old king."

This stopped them both in mid-argument.

"How is he connected? He's a Norman!"

"His Lady—Theresa—is meant to be a direct descendant of the great king."

Sharrock got up and began to pace.

"You find this disturbing and convincing?" Lady Eloise asked him.

"It makes sense, My Lady! Not that I think that the Duke cares much for rights, but I could see how he might cobble together a very useful alliance of old Saxons and citizens who find the Prince offensive. Out of that, he could create enough opposition to be a threat. So again, it raises its head, so many years after the old invasion."

Then, he smiled ruefully.

Sharrock added, "Grievances die hard, particularly when they are those of a conquered people."

"No!" She gestured with her hand. "No. I am not advocating that we should return to ancient times and restore old kings, particularly when they are as snivelling as our present crop and as for the Duke! Well, despite his fortunate and not very happy marriage—a pig dressed in fine livery is still a pig."

Seeing the look on Bella's face, she smiled and continued. "Yes, Bella. I do have opinions beyond those that civility and my station demand of me, but not beyond these walls. I have known the Duke to be ambitious and avaricious, but I did not think his greed took him to treason. It seems I was wrong!"

"So, you believe me, then?" exclaimed Bella.

"It seems that, unfortunately, we do. Now, we must decide how to proceed. What is your opinion, Sharrock?"

"In a sense, our decision is made for us, milady. Although it is not yet generally known, the Prince is to visit here soon—invited by the Duke with promises of great banquets and a tournament named after His Highness."

"When is he due?"

"I don't know, but I think within a week!"

Bella and the Lady Eloise exchanges glances and saw the other's eyes also held their own idea. They both mouthed the words, "Treason!" and "Betrayal!" at the same time.

It was then, that the old teacher understood what they both meant. "You don't mean…surely, no. Not in his own castle. It would look far too obvious."

"What if he found someone who, for the promise of riches and estates, was prepared to kill the Prince while it looked as if all due precautions had been taken by the Duke?" Lady Eloise proposed.

"Then he could weep and grieve and claim it was not of his doing," concluded Bella.

"What should we do? How might we stop this?" Sharrock asked with wide eyes.

"Bella, I need your permission to tell my husband—your guardian, what you know. Our few men are no match for the Duke's, but he may be able to warn the Prince or even guard him closely." Lady Eloise could see that Bella was perturbed by this suggestion. "What's wrong, Bella? Why does this displease you?"

"No!" she replied. "I think it's a good plan. I just wish I could get word to Seth and Hewitt to tell them of what we know. It's just that, Seth has been a part of it from the beginning."

"Where is he now? Do you know?"

"No. Since the escape I haven't heard from him."

"Perhaps, quite wisely, he had decided to move to where the danger is not as great," murmured Sharrock.

"Bella, perhaps we can contact him. Is there anyone who might know where he might be?"

"Yes, there is. I have to trust you. It's the blacksmith in the square. If anyone knows, he would."

"Well. We must have you buy fruit with the maids today in the square…" Lady Eloise would have continued, but she saw the smile begin on Bella's face. "Ah! My plan is so good I can see you have already trialled it yourself. And all this time I thought you were showing an interest in the proper running of a home! My! My! How foolish I have been!"

Bella felt overcome with shame and remorse when Sharrock intervened.

"Come, Eloise. Perhaps the deception was necessary at the time. While not to be in anyway approved; it may have served its purpose. I suggest you both stay while I fetch His Lordship."

He swept out of the room.

The silence still lay heavy between them.

"Lady Eloise. I must apologise—" But she was cut off in mid-sentence.

"It is not *you* that should apologise. I am sitting here, realising that for several years I have seen things about the Duke and his flattery of my husband which have not been proper, but I have been too taken in by it all to be anything other than receptive. I am not proud of myself. I think he has wanted the prestige of our name alongside his own to add a degree of credibility and nobility to his less than admired one." Lady Eloise sighed heavily as she continued, "Dear girl, I have been taken in. And what is worse, I have allowed my own kind, but ineffective husband, to also be taken in by a calculating and cruel rogue. Ah, dear! All this for a few dresses, a banquet or two, and the chance to be thought someone again."

Lady Eloise looked suddenly very old and very frail.

Bella crossed to her and took her hands in her own again.

"I'm sure your motives have always been pure. Your character knows no other way!"

"Very kind of you, my dear, to say so. But I will own what are my own mistakes. For too long I have denied the evidence of my own eyes and ears," said Lady Eloise. "I only hope that my own dear husband will not be too shattered by the news. I'm sure that he, too, has enjoyed being feted and praised in the last few years when truly our strength and power were waning. You must know that our castle is in ruins and our lands overgrown and poorly tended."

It took a long time, but all too soon the door was swung open. Sharrock re-entered with Lord Alfred, Lady Eloise's husband and Bella's guardian.

"My dear," he addressed his wife. Upon seeing Bella, he included her in the greeting. "My dears. What is wrong? I feared you were ill. I could get no more sense from Sharrock than I could have from a sheep. He simply said that you wished to seem me quite urgently. I was forced to make my apologies to our host when plans for the tournament were still to be finalised. Apparently, the Duke intends to name the joust after my late father with the Prince to invest the victor with his prize. I am so looking forward—"

He caught his wife's eye and was flustered by what he saw. "Eloise. What is it? What have I done? Have I gotten too swept away by all this glitter and flattery?"

Lady Eloise smiled lovingly.

Softly, the older woman said, "Dear Alfred, hearing you say that has set my mind at rest. Our own dear girl, our Bella, has something she must tell you and we require your advice and wisdom."

Bella watched as the old man with his crop of thick white hair, worn long as was the custom, sat on one of the window chairs and watched her with his pale blue eyes. As she began, she prayed he would also believe her and that what she told him would not destroy his world.

Several times during her story, he tried to get to his feet or attempt to speak, but each time Lady Eloise prevented him from doing so by laying a gloved hand on his arm.

When Bella had finished, she could see the changes in his face. His mouth was set in a tight, firm line and she could see his jaw now jutted out, straight and solid. He asked several questions in a clipped tone and took him time to digest her answers.

Lady Eloise was the first to enquire, "My Lord, it gives us no pleasure to tell you this. It seems that we have been taken in by a wicked and deceitful host!"

He sat a moment longer as if transfixed. Then, Bella saw his face relax and a weary calm settled on his face. He half-snorted and half-sighed.

Bella asked, "Do you doubt me, My Lord?"

For a moment, he was away somewhere. The next, he smiled at her.

"No! No! Not at all. One the big things I always knew that, you were trustworthy. Just not always on the reason your dress was muddy or the dog was one pup shy; I'm smiling because I realise my own vulnerability and stupidity. I found myself wondering if we could stay quiet about all this and end up on the winning side. The thought itself is an insult to my family and lineage."

Lord Alfred bowed his head.

"You are far too hard on yourself, My Lord," began Sharrock. "Who would not wish to see his family name again toasted and admired? That is no crime!"

"Good names grow from good deeds—not from flattery and pomp."

He crossed to his wife of many years.

"My dear. I owe you an apology…"

"None is needed, My Lord," she began.

"Ah. But I insist. For this way, I shall not be weighed down by guilt and shame. I need to apologise because I have been taken in by praise and adulation and in the process, I have stopped being who I really am."

"And what is that, my love?"

"An old man with little wisdom and doubtful integrity, who has seen his family fortunes sink, and who has been powerless to prevent that. This Duke seemed as if he might be a way to mend that had been broken. In the course of this, I have endured the sight of coarse behaviour, unnatural greed, and treatment of servants that required my intervention, but I was too cowardly to do so, and it has come to this."

Bella felt she must intervene, or the Lord might ramble away for hours. "My Lord. Lady Eloise. What can we do?"

He almost jumped at her voice, as if he had forgotten her presence. "We must warn the Prince and do what we can to protect him. I will go to see Gloucester myself, as he is the one who effectively controls the Prince's army and bodyguard."

Lady Eloise saw Bella's concern.

"My Lord, I think that we should let Bella be in touch with the young man who first noticed the plot," she suggested. "I think that the Duke and his henchmen will be very alert to anything that looks like opposition. Suffolk must be told, but perhaps we need not hurry and draw attention to ourselves."

She explained how Bella would contact Jeb and then they might be in touch with Seth.

"I hardly think that we should base our plans around the ideas of a small boy who has no idea of diplomacy and to whom no doors are open," scoffed Lord Alfred.

It was Bella who intervened. "My Lord. He knows more of the Riders than we do. He is with Hewitt who knows of plans hatched by the Duke. I beg you to let us have a day or two!"

They could see him consider and then agree.

"And what would you have of me?" he asked.

"My Lord," Lady Eloise began gently, "you must act as if you know nothing. You must go back to the Duke's table and pretend that you find him most witty, amusing, and transparent of men. He must suspect nothing!"

"As I have played that part so well for several years, I should know the lines by heart."

They attempted to placate him, but he would not accept that.

"I will return to the jousting planning. I will wait several days and that is all!"

Lord Alfred bowed stiffly to all of them and left.

"He'll be hard on himself for some time!" intoned Sharrock.

"Yes. And we must not make it worse by failing to act." Lady Eloise turned to the young girl. "Bella, you will ask the maids if you may accompany them. Sharrock, you and I will devise ways of getting messages to people safely in case our real plans are discovered. We will help none by having ourselves killed—accidentally or not. I think we may safely assume that we can no longer trust to send letters with messengers and know that they will not be intercepted. We must act with great caution."

Several hours later, the Lady Bella, also known as Tess, moved through the market showing much attention to the smell and texture of vegetables she was learning to know by name. She slowly and carefully moved to examine some small string puppets that serendipitously happened to be displayed on the stall closest to the forge.

Between blows of his hammer on a horse's foot, Jeb muttered a greeting without looking at her.

Again, Bella began a conversation with a particularly dirty looking potato while holding it to the sky as if she were searching for flaws.

"Where's Seth?" she sang to the humble King Edward.

"Is it safe to talk?" asked Jeb between blows.

"Yes. It's safe."

"Then, he'd like to know you're safe. He's in the forest with Hewitt at Hestor's cottage."

"Can you show me the way?"

Others passed by and Bella' potato became a sack of corn that she could only pass her hand through.

"How will we get there?" he asked.

"Horses. I will be here tomorrow morning; early!"

"Horses?" enquired Jeb, faltering in his rhythm.

"It's safe. Trust me. I can't talk more."

"Tomorrow morning it is then, lass." As he straightened his back and turned it upon her as if he didn't even know that she existed.

***

At the cottage, Hewitt was impatient to be gone, but Hestor urged him to wait.

"It'll get no worse by your waiting for a few days. Give Jeb a chance to tell us more," she told him.

So begrudgingly, he stayed. She was bemused to see Seth; without prompting, begin on the large job of weeding and turning the remains of the garden beds. Their manured soil had become a jungle of tall and very healthy weeds.

"You asking for inspiration, Seth?" she teased.

"No. Just gardening."

Handling the spade was still very difficult for Seth, and Hewitt was not willing to see the boy struggle. They were both dripping with sweat when Hestor found them.

"Well! Well! And not even for punishment. What's become of you? I'll have to think up a whole new punishment!"

She watched them for a moment with a smile.

"I only came to warn you that we'll be having visitors soon. No. Not to be anxious. They're not foes. But they'll be calling soon. I'll find some food!"

Hewitt had considered asking how she knew but thought better of it and turned back to exercising his hoe.

When she was out of earshot, he enquired of Seth, "How does she know? How could you be that certain? Do you know?"

Seth shrugged. "I don't know. She just does!"

"Is she ever wrong?"

"Not that I can remember," answered Seth as he yanked a weed taller than himself from the garden bed. He hurled it onto a pile they were creating alongside the beds.

"Do you think we could all learn it?" Hewitt enquired after another row of fallow earth had been created.

"I think so. I forget it when I'm in the town. It's like there's no real place for it there. And then, when I'm here or when I'm in real danger—that's when I remember."

Hewitt shook his head. "I'm not making fun of you. I just don't know. But I tell you, you've got me on edge to see if they come."

They didn't have to wait long. They'd barely cleared half of the largest bed when they heard horses.

Seth looked up and smiled at Hewitt knowingly.

Hewitt held both hands up, palms toward Seth in mock surrender. "I'm convinced."

There were four horses. Three of them had riders aboard—Tess, Jeb and a young man in light armour. Tess and Seth were delighted to see each other. Jeb could only smile at Hestor as the two young people embraced, laughed, and then became self-conscious at their antics.

Tess stood back, straightened her tunic and attempted to look calm and unemotional. "Seth, Hewitt, Hestor—this is John, who is a very trusted steward of our family's."

The young man nodded to them. Having established the right of John to be among them, they dismounted to refresh eat and talk. Hestor showed them into her cottage.

For the next several hours, they shared news, plans, and what had happened since they last met. They heard of the escapes, the plots, and schemes—and most importantly—of the arranged visit of the Prince to the Duke's castle.

"Do you honestly think that he intends to do harm to the Prince?" enquired Jeb.

"We don't know, but it seems very likely. No doubt they would find a way to blame it upon someone else. Then, with the death of the Prince, there would be a vacuum that the Duke and his allies would have to fill—for the good of all, of course!" said John.

"Of course!" muttered Jeb.

"You may have other plans. Seth. Bella, was insistent that we talk to you and Hewitt before we did anything further. We plan to have Hewitt travel north to see Gloucester and alert him to the possible danger while I will accompany Bella back to the castle, and there to ready our party of soldiers—small as it is—to safeguard the Prince, if and when he does come," John explained.

"Why not just warn the Prince direct?" enquired Jeb.

"We think that he would either laugh at us if we could get to him or that he might even make a joke of it, tell the court and so not only warn the Duke, but identify us as well."

"Is he that silly? said Seth.

John gave him a look. "It does not do to speak badly of those who rule. But yes, if any of the reports are faintly true, then he and his chosen few; all bored, rich and sycophantic—"

"What does that mean?" interjected Seth.

"Sycophantic. It means those who surround him spend their time praising him and telling him what a great and wise ruler he is," informed Hewitt.

"Oh! And he believes them!" exclaimed Seth.

"Indeed, and so surrounded by his gaggle of fawning adoring sycophants," continued Hewitt, "the Prince not only does nothing, but spends his time trying to find new things to eat and drink or new clothes to wear. Even worse…he also believes that he is loved and lauded throughout the land. The older nobles have either learnt to play the same game, which is to administer and then tell the Prince how well he is doing or they're retired to their estates too despairing to stay about such foppery. It's a bad time for us all."

There was silence after Hewitt had spoken.

Hestor broke it:

"Well, it seems that you must try to talk sense to this Mister Gloucester. That makes sense but come now, Seth, I can hear you plotting from here. I can see the thoughts in your head scurrying about like a nest of ants."

They laughed because what she said was true. Seth's eyes had become slightly hooded and a tiny smile escaped at the corners of his mouth.

Tess knew him well. "I bet that you'll want to come back to the castle and try to see the Prince, won't you?'

Everyone expressed their dismay and disapproval.

"You'd not be that silly?" exclaimed Jeb, but with a look at Seth's face, he relented a little. "You wouldn't, would you?"

"Seth. You might endanger Bella and Lady Eloise. Have you thought of that?"

Seth took a deep breath.

"I wouldn't do anything to harm them. It's just that…" And he ran out of words for a moment.

"Go on. Spit it out," encouraged Hestor.

"I know you'll think I'm making it up but I'm not. Last night I had a dream. In it, Tess—I mean, Lady Bella and I were sitting in a richly decorated room, and we were telling this young nobleman about the Riders. He was blonde-headed, with hair to his shoulders, a pale complexion and was dressed in long silk robes like a women's dress. And he had really smooth hands with rings on every finger. And he was listening to us. He believed us."

"Sounds like the Prince. That's the way he dresses." John grunted. "Seth. Having a dream—good as it was, is hardly the evidence we need to convince us that you could take such a risk. It was just a dream after all!"

Seth looked with earnest gaze to Hestor.

"I don't like it. It seems too dangerous to me. I've just gotten you back, Seth," began the older woman. "But I've always taught you to trust yourself and I can hear that you believe this dream to be a true one. If you can tell me—tell *us* how you could safely get to the town and then the castle, then I'll think about it."

"They know you, Seth," ventured Jeb. "I'm with Hestor. I'm not meaning to be unkind, but they'll be looking for every young boy with a limp for miles around. You may as well just go and throw yourself into a river as do that."

"I know how to do it!" said Seth. "You see, it was in the dream. I could see myself and that was a shock. I was all dirty and covered in old clothes and I had my crutches with me. I was a beggar child!"

All about him, people took breaths, but in Bella's face, Seth could see only excitement.

"It could work," said Hewitt. "I'm not saying it's not a risk, but they've seen you with a stick or a limp, however not with crutches and in very differed sorts of clothing. Beggar children are everywhere. No one pays them any attention. But how would you get close to the castle?"

"I'd be begging with a patch over an eye. I'd sit out under the walls with the others. I could do it. I know I could!"

"That's all fine. But how does a beggar child get an audience with the Prince? Tell me that," broke in John.

Hestor glanced at Jeb. Jeb smiled at Hewitt, and he smiled at Seth and back at Hewitt.

"How does a chicken and a giant get a prisoner to turn into a jester and be chased out of the castle by those guards who were meant to be watching him? How indeed?"

John heard the full story.

"John. You find it encouraging! You, who have been so unhappy about taking the advice of ones younger than yourself!"

He blushed.

"But now I need to ask you because I will not be there, and Jeb will not be close to the castle—are you happy to help look after these two and help keep them safe?" Hewitt asked.

Seth and Bella chorused their disapproval.

"I know! I know you can say that you both have and can look after yourselves. But I need to be reassured in my mind and a willing John would help do that."

All eyes were on the young steward.

"I would be willing to help in whatever way I could. I don't fancy myself in a chicken suit, though!"

This was said with a straight face.

"Then I think this is settled if it also meets with your blessing, Jeb and Hestor?"

"I think I am of more use here. But we'll see what tomorrow brings!" chuckled Hestor.

"We have brought food and provisions for all of us and for the horses, which we best attend to before it becomes too dark to see," said Jeb.

Seth went to the garden. Hestor, to see if she could find sufficient bedding for Seth and Jeb to sleep in the small shed. Tess joined Seth in the garden.

"Maybe I'll never get it all finished!"

"I think you will!" she brushed a tree stump clear and sat down. She asked, "Are you scared?"

"No. Not really. I was when I was in the guardhouse and I don't want to go back there. Are you?"

"I'm excited, but I know now it's not just a game. That people could die. It just feels that we can't not try to change things for the better. Is that how you feel?"

"Sort of. Just that it's something that was started and that we've both had a part in." He paused. "Tess. There's something I need to tell you."

"What's that?"

"The dream. It was a lie. I just made it up so that I could come to the castle!" said Seth.

Tess was thunderstruck. "But…but, how did you know about the Prince?"

"Hewitt told me one day!"

"So, it's all just a make-up. Not a dream at all!"

"Well, not totally. Like…like it's what I keep seeing in my mind. If I can do that, then maybe that's what we'll do. I just didn't want to lie to you."

"Well, that's something. I'm just amazed. It used to be me that was the liar," snarked Tess.

"Yes. But then you turned into a lady," mocked Seth.

She thought for a moment. Then, as his back was to her, bent over the garden bed, she gathered a pile of the discarded weeds and flung them over his head while pushing him face forward into the bed.

19

Beggar Seth

It was not even light when the preparations were begun in the small cottage. Outside, horses were readied, as inside, bags and trunks were made secure. Food was heated and Hewitt pulled on a heavy cloak to guard from the cold at the start of the journey. Now there was very little excitement; only the hush of knowing that soon, there would be partings and then the beginnings of endeavours whose outcomes they could not foretell.

With the breakfast over, hugs and handshakes were exchanged, and he rode into the greyness of the approaching day.

"No good gawking or worrying. It hasn't happened yet, and it probably won't—so spare the agony. Let's get you lot on the way before the sun is really up!"

They cleared up and prepared as best they could. It was just as they were about to go that Hestor called Seth aside. She lent on his shoulder as they went.

"Now," she started, "I'll have you know that I'm a little older than when you lived here. And no doubt, a little more silly, but I just wanted you to know that I still don't take kindly to people telling whoppers to me, even if it is for a good cause."

She felt his shoulders stiffen under her hand.

"No. Don't carry on. I know why you did it. But remember for next time, mostly we don't see ourselves in dreams. Mostly we see it through our own eyes, not as if we're separate and standing outside looking in."

She lightly cuffed him over the head.

"I'm sorry, Hestor. Truly. I just didn't know—"

But she cut him off. "Shhhh! I don't need to hear all that. And I had a sense that it was almost a premonition! Yes?" And she chuckled loudly. "I'm thinking that maybe you should do the rest of the garden before you go—just to make up!"

Seth looked horrified until he saw her smile.

"Get on with you! You look after yourself and don't get any smellier than you have to."

It was a subdued Seth that said goodbye to her later that morning.

"Don't you go missing me!" she shouted at him as he twisted in his saddle. "Remember now. I'm here having a good time with Tiny, so you have a good time looking after your Prince or whatever it is you're doing." Then as they were almost out of earshot, "And also—I expect clean clothes, or I'll set Tiny on you!"

Jeb shook his head in amusement. "She's a one, your Hestor!"

They paused after several hours to rest the horses and themselves. They stretched, ate a little, and planned how they might most safely re-enter the town. Bella had several jars of Hestor's potions that were both particularly useful, providing a valid reason for her journey outside the town in the company of a trusted steward and guard. Jeb and Seth would accompany them to the edge of the forest and then wait 'til nightfall before completing their journey.

"He'll stay tonight with me and tomorrow morning. I'll take great pleasure in finding some evil smelling clothes and then rolling him in the cattle yards."

Seth looked on with disgust.

"You've got to be authentic. We can't risk you looking too clean." All this, with a huge conspiratorial wink Jeb sent to Bella.

At the edge of the forest, the group parted.

"You'd better toss me a coin!" reminded Seth to Hewitt, John, and Bella's retreating figures.

It was dark when they came to Jeb's forge. They had come the last part of the journey on foot, leading the horses, so that they would make as little noise as possible. Dogs barked at their progress, but mostly it was still and quiet.

"I supposed one good thing with Mr. Fancy Belt up at the castle, is that we don't have to worry quite so much as we used to. I'm a bit sick of having to put my door back on. All I've done since I've met you is dress up in silly clothes, ride horses, and put my door back on."

"Don't forget climbing trees. It's a break from black-smithing?" said Seth.

"Well, it's certainly that. That it is! Still, I'm starting to see the joy in a well-made shoe and having my door stay in place longer than a week."

The hut was cold, and they didn't even bother to light a fire. They stabled the horse, and then shivered for a while under every blanket they could find.

In the morning, Seth was loathe to climb into the clothes the Jeb brought him. However, he made porridge while Jeb began the forge fire and had the small eye patch made by a friendly tailor a few doors away. Jeb was bright and boisterous, but Seth knew he was anxious and would show it by being loud and cheery.

Finally, Seth was ready. Dressed in the rags, the dirt smeared eye patch, and faintly small crutches, he didn't need any further disguise.

Seth noticed Jeb and the tailor examine him.

"We'll put a bit of ash from the fire in your hair. All those baths have made your hair look a bit too clean and healthy. Also, rub your hands in the dirt in case your nails look more like a scholar's than a beggar's. Here's an old cap for your collection and remember, dear boy, not to take any chances. Sit there. Be a good beggar and let Bella and John look out for you. I'll have a clean shirt and a decent meal ready for you when you get home. Watch yourself now!" fussed Jeb, fretting over every detail.

Seth adjusted the patch and felt the familiar pressure under his arms of the crutches. With Jeb keeping an eye out, he swung out the door and onto the path that led to the castle.

By the time he was climbing the hill to the castle gates, Seth felt that he really was a beggar boy on crutches. The other beggars who crammed the causeway edges, each with their own space, held no great sympathy for another who might take the meagre offerings from them.

"Move on. You, young git. Don't stop here!"

"Oi! Where are you from? Don't you go crowding our territory now. Keep going!"

They were the most ragged, miserable bunch that Seth had ever seen. Certainly, they'd always been there, but up until now, he had never noticed them as clearly. They were all ages; women without teeth surrounded by wailing children, blind old men with bandages over vacant eyes, sick and destitute young women with sores on their faces and arms—the poorest of the poor.

Seth shuddered and kept moving, in the hope that he could find a place closer to the gates. Except, the closer he came, the shriller came the chorus of complaints.

"They're taken. Get out of it!"

"You can't push in up there. These places have been got for years. You stop there!"

He didn't because he couldn't. Luckily for him, when Seth came to the gates, the guards took pity on him and forced the others to make some space. They forced the other beggars back with the wooden handles of their pikes.

"Make some space. You've got another to join you. Make him welcome, you lot, or we'll drive you all off."

This was sufficient threat. Despite jeers, insults, and promises of retribution, Seth found a spot not far from the main gateway where he was able to watch what happened. And importantly—who came and went.

It was one of the longest and most trying mornings of Seth's life. Mostly, people sat and enjoyed the weak sunlight. But every time a traveller or visitor came to the castle, then the beggar folk set up a caterwauling and crying out that made Seth cower until he realised that he must also do the same. He gibbered and held up his hand; occasionally a few coins came their way, though not to Seth.

"Stand on your crutches and sag a bit!" came a voice at his elbow.

Seth looked down into the bandaged face of a man who was missing one arm. He thought he saw an eye move beneath the filthy bandage.

"Aye. It was me that spoke. If you want to do this properly, then you have to pull at their hearts, such as they've got. You're young. You're on crutches. You might also have lost an eye. Who knows? But you've got to play 'em son, or you'll starve."

Seth was about to reply, but by then the eye was stationary. It was as if no one had spoken. The man smelt awful.

He followed the advice. A column of guards escorted a noble family into the castle, Seth caught the eye of a lady by suitably sagging and looking woebegone. She gestured to a steward who flung a few small coins in his cap as the rest howled with envy. Shaken, but pleased, he sat again.

"No honour among thieves here," came the voice at his elbow again.

When he was sure no one else was looking, he slid one of his coins into the tin of the man alongside him. A few minutes later, he heard a muted thanks.

The rest of the morning was as before. He scored a few more coins that he shared. Then, with few visitors except the movement of soldiers, the beggars and Seth settled down to wait and argue amongst themselves.

"Sometime about noon, life can be a little luckier." It was the armless man again. "Some days, they come from the kitchen, pick a few and give us the leftovers from the lunch. The main thing if you're picked, is to cram in your pockets what you can't eat and be as thankful as you can. Practise your curtsey, if you know what I mean."

By the time a maid appeared from the kitchen, the beggars were beside themselves with hunger, misery, and anticipation. They began yelling and waving as soon as they saw the girl walk from the back of the kitchen and towards the gate.

"Me. Pick me. I've not eaten for days."

"Look at the children. Have some mercy!"

The girl looked as if she would rather not look at any of them. With the guards beside her, she picked two of the more healthy-looking beggars who whooped and set off for the kitchen while the girl appeared to be looking for someone. Seth's excitement rose when he saw her recognise him and then point him towards the kitchen. Again, he heard the howls of protest:

"He's new. Not him! He's not one of us!"

But it made no difference to her choice.

Seth made his way, following the two beggars. He turned a corner of the building and saw the two of them being ushered into a doorway.

By now, the kitchen maid was alongside him. "She asked me to look for you. You're to eat inside."

Seth nodded and tried to look as humble and grateful as he could. With as much good grace as she could muster, the girl held the door open for him while staying at a distance. It was as if he was a leper or had the plague.

The two other beggars were already seated at a small table and were wolfing into the meal placed in front of them. Seth sat at their side, picking into the plate of food placed in front of him. On it was thrown all the off cuts, leftovers and burnt pieces off the main hall dinner. Pieces of roast, overcooked parsnip, broken drumsticks—Seth ate what he could, the rest he stashed in the folds of his ragged tunic. What he couldn't finish was eyed, and then taken by the other two until his plate was empty.

"You two—out. Leave the plates. You. Stay here." This was shouted at them by a huge, red-faced lady who was obviously one of the chief cooks. She waddled over to her huge stove while keeping an eye firmly on him.

Seth sat as his plate was wrenched away and a moment later, Bella swept into the room as if she were a princess on an errand of mercy.

"Boy. This is for you." She placed an old, well patched cloak before him. "We can see that you can't walk. It may keep you warm."

The cook knew her place. She curtsied and remarked how kind the young lady was to think of the poor and helpless.

"You look great," whispered Bella. "Really horrible." Then with a smile, she was gone, leaving Seth somewhat devastated.

The cook was yelling at Seth before the door had properly closed. "Right, you. Take your one eye, your crutches, your precious cloak, and you get your filthy body out of my kitchen. If I had my way, you'd never get past the gates. Handouts like this just make you worse. You need a job like every other honest folk."

Seth resisted the temptation to offer to stir one of the pots with his crutch. The cook, in tone and manner, reminded him of his dead aunt and that was enough.

Quickly, he collected what was his. With much touching of his forelock in respect and appreciation, Seth pushed open the door with one crutch and escaped the cook's continuing harangue about the uselessness of charity to beggars and thieves.

He was screamed at when he emerged, and as quietly as he could, he made his way back to his place. He waited until a passing merchant distracted the other beggars again before he leaned over and placed much of his saved food by the blind beggar. Seth was about to tell him of its existence when—to his surprise—he found that the food was found without any problem at all.

Seth was astounded.

"There's none so blind as those who cannot see," the man muttered under his breath. He ate quickly without a fuss. At the end, he turned his head to the road and said as if speaking to mid-air, "There's some that are grateful. Some who are not! I'm one of the former, lad. If ever there were something you want seen that no one would think is seen, I could be your man."

Seth still had food left and he thought of the monstrous woman with many children. He was moving to pass to some to her when he felt a hand on his wrist.

"Don't do it, lad. Give her anything, and she'll not take it in quiet gratitude but will let all know where it came from and why you must get her more. I know that sounds hard but trust me on this one! Gratitude doesn't come easily to all. It can just feed greed and neediness."

So, he didn't. Seth knew that the last thing he needed to do was to draw any attention.

As the day grew colder and the chill began in the afternoon air, then most of the beggars moved off to find places of some shelter for the night. The woman screamed a few parting insults and threats at Seth before she and her brood made off—like a bedraggled chook surrounded by darting nervous chicks. There was now some distance between Seth, his armless friend, and the rest.

"Where will you sleep tonight?" Seth asked.

"Where I normally do, unless the cattle are being penned for sale. It's at the back of the inn. Most nights, I get a bowl of stew from the cook there. He thinks I know his dead brother from the wars," replied the man.

"And you didn't!"

"Who knows, lad. I've known a lot of people in my life, and he could have been one of them."

"Were you in the war? Is that where you lost your arm?" Seth's unpatched eye widened.

The man grinned.

"Now, saying that would be a trade secret, and might strain our excellent relationship, if you know what I mean. Thank you for the food. If you don't mind, I'll follow you down the path, drawn just by the power of your voice along the way." The tone was mocking.

So, the crippled boy on the crutches led the armless, 'blind' man down the embankment away from the castle.

Seth asked for the man's name, but he just smiled. "Names can be trouble, young'un. No offence, but I don't go by any name anymore."

Seth made his way back to Jeb's as quickly as he could. He was both drawn to, and scared by, his armless friend, who seemed such a mixture of the honest and the deceitful—so unlike Jeb. He changed out of his rags once he was in Jeb's hut. That night, they talked as they ate.

"Well. You've landed on your feet, young'un. That's right and no mistake. You got fed, with some leftovers for me. The bones that'll make good soup and…even a coin or two. You've got a friend, strange though he might be. And the Lady Bella has a plan arranged so that she might see you when she wishes. All that in a day! All I've done, is to take some shears from a plough and straighten them. Maybe I should give up the forge and begin begging."

"I just hate having to smell that bad," grumbled Seth.

"Scared it'll frighten the Lady Bella off?"

"Jeb!" he gasped. "…She is very pretty, don't you think? It's not just me."

Seth's question made Jeb almost choke on his food.

"What's funny? It's just a question." Seth grimaced.

"Keep your shirt on. Particularly that clean one! I'm not laughing at you. And yes. It's not just you. Tess or Bella, or whatever she calls herself, is a very striking young lady. Not one of your delicate blooming flowers, but strong and determined and full of life."

"She'll grow up to marry a nobleman, won't she?"

"Oh, yes! Probably looking for one with money, considering the state of their finances and estates. But—and this is worth re-membering lad—I don't fancy anyone being able to marry her off to anyone she didn't fancy! Does that answer your round about question? Put your mind at rest!"

It didn't at all.

That night as they lay in bed, a quieter Seth was now more selective with his questions. "Can you get to be a knight, or do you have to be born one, Jeb?"

"There's tales of common folk rising to be knighted."

"Do you believe them?" asked Seth.

"I don't disbelieve them?" answered Jeb. "I've just never met anyone who got to be knighted. But that doesn't mean it can't be done."

"Would you have to do something very special to be knighted?"

"I don't think the Prince does it for shoeing horses, if that's what you're asking?" The blacksmith smirked.

"So, you'd have to do something pretty special—like save the kingdom. Or risk your life to save the Prince—something like that?"

"With this new one, you might be better off making him a new hat or designing a cloak to match his horse." At Seth's expression, Jeb added, "That's a joke, Seth. Just in case you're doing some hat sketches there in your mind."

"I wasn't. I was just thinking!"

"You weren't at all. You were plotting how to be knighted so that Bella wouldn't think of you as a smelly beggar and Lord Alfred would think you were the best thing since quilted codpieces. Right?"

"Sort of!" huffed Seth.

"Well, just think of it this way. You're racing about trying to impress someone, actually means you think they're the sort of person that needs impressing. Shallow-like. If they're as good as you think, then you won't need to go fighting dragons to show 'em how brave you are because they already know it. And if it's the nameless girl we think it is, then for goodness' sake—you've already saved her from the Riders, dressed up as a chicken, and helped a man escape from the dungeon right in front of her. You've done your impressing, if that's what it takes. I reckon you need to sit back on your hands for a while and see what she has to offer," Jeb said, wisely.

Seth was impressed. "Do you really? But she's Lord Alfred's ward! And she thinks I'm stupid."

"Don't matter? Being stupid never stopped me being happy, now. You know what they say about cats?"

"What?"

"That you don't make friends with a cat by chasing after it. You have to stay still and wait for it to come to you," advised the blacksmith.

"What if it doesn't come?" asked Seth.

"Well, I guess it's not your cat, so you throw rocks at it."

Seth laughed so hard he thought he might wet himself.

"Now, no rocks at young ladies. Just settle yourself. You've got a big day of begging tomorrow."

Seth went to sleep much relieved but still wondering at the possibility of being knighted if he exposed the Riders, saved the kingdom, and rescued Belle from drowning, even if he couldn't swim yet.

***

After a night in clean clothes, Seth found it hard to return to his rags. He also found himself closing the eye that he had the patch over before it was even put on. After a good breakfast, he snuck out of Jeb's home and up the road to the castle.

"I'll think differently about beggars once this is over," were Seth's last words to Jeb upon leaving.

Again, he had to run the gauntlet of enraged and misery cloaked cripples and destitute orphans. He sat down, put his cap out and prepared to wait. In the morning, there was little movement in or out of the castle and little conversation amongst the beggars. For his greeting from his blind man, he had received just a grunt. If possible, the man smelt worse—a mix of animal manure, alcohol, and wet straw. He dozed next to Seth.

About noon, trade picked up a little, but today was not a scrap day at the cook's kitchen. Now, there was a despairing and desperate note to the calls and wails of the beggars as they tried to gather the attention of the passersby.

Seth could barely bring himself to join with any enthusiasm, until he heard a call of advice from alongside him, "Don't hold back. They might find out you're well fed and you'd be really in for it."

He took the advice offered. Seth went back to hanging off his crutches, looking piteous and calling for alms with as much despair as he could muster. He gathered a few coppers. As before, he quietly shared them.

By now, he was aware of how hungry he was, and of what that would mean later in the day. It was halfway through the afternoon before Seth was forced out of his reverie in a sudden and surprising way.

A sergeant-at-arms and two guards strode from the walls and pushed their way among the beggars producing a hullabaloo of complaints and curses.

"Where is he?" called the sergeant. "The boy with crutches. The crippled one. Where is he?"

The monstrous woman with the brood was beside herself with glee as she rocked to-and-fro and pointed Seth out.

"What'd he do? What was it?" she bellowed showing a mouth almost completely devoid of teeth.

By now, the two guards had Seth under the arms and bodily lifted him from the ground. Seth's protests were swept away in the cries of delight and triumph that went on about him.

The last thing Seth remembered before clutching at his crutches, was a hoarse whisper from alongside him, "Sometimes things aren't as they seem!"

And then he was carried, crutches and legs dangling into the castle proper.

He heard the sergeant yelling at those at his feet, "Don't forget it. We leave you here only because we choose to. Anymore trouble and we'll move all of you on."

Seth tried to protest again, but received a cuff over the ear that half-knocked him senseless.

"Shut up. Steward will know what to do with you."

He was half-carried, half-thrown up the kitchen steps and beyond to a well-lit room behind the dining room. As he began to claw his way up from the floor, he recognised the man before him—it was John.

He said nothing as the guards were thanked and dismissed. He gulped in disbelief as John produced a belt and began to beat a leather covered chair alongside him.

"Yell as if I'm beating the tripe out of you!" John whispered, urgently.

Seth hesitated.

"Do it. Don't think. Just do it!" hissed the steward.

So, he did for the next few minutes. John flayed the chair and Seth yelled out as if his hide was being beaten from his body. Then, he stopped.

"Snivel a bit," ordered John. "As if you've had a beating."

Seth found that he could do this quite easily.

"Now," said John. "Rest on this much beaten and punished chair. You'll find a bowl of soup on the table. Eat it quickly and I'll tell you what we know."

Seth took no further encouraging. He sat and began spooning the soup that was as thick as stew into his mouth while he kept his attention upon the steward.

"The Prince is coming this weekend. The jousts are to be officially declared open by His Highness, and that night there is to be a lavish banquet and feast in his honour. From what we know, the Prince and his followers will eat and drink well, then fall into elegantly prepared bedrooms at some time in the early morning. Then at some time that morning, he will stagger to the chapel to give his royal blessing to the early mass. If… anything is to be attempted against him, then the night of the feast is the most likely. Everywhere else, he is too well watched and guarded. Beyond that, we don't know."

Seth gulped hot soup and gnawed on fresh bread.

"The only other news is about the informer—Tad. He's in very thick with the Captain. He's not been seen to leave his side for the last few days. As thick as thieves or something even worse."

"Do you think that…" The bread got in the way in Seth's mouth.

"We do," John pressed on. "It makes sense, doesn't it? He's already had a taste of the good life and no doubt he's been promised something wonderful if he'd rid the Duke of the one thing that stands between him and his ambitions."

"What if a group of Riders burst into the Prince's room and killed him when the castle is sound asleep after the banquet?" asked Seth.

"There'd still be guards on duty."

"What if they were replaced with men less sympathetic?" Seth probed.

"I have 20 men I can keep close on the night. It would be good to have someone closer," answered the steward.

"Maybe I could hide in there. I'm only small. I could. Really, I could."

Seth could see John's resolve weakening.

"Think about it. Risks there!" said Seth.

"You'll have to be getting back. We'll wait 'til the Prince comes. I'll stay as close as I can to him and have Bella seek out the lie of the land—where the Prince will stay and where you might be able to slip close to him. Now, practise your limp. Cry a few tears as you go. I'm sorry, I can't order the guards to be kind to you, but I can tell them to put you back where they found you. Or would you like to be thrown out completely?" John left the decision up to Seth.

"No. Just put me back or else it will be too hard for me to be near the castle and see what happens. Thanks for the soup."

"Take care, young one!" He ruffled Seth's hair and smiled at him. Then, John changed his expression and tone to shout for the guards, "Guards! Come! Take this lying, smelly child back to where you found him. Perhaps now he might know the meaning of the word gratitude!"

Again, Seth found himself lifted and carried across the courtyard to be sent sprawling at the gates. Wearily, and as if in great pain, he hoisted himself onto his crutches and limped back to his place as the cat calls and jeers resounded around him.

"Teach you! That it will. A good thrashing is what you needed. Fancy giving us a bad name," frothed his tormentor.

"Shut up, you great tub of lard!" he heard himself yell at her, and then was horrified to hear what he'd said. If she was furious before, now she was roused to boiling point.

"What did you call me? What was it? I'll break your crutches and shove 'em down your throat—you useless little faggot."

And like a galleon in full sail, she strode across bodies to make good her threat.

Seth realised he had a real beating coming.

It was hard to know what happened next, unless you had some idea about the present blind, one-armed beggar. Sufficient to say, that as she roared towards Seth; somehow the beggar twisted to escape the noise and, in his writhing, he connected with her leg, and she went down on top of him cursing and screaming. By then, the guards had come, half-serious and half-amused by it all. They poked her with their pikes and turned her back like they were dealing with a wild animal.

"Go on. Back you go, Emma. No fighting. You start anything and we'll have you all out. Just cut it out, you old cow!"

"Watch who you're calling an old cow. I'll have your guts for garters…" she growled.

But Emma knew she was beaten. Still seething, she dropped back in her spot to be covered by crying and disturbed children.

Seth let himself down shakily.

"Don't you rest too easy! You…you…crippled boy there. You'll get yours, that I promise! I'll break your other leg—and your head as well," she raged.

But by now, all the beggars knew their positions were precarious and alliances were easily strained when that occurred. She was hushed and calmed while still red-faced and abusive.

"Was that an accident or did you mean to trip her?" Seth whispered to the one-armed beggar.

"Depends really on who wants to know. To most, I'd say it was just the actions of a poor, blind beggar who was suddenly frightened by the noise about him and the pounding of feet. Wouldn't you say that's what you saw?" replied the man.

Seth nodded. "That's certainly what I saw!"

"Good, then. I like to pay my way."

The few coins Seth had gathered made their way into the tin alongside him in the next half hour.

"What's *really* happening, lad?" came the enquiring from alongside him.

Seth weighed up what he might say.

"I'm foulmouthed. I'm a drunk and I'd steal anything that wasn't nailed down, but I'm trustworthy," offered the man. "I don't betray those who help me, and you have when you had no need to. So, tell me what you will or not. It's the same difference to me. I don't blather when I'm drunk, so you're safe there."

Seth pondered and then risked it. "The Prince is coming."

Seth thought for a moment that he had made a huge mistake. The demeanour of the beggar changed. It was like seeing a snake lying in the sun, all limp and unmoving, suddenly uncoil, rise on its tail, flare its head as if to strike and then as quickly slump back to being just a small coiled shape. Suddenly, in the place of a blind beggar he'd seen the shape of a man—not a dirty, smelly beggar; but a warrior.

Seth was quiet; he was scared. He was even scared to ask, but he had to, "What is it? Why did you do that?"

"You'll have to tell me. I'm blind, remember. I couldn't see what I did."

"You straightened up when I said the 'Prince,' as if you were someone else or as if you were going to strike someone," Seth explained.

"Did I, then? Well, well. After all these years. You'd think I would have gotten over it, wouldn't you?" the man muttered.

"I don't know what you're talking about?"

Seth could hear hesitation.

"Just keep it nice and quiet. I don't want everyone listening. Do you know what a broadsword is, lad?"

"Of course. It's a big sword that you need two hands for. The best fighters use them, and they can cut a man in two, even bring down a horse," said Seth.

"Aye. That's right. How many hands do I have? Tell me how many you see?"

"You've just got one. Your left one!"

"Ever wondered where the other one is, eh?"

Seth bit his lip. "Yes, but I wouldn't …."

"Been brought up, not just dragged up. Too polite to ask. So, I'll tell you. I was a swordsman. Not just any swordsman, but the best in the King's own guard. I went everywhere that he did. He'd even nod at me as he passed. I'd practise for hours even when everyone else had gone to rest after training. I was good, lad. I was really good…" his voice trailed off.

Seth wanted to know more. "What happened? Did you get beaten in a fight?"

He snorted. "Never. I wasn't bested in all my years. No. Not beaten. Beat myself!"

Seth looked around, but no one else was listening or interested.

"I started drinking. Just a bit. Not on duty, but in my time off. Then it changed, and I started drinking all the time. I got caught. Not just caught but really, *really* nobbled."

He paused for a moment as if deep in thought.

"I was on guard outside the King's chamber. Only the hard picked got to do that. A great honour! I didn't know I'd drunk so much beforehand. I went to sleep on the watch and they found me. Dragged me up in front of the commander who I'd known for years. I expected that they'd throw me out of the guards and I'd go back to being just a soldier at the front or shipped off to fight the Picts. But no. No! Somehow the young Prince heard about it all. Who knows how or why—but he persuaded his father, the King, who was very ill by then, to make an example of me. To impress upon people how important the duty was to protect the King."

"They chopped off your arm!" Seth said it as quietly as he could while he felt the horror of it all.

"Aye. As you said. They chopped off my arm before the whole body of the guard. Ladies in attendance, like a festival or an occasion. Did it hurt? They kept me so full of grog. These men I'd lived and worked with for years. They knew it was unfair but what could they do but try and keep me drunk." The man grumbled before he continued, "I remember fainting and coming to later on. It was a clean axe. I didn't die. Just couldn't use a sword anymore or earn a living. And that's my story. Here I am. Still drinking and begging so I can drink. So, lad. The Prince and I go back a long way, although I've not seen him since that day he stood up, dressed to the nines like a popinjay, and demanded that I be punished. You could say that I'm looking forward to seeing him. I hope he falls off his horse as he's passing and I'll bite his throat out before they get to him!"

For Seth it was all too monstrous. After a while and most hesitantly he said, "I'm really sorry about your arm. I would have liked to have known you also, before, when you were a swordsman!"

"I believe you. And I know you're no beggar, but no one will hear that from me. What you're doing here, I haven't got a clue."

A few travellers passed.

A troop of horsemen came in from a hunting party with a deer, several pigs, and hares draped over saddles. The beaters carried ducks and pheasants that had also been taken. The beggars stared at the huge deer hounds that strained on their leashes. It was chaotic, but it gave Seth time to think. By the time some order had returned, he had decided what to do.

He moved a little closer to the beggar who had once been a proud and trusted guard of the king. "I've got to tell you a secret and ask your help!"

"And how's that? Are you wanting me to show you where you can get the foulest and strongest brew in the town? That I could do!" The former swordsman snorted.

"It's strange," observed Seth. "You want to kill the Prince, but I want to save him, and you might help us to do that. No! Just listen. I don't think much of him either, but it could even be worse. That's why I need you to listen."

For the next hour their begging lacked conviction. The two were deep in conversation and argument. They were still at it when the cold began to descend and other beggars began to decamp.

2 0

Hiding

"**D**id you talk him around?" Jeb asked Seth that evening.

"I don't think so, Jeb. I'd never heard anyone hate so much. He doesn't want to see anyone else kill the Prince," Seth explained.

"Except him?"

"One day, when he stops drinking. So, he says. It's all that keeps him going."

They were lying back with coals in the fire still glowing.

Seth's feet squirmed, uncertain. "Do you think I shouldn't have told him? Was I stupid?"

"I think you'd better learn to trust your own judgements. You said you thought he'd be a good ally."

"He sees it all, Jeb, and he doesn't miss anything. When I told him about the Riders, he just went; 'Oh. That's where they were going!' He'd seen them."

"So, he's not blind?"

"I don't think so. But I don't know. I suppose the good point is, that everyone else thinks that he is."

"… And they won't be too careful in front of a blind man." Jeb rubbed his chin thoughtfully. "You know that they'll clean the town up before 'his nibs' gets here. They might move all you beggar's off somewhere so that he doesn't have to see you all. They do it for every king, in case it upsets their digestion."

"So, it might be tomorrow that I'll need to hide in the castle," concluded Seth. "Bella and John might want to risk it on the day of the tournament."

Jeb hesitated, sighed and began. "Seth, you sure you're not reading too much into the Prince coming here? It seems to me, that you're taking a mighty big risk on what is a pretty big hunch. You could get yourselves all killed for nothing. That's all I'm saying. How's it feel now? Knowing or just being heroic; heroic could get you killed?"

He took a moment to consider. "When I'm really quiet, then it feels like it's true. And Hestor told me I had to trust to that. She said when you're really, really still, then you can know what you have to do."

"Well, I've never stopped long enough to know that one," Jeb chuckled. Then, seriously, he added, "It's just that, once the Prince is in there for the night, they'll raise up the drawbridge, lower the portcullis and I won't be doing any rescue missions unless I manage to fashion a pair of wings in the next few days. I doubt if even 'chicken boy' could do much. You know that?"

Seth nodded.

The next morning the news was out. It was official; the Prince was coming. As such, the town was to be cleaned up in his honour. In the square, officials from the castle were organising work parties and ordering people to observe curfews, take their rubbish to the river and to get their best clothes ready. On the Saturday they could attend at the jousts, and that night there would be huge spit roasts for all.

Seth was anxious that he might be turned back from the path to the castle. Except, as he neared the gates, he saw that amongst all the bustle and the preparation, the beggars still occupied their normal places. No one had moved them and there was the hope of charity in the air.

This did not extend to all—his one-armed ally looked worse than ever. His skin was the same colour as the dirty bandage that hooded his eyes.

"His Highness—Lord Fop, is on his way," grumbled the man.

"I told you. Are you with us?" asked Seth.

"The mongrel that took my arm!" he spat. "You're thinking that he might have changed. I don't want him to at all. I want him to be worse so that I don't have to be ashamed to hate him. I want him to be the mongrel I once knew."

Their lunch came in time to save Seth. He helped the Prince's most unlikely supporter to his feet and led him into the castle courtyard. Food was brought out to them. Potato and leek soup with chunks of slightly stale bread.

"You. You with the crutches! You don't eat out here where you can steal plates again. You eat in here where we can see you. Move it!" shouted a guard.

On the end of the long kitchen table sat his soup and his bread. Alongside it, sat Bella.

"You be right there with that smelly one, Lady Bella?" called the incredulous red-faced cook.

"I'm fine. Thank you. If he's impertinent, I'll take away his soup."

"As long as you're right. Can't be good, you mingling with those below your station, miss. Charity gets you nowhere in this world."

"Thank you, cook," Bella dismissed her with a practised smile.

For a moment, Bella smiled at Seth; not the kind of smile of someone who saw a friend in ragged clothes, but the smile of someone who was glad to see him.

"Don't smile back," she warned under her breath. "Cook will be watching. Eat your soup!"

"I think I've never been told by so many people to eat my soup," Seth muttered.

"Well, you need instruction. Maybe then, you wouldn't be in so much trouble. Listen carefully," Bella started. "Tomorrow, the courtyard will be open to the crowds. There'll be jugglers and the like. Come, and I'll find a way of getting you into the castle. John will have his men hidden all around the chamber, just in case. There's no word from Hewitt or Lord Alfred."

"We're on our own then," he surmised.

"Are you still going to try and hide in his chambers—that silly idea of yours!"

Seth closed his mouth. He knew some arguments weren't for winning.

Bella persisted. "Aren't you afraid or are you too silly?"

"Bella, are *you* afraid? You asked me that once." He snuck this out of the corner of his mouth as bread followed soup.

"What do you mean?" She raised a brow.

"I mean like in the forest, with the Riders and all. Are you scared like that?"

"No. Not of that. I'm only afraid that all this might end, and I'll wake up back in the village with cold potatoes and pigs. That's all I'm afraid of—that I'll lose this."

Seth chewed on his bread, and then spoke hesitantly, "When you're really rich and married to some knight or Earl, will you still talk to me?"

Bella stared at him as if he was some creature newly escaped from the marshes. "What? What are you saying? What goes on in that head of yours?"

"Nothing. Just, I was wondering," he murmured.

"Well. Just eat your soup and stop being stupid or I will call cook over. Really. You really are the weirdest boy I've ever met. I just hope you don't get any weirder." Bella rolled her eyes, good-naturedly.

It felt like some sort of strange praise— 'weird' was better than 'stupid,' he ate his soup until Bella had to leave. She called as she went, "Finish your soup. Don't take the plate this time. Thank you, cook! I'll tell Lady Eloise how helpful you were!"

Seth left before the cook decided to tell him how useless and awful he was. He was tempted to steal the bowl but thought better of it. Instead, he made his way back to the gates.

He noticed the children laughing and the mother, Emma, almost happy. He felt sad to know that the one-armed man was right—they'd have few such days of joy or contentment. There was no ease to come for them. He knew that hope for better days was for other folk, but not them. Seth didn't really want to stay; however, he thought he better not appear as if there was something else he should do, or some other place he could be.

"Why don't you go off home," suggested Seth's one-armed ally. "I've got nothing else to do until the inn gets going at dusk, and they'll be a few along who might give money to an old soldier. Don't wait about unless you have to. I've told you; I'll keep my blind eye open. If anything happens, you'll know."

"Tomorrow I won't be dressed in beggar gear. I'll be dressed in my normal clothes," Seth informed him.

"Well, that's nice for some. I'll still be here in the same clothes, with the same arm and the sound of my tin. So, you'll not mistake me for someone else, now, will you?"

Seth was confused by his words until he looked down and saw the same mocking smile. Quite gently, the man spoke to Seth, "Off you go. Don't spend more time here than you have to. Also, lad, if I don't see you again, good luck with your life. You're a plucky one!"

"I'll be back! Honest!" insisted Seth.

"Maybe. I'd just rather not take the chance. Come here, lad. Before you go, I've got something for you. Don't look now. Just take it. And lad; one more thing! I did used to have a name. I was called Garvin. I'm told it means, 'the sword-wielder.' Funny that! That was my name, and at one time, I was proud to own. Good to have met you!"

The 'blind' beggar—Garvin, pushed a small parcel wrapped in layers of Hessian into the confused boy's arms, took his hand and pressed it briefly.

***

Seth made his way home, quite slowly through the crowds that were coming into the town for the day of the tournament. He wanted to see what it was that he'd been given, but he also wanted to get to the shelter of the hut before he looked. He paused by the forge where Jeb was working on armour for the following day.

All about, were knights and their squires; mostly squires bringing their master's arms or armour to have finishing touches and edges made. Seth knew Jeb would be busy as long as there was light. Seth slipped into the hut, laid his crutches down and unwrapped the present he'd been given. It was quite heavy and hard, like metal. He unrolled the last flap of Hessian and a leather scabbard, brown with much use, lay in front of him. Carefully, with his heart pumping, Seth put his hand around the handle of the instrument and pulled it free.

It was a knife. It had a wooden handle that was inlaid with metal patterns and swirls. The blade was sturdy and strong. Seth knew that this was not a ceremonial tool, such as nobles carried to show their wealth, but a knife that had been made to be used. It was a tool, not an ornament.

Why Garvin had given it to him, he had no idea.

At this point, there was no room for stupidity. So, he waited. He made soup and waited for the sun to go down and the forge to empty of its customers. Seth made sure there was a jug of fresh water ready for Jeb when he came in.

Eventually, he did. Seth almost waited until he had drunk his water before he showed him.

"He gave me this!" Seth exclaimed.

Jed didn't even question him; he just held the knife in his two hands and rolled it over to better examine it.

He whistled between his teeth. "Well! Well! What have you got here?"

"I didn't know. I've never seen one like that before. Is it rare or special?" wondered Seth.

"It's both these and more. If you need proof of your friend's story, then this could be it. It's a broadswords man's waist knife. They all carried one because with the weight of their broadswords, sometimes they'd get dispossessed in battle, and then the very best of them would have a knife like this at their waist so they wouldn't be completely defenceless," Jeb explained. "This one is a beauty, Seth. Not just the workings on the haft, but the make of the knife. Feel it in your hand. It was made by a real craftsman, Seth. Someone who really knew his trade."

"Could you make it?"

Jeb laughed a little sadly. "Not in a year of Christmases. I do what I do well; don't misunderstand me. But, this is made by a man who folded metal over metal over metal until he had a beauty. I'm a bit scared to let you have it, Seth. It's not a toy. This was made to kill people."

"Why would he give it to me? Why me?"

"Ah! Well, that's hard to know exactly, but I'd say he was paying you a huge compliment. He was both thanking you for your kindness and giving you one of his most precious things. Maybe the only thing he hasn't sold or pawned for drink. It's a great gift. You should be proud." Jeb offered the knife back to Seth.

"Jeb, I can't keep it. It's his. Why would he give it to *me?* He might need it again." Seth knew by Jeb's silence that he was holding something back. "There's something I don't know, and you do. It's about the knife and why he gave it to me."

Jeb sighed. "Seth, I might be horribly wrong. I think he gave it to you because he was saying goodbye to you."

"He wasn't saying goodbye! He's waiting for the Prince. He told me his name," Seth insisted.

"That's *why* he told you his name."

"But he'll be back tomorrow. He told me! He did. Why would he go away?" Seth desperately asked.

Jeb crossed to Seth, put the knife in the scabbard and picked the boy up.

"He might be there tomorrow. But I think you just did a great favour to that man. We'll see what tomorrow might bring. Either way, you should be proud of such a gift. You hang onto it."

"I don't understand, Jeb…"

"You will, lad. There are some things that make themselves plain as time goes on! Some things, you can't force. You do and you break them."

Jeb's forecast was true. They had just breakfasted the following morning, after Jeb had added wood to the forge when there was a knock at the door and an unfamiliar face appeared.

"I'm sorry to be disturbing your morning meal. I'd be looking for a boy with crutches. I was told to look at the forge."

"What you wanting to see him for?" Jeb asked, protective as ever.

"I've got some sad news for him. A friend of his died last night in the cold."

Seth was up and alert in an instant, fear gripping his heart. "Who? Who was it?"

"I don't know his name. He was a one-armed beggar who used to sleep at the back of my inn. I'm sorry to be telling you, but a few days ago he asked me to tell you, as if he already knew.

I was to thank you and to give you this. He said you already had a part of it!"

It was a broad leather belt. It had once held at least one scabbard. Jeb thanked him and showed him out.

When Jeb returned, Seth was sitting stone-like at their bench table with the leather belt wrapped around his wrists.

"You were right!" he said between tears. He sniffled and wiped his eyes and nose on his arm.

"I'm sorry to be so," Jeb said, sadly.

"What did you mean last night when you said that I'd helped him? How did I? He's dead."

"Oh, lad! He was waiting for you or someone. He'd sunk so low that he'd given up even *his name*. You gave him back the strength to respect himself again—just your kindness, and the fact that you trusted him. He knew he was worthy of trust again. You've done well, lad. Come here and I'll give you a hug, and then we better make sure that they bury him in a proper grave—not just toss him out. There was a great man there once. He deserved better," consoled Jeb.

A pall had descended on their small hut.

Jeb tried best to cheer Seth up, but he would not be so. He sat and held the belt with the knife, saying nothing.

"I'm worried about you, boy. You've not asked a question in over five minutes. Perhaps your brain is melting," Jeb said, trying to lighten the mood.

Normally, Seth would have laughed but he felt too sad.

Jeb knew that he must attend the forge soon. "Seth, it's fine to be sad and to miss this good man who sunk so low. You take your time."

Seth nodded. He knew Jeb was right, but he just felt heavy, as if he could sleep for a week. "I'll be all right. I just need to stay still for a while. You know!"

"I do. You know where I am if you need me. You can dress in your real clothes today. I'll be keeping the forge going all day to belt the dents out of the armour that the knights have inflicted on each other. Come and see me before you head up to the castle."

Seth sat on the bed once Jeb had gone. He missed this strange, flawed man whom he had just met. He missed his mother, and Hestor in the forest. He missed his father who was away, somewhere that he didn't know.

Seth cried some more, feeling small and alone. Gradually, the first rush of his sadness was blunted a little, until it was a slow, deep ache in his guts. He believed Jeb when he had told him that he had helped Garvin in some way. But it was in a way that he didn't quite understand, and he was still faced with the overwhelming reality of the man's sudden death. He couldn't sit alongside Garvin anymore and gag at the powerful stench that accompanied him, nor talk to him about his plans. His world felt a little emptier.

"Maybe I don't even care about the Prince, anymore. Maybe that's why he left the knife with me, so that I could do what he always wanted to do. What do I care about the Prince or the Duke? Nothing changes," Seth muttered, crestfallen.

He ate a little bread and cheese. He wiped his face and put on his clothes. He had decided what he must do. He wouldn't tell Jeb, for fear that he would stop him. Among the few belongings, he had he found what he wanted, and he made off for the inn.

Seth's heart thumped, he was both scared and a bit excited. It took him several tries to find the right inn, but eventually, he recognised the man who had knocked at their door a few hours before.

"Excuse me. You're the man who brought me the belt," Seth initiated.

"Oh. Aye. You're the lad. I didn't recognise you there for a moment. What can I do for you?" asked the innkeeper.

Seth took a breath and looked him squarely in the face. "I've come to see him!"

A frown leapt onto the man's face. "Oh! You wouldn't want to do that, lad. He's all stiff and grey from lying in the cold. It's not a sight for lads like yourself."

Seth was prepared. "I've got a promise I also have to keep. It won't take a moment. I've seen dead bodies before. Honestly. It'll only be a second."

The innkeeper looked sceptical; but, in the end, he allowed him.

"All right, then. But don't you stay too long. Morbid—that's what it is." He shook his head. "It's not a pretty sight!"

"He wasn't when he was alive," ventured Seth.

The innkeeper's eyes opened wide, and he chortled. "You're right, lad. He was your friend. It's right you have the chance to say goodbye to him. He's wrapped in an old blanket in the shed furthest. Anyone stops you, tell 'em that I said you could. Come and see me before you go."

Seth didn't know what he expected, but it was different in some way. He slid the blanket from the body and sat alongside it. The body was quite rigid, and the face had sunken that the skull showed through. Seth unwound the bandage from around his eyes and saw that they were closed. Maybe he saw, maybe not.

He sat alongside the body and thought that it looked like a shell—that the life that had been there had gone or disappeared. He felt somehow better for that. Seth almost didn't do what he had come to do, for it was obviously lifeless. But he did it anyway, because somehow it felt both right and silly. So, he did it as he had planned. He unwrapped the most precious thing that he possessed which was his mother's ring, given to him before she died, and he tried to fit it on one of the rigid fingers. The only one it fitted was the little finger, so he slid it on as far as he could.

"Garvin, this is my mother's ring," Seth told him, softly. "Thank you for being my friend. I hope that, wherever you go, you'll find your arm and be a fine swordsman again."

He felt silly saying it aloud, but he felt that he had to say something. He covered up the face and he left to return to the innkeeper.

"You all done, then?"

"Thank you. We're willing to pay for a proper grave. Jeb asked me to tell you. Seeing he was a friend and all."

"I can do that. We'll split the costs. I have to tell you," started the innkeeper, "I liked him, and I felt sorry for him. I know he had his pride, so I made up this story about my brother in the war and how they might have known each other. That way it wasn't charity, if you know what I mean. I'll miss him, poor man."

He put a hand on Seth's shoulder.

"It's good that a lad of your age could see the goodness in the man, still. Here, it's not much, but the biscuits are freshly baked this morning."

The biscuits were good. They helped Seth with the loss and doubt he felt at what he had just done. He remembered yet another Hestor saying: *Just do it, and if it's right, you'll know. Good seeds grow into great trees. Rubbish just grows into weeds.*

By the time he reached the forge, all but one of the biscuits we're gone, and he felt better. Seth gave the last biscuit to Jeb who came over to him.

"It might be just a silly thought. But as the knife was given to you, then take it. It might be lucky. Take good care."

Seth followed Jeb's advice. The knife was too big to hang about his waist and the belt was a man's. Eventually, Seth made a thong with a leather lace and hung the knife inside his shirt, strung about his neck.

***

Seth felt safe in the crowd. People had come from miles to see the Prince and to view the games. There was no turning against the flow or changing direction until they were all inside the castle walls. There, a stage had been set up and people watched as troupes of dancers, jugglers, actors, and singers plied their trades. Seth wished to stay in the body of the crowd to avoid detection, but at the same time, he wished to see if he could find his way to the main door as quickly as he could.

Sharrock was waiting for him. "Come. We'll get you out of sight as soon as we can."

He helped Seth to food and drink. Then, drew him over to the window ledge where they could see out over the external walls, and the trees where Seth had hidden a few days before.

"It's under the bed for you!" Sharrock told him. "Is that the case?"

"Probably the bed. I've done it before!" said Seth.

"Ah, yes! Indeed you have. Under a bed, not far from here. Audacious!"

"What?" he asked.

"Audacious! It means brave and quick thinking," explained the teacher.

"Like Achilles?" Seth enquired, hopeful.

"No." Sharrock shook his head. "Achilles was more like a bull. Strong, certainly, but perhaps not so nimble of brain. The ancient heroes mostly were like that—even Hector. Big, strong fellows who could throw a spear a mile and wield a sword all day; but, not so bright at dealing with the gods and goddesses. Paris was tricky, rather than audacious."

"Oh!" said Seth. He pondered for a moment, then thought that the time was as apt as ever to ask. "I've wanted to ask you, because I know you're wise, what do you think happens to us when we die?"

The kindly old man looked into the young face and saw that the question was heartfelt.

"Well, Seth," began the wise mentor. "From the church, we are told that upon death, our souls travel to purgatory where we wait to be judged. Upon that judgement, we either are allocated our place in heaven with God, the father, and Jesus, the saviour. Or we go down to Hell—to Hades, where we must pay for our sins and evil deeds, until such time as we are forgiven."

Seth looked at him doubtfully.

"Do you believe that?" he asked.

The old man feigned indignation. "Of course. It's what the church has told us. That is the word of God made clear though the descendants of Christ. That's why we must be good. Why you must be good."

Seth didn't look convinced. "I know you say that, but it sounds funny."

"What is funny?"

"Well, when you talk about Hector, Achilles, and the wars; you talk really wonderfully, as if you were there— exciting and all. But when you talk about Christ, it's different," Seth observed aloud.

There was a ghostly silence, and Seth thought that again his tongue had led him into trouble. He lowered his head and waited for the lecture or the cuff to the head. None was forthcoming. When he finally looked up, there was a huge smile playing on the face of the grey-bearded scholar. He was even noiselessly chuckling. As he watched, just faintly amazed, he saw real tears of merriment come to the eyes of the old man.

Seth stood with mouth open, wondering what he might do.

"Are you alright?" he finally asked.

Except, all Sharrock could do was to motion him to sit down while he doubled up with pained amusement and held his chest.

Seth crossed the room to pour a mug of water from a nearby pitcher. He held it out to the older man, who eventually took it, and—while spilling a lot of it—got some down his throat.

"Thank you. Thank you, Seth!" Sharrock managed between breaths. "Come sit by me. I'm not dying, just wheezing. I must not have laughed like that for some time. My body wasn't sure what to do with it all. You must be careful, Seth."

"I didn't mean to. Honestly. I was just…"

"You were being a very honest and insightful young man. As such, I must treat you with the respect due to someone of your perspicacity."

"Of my what?" replied Seth, bewildered.

"Perspicacity! It means insightful—seeing things that perhaps other people don't," the old man explained, excitedly. Then, he continued, "I shall answer your question as well as I can. I shall tell you a story. Mind you, it is just a story. It is not about anyone in particular, but it is quite a story, and it may explain some of this to you. How shall we start? Perhaps with a formal opening.

"There was once a young boy, younger than even you, and he was brought up in the country by loving parents who had lived on their land for centuries. Every tree, every bush, every rock on their land was known to them. Strangely, they were not rich; but they were not poor, and they made a living from working their land and teaching the children of the noble families that bordered their small holding. Their learning came from an uncle who had been a monk, who had grown sick and come there to die. He didn't die, instead, he taught them all to read and write. They passed on that knowledge deliberately to each of their descendants. Not many people at all knew how to read or write in those times.

"Now, the new king was Christian and so the whole country became so. Those who disagreed became very silent or else they were killed—a good reason to stay silent.

"The dying monk who didn't die was a Christian too, and so, the family became Christian and went to church. And that was that. They learned to write, and they became Christians. But—and this is the interesting bit, Seth—there was more than one religion in the house. The mother of the boy had for years spent time in the forest and she knew the old women who knew about herbs and crystals and magic. She knew she had to be quiet about what she believed or else she might be persecuted as a heretic—"

"—And burnt as a witch," interrupted Seth.

"Indeed," agreed Sharrock, before he continued his tale. "So, the young man grew up to go to church and to love the baby Jesus and Mother Mary. But, as well he was shown the ways of the forest, the fairies; and the terrible Old One that could still be brought to life in the forest, if you knew the right charms and were strong enough to ask his help."

"Like the Horned King," supplied Seth. "The one with antlers and a pack of hounds that could tear your throat out. Him?"

"Well, you're full of even more surprises. But yes, like him!"

"Did you—I mean—did the boy ever see him?"

"Not him. But one day, the boy—feeling very confused by it all; and being a boy, went into the forest to see if he was brave enough to sit and ask the creatures he'd heard about to make themselves known to him. He needed to know if they were real or were they just made-up stories. Like another boy we know." Sharrock winked, knowingly.

"And he did?" Seth asked eagerly.

"He followed a trail into the forest. He knew to follow the signs, of the birds, and watch for the timid deer that might mark the way. He'd been taught to take the white quartz crystal with him; to magnify the light he carried within him."

"What happened?"

The old teacher described, "He followed a path, to a part of the forest that was very old, and very ancient. He saw wolves and other beasts, which frightened him, didn't touch him as if somehow, he was to be spared. He came to a huge oak tree that covered an area half the size of the courtyard outside. And he sat there 'til nightfall. He vowed he'd not move 'til he knew if the stories he'd been told were true or not."

"And then..." Seth ventured.

"And then he spent the worst night of his short life, where his mind imagined all sorts of creatures and monsters creeping up on him out of the foggy gloom," Sharrock grimly retold. "Every twig cracking was a dragon. Every leaf that fell was a serpent coming down the trunk. Each scream and call were the sound of orphan children who had starved in the woods and were now coming to rake his face with their tiny, claw-like hands. Despite this, he stayed until he knew that he couldn't run—could only wait until he knew something that was felt and true, and he could *believe* in."

Sharrock paused dramatically. He knew he had his audience. "After a very long time, he knew that there was a powerful change happening in the forest. The birds stopped. The trees no longer moved in the wind. All went quiet, the boy was more frightened than he could remember being. He would have cried but he didn't dare to because, whatever was coming his way, might hear him. So, he stuffed his cuffs in his mouth and waited with his bowels churning, his eyes closed. Then, he realised that something huge and strong smelling stood just in front of him."

"Not the baby Jesus?"

Sharrock had to hold back his smile. "No. Not the baby Jesus, but the God of the Forest. Pan, the Romans called him. He was part human and part goat, with horns on his head and a pipe that played sweet music. The boy held his breath convinced that he would die, when the creature knelt down and sniffed the boy's face. When the boy opened his eyes, he saw two huge brown smiling eyes looking into his own. Although his hair stood on end and his heart thumped as if it might burst, he was no longer afraid. In fact, he was amazed and even exhilarated. He was told to hold out his hands, and into them was put a small statue—a talisman—a carving of the Horned God."

"And then….?"

"He was gone. And the boy went home on shaking legs, still grasping the gift and in a daze that troubled all the family, except his mother, who recognised the telltale signs of awe on the boy's face," Sharrock finished with a fond smile.

"What happened to the boy?" enquired Seth.

"Oh, he did what most boys do. He grew up, but he didn't forget."

"But he couldn't tell, could he? Because if he did, then people might think he wasn't one of them. So, he'd have to pretend to forget, wouldn't he?" Seth guessed.

The wisened mentor shrugged, noncommittally. "Perhaps. Although, I believe that the old gods have ways of reminding us of their continuing presence."

"Like what?"

"Well—like wind in our faces, birds that call to us, and small boys with inquisitive minds." The old man looked at Seth, smiled and nodded. "Thank you, Seth, for the timely reminder!"

"You're very welcome," Seth formally replied. He waited for what he thought was a respectful time until he said, "So, it's not really clear then, where we go when we die?"

Sharrock chuckled, nodded and replied, "Perhaps it depends upon which gods we follow. For now, we should prepare for the return of the ladies. They will want to change into new costumes for the banquet."

"Does Tess—I mean, Lady Bella, does she get to go?"

"I would think so. Oh! Perhaps you might like to see her fully dressed before her first big banquet." Sharrock's eyes glittered in silent knowing. "It is very important for a girl—for her to look her very best."

"I'd like that, I think," Seth said, softly. Then, a thought came to him. "One last question. Can you be both? You know, can you be a Christian and believe in old gods, as well?"

"How do you see them as different, Seth?"

"All the words I hear in church are about gentle Jesus, being loving, and turning the other cheek if someone hits you. With the old gods, you wouldn't turn the other cheek. You'd chop their head off," he contemplated, aloud.

"To answer your question," began the old mentor, "I think the early gods were those that we needed at that time. Perhaps, gentle Jesus may be for later on. But they're similar, Seth. Both urge us to value truth, goodness, the power of friendship, and love. I once saw a line of monks go unprotesting to their deaths—killed by raiding Norsemen. It seemed to me, that very few were happy, and they may have been better off wielding a sword or throwing a spear. Such a waste!"

They didn't have much time left for further talk.

Lady Bella breezed in. Her face flushed from the jousting and the promise of the banquet. "It's just as we thought. It's like we almost know their plans!"

"Why? What's happened?" asked Seth.

"We hear everything at the jousting." Bella explained, "The Prince's own guard have been relieved of their duty for the night, and handpicked men of the Duke have been given the honour. If that wasn't enough—wait until you hear this—the Captain has had the spy, Tad, presented to the Prince. To reward him, Tad gets to accompany him everywhere, with his personal steward. And guess what? Tonight, he even has the privilege of sleeping in the same quarters as the *Prince!*"

Face determined, Seth remarked, "So, he's the one…"

Bella knew that look. "You can't go there, Seth. It's not safe."

"We need someone inside or else it's too easy," countered Seth.

"Seth," interjected Sharrock, "I think Lady Bella is right. It will be almost impossible to guarantee your safety."

Before they could argue further, Lady Eloise returned. She was welcoming to Seth and then quite firm.

"We need time to dress for dinner. We must look our best whatever the outcome of the night," she stated, regally. "We do not dress in front of young or old men, so Bella, you will conduct these two across the hallway to where there is adequate room in the classroom. I will have refreshments sent there as soon as we are ready."

They were going, when Sharrock enquired, "Lady Eloise. Seth was wondering if he might see you both before you go to the banquet. He's never seen a lady fully dressed in formal attire."

"Well, I suppose there's no harm in it," she considered. "Bella, what do you think? Can you bear this young admirer gawking at you before you go to the banquet with the Prince?"

"If he promises not to make fun of me."

"Seth?" enquired Lady Eloise.

"I promise. Cross my heart and hope to—"

"Don't spit on your hand, lad," cautioned Sharrock.

They talked as they waited for the women to finish dressing into their formal outfits.

"I have to be there," Seth muttered, still determined.

"I don't know if we can get you into the Prince's chamber. There will be guards," warned the old teacher. "Do you have a resourceful plan? Am I to make a small wooden horse in which to hide you?"

"I think that you'll have to take me to look, you know. I'm just a young boy who simply wants to sneak a look into the Prince's own room. Just for a moment. No harm in it! If it's too dangerous, then I won't stay. I promise," Seth insisted.

"The rustic young man whose only wish is to spend a moment in the hallowed surroundings of the Prince of the realm? Is that our line? That might get us through the door, but how do we manage to stay in there?"

Seth shook his head. "I haven't worked that out, yet. Somehow, the guards have to think that I've already left or forget that I ever went in."

"You'll inform me, no doubt when you have!" chuckled Sharrock.

Thoughtfully, Seth said, "Somehow we have to confuse them."

Tess, now totally transformed into Lady Bella, came and whirled about them in her finery which made her look much older than she was. Seth had hoped that he might hate all the finery, but she positively glowed with excitement and anticipation, her face flushed with the joy of it all. Seth was admiring, though sullen. By the time she had whisked her way out, he was downright glum.

"You were unsure of the colour?" Sharrock gently teased him.

"She looked really beautiful. Really…"

"…Grown up?" he finished for Seth. "Is that what you were about to say? That she looked grown up and years older than yourself?"

Seth knew that lying was of no use. "She looked really grown up. I look like just a boy." He almost choked on the last word.

"Never fear, young Seth. It happens. Girls grow into womanhood, while we're still climbing trees and spitting on pigs. The good news is that, eventually, we catch up. It just takes a while! Just a few years. Twenty or thirty!"

Seth frowned. "What if I don't have a few years? By then, she'll be married off to some nobleman's son or knight while I'm still a boy on a stick."

"What a grim picture! But the future is always uncertain, so I suggest that we go to the Prince's quarters. Also, I have an idea—flowers!"

"Flowers?" Seth repeated doubtfully.

"We may need to visit the maid's quarters first to talk to the steward. He's an old friend."

Not long after, the guards at the Prince's door were cursing their luck at being on duty when a banquet was on. They were trying hard to remember what an honour their selection had been, when they heard footsteps approaching, revealing a cavalcade of stewards and maids carrying armful after armful of flowers appeared.

"What's this, then?" demanded one of the guards.

Sharrock led the group to the door where he smiled politely, but firmly at the guards. "Flowers for His Highness's room—a gift from the Duke and the admiring folk of the town. If you would open the door for us, that would be greatly appreciated."

Keys were fumbled, and then found. As soon as the door opened, the servants bearing flowers began rearranging the room—moving pieces of furniture to allow tall vases to be installed, clearing benchtops and tables to accommodate the profusion of flowers. A small army of helpers moved and positioned vases, while others shortened stems and carried water from the central well. Amongst all these, between voices and orders rang out, a boy limped about in the rooms as if he had some tasks to perform, whether it was steadying a vase or holding a jug full of water.

The guards lost interest very quickly in all this coming and going.

Sharrock pretended to be helping the servants, when in truth, he was ensuring that there would be a moment for Seth could find a suitable hiding place. If that did not exist, then he was hard-pressed to herd an unhappy Seth from the room. He watched Seth, slowly and cautiously, check the rooms and saw the moment of disappointment cross the boy's face as he realised that each bed was solid to the floor. In place of the empty space, there were cupboards that held quilts and eiderdowns. Their eyes met, and then both glanced at the massive wardrobes that took up one complete wall of the first room.

"Boy, check that there are no dirty clothes that need our attention. Be very careful in the wardrobe not to disturb what you needn't. The last thing the Prince needs is you running your grubby hands over his suits of silk!" Sharrock ordered in a fake, stern voice.

To appear as if he was supervising a young and badly trusted steward boy, Sharrock crossed the room. Inside, the wardrobes were more brightly coloured clothes than Seth or Sharrock had ever seen. There was row upon row of doublets and tight-fitting vests, each with a cloak of matching colour and design.

"You sure?" he asked.

Seth nodded once. "Sure."

"Good luck. May the Trojans not find you," whispered the old teacher.

Sharrock looked to see if anyone was noticing, but there was still too much confusion of stems and bodies for that to happen. Quietly, he closed the massive doors and swept about the room.

After half an hour, the rooms were hugely decorated with stand after stand of beautiful blooms. There was much admiration and clapping of hands. Everything not needed was picked up and taken away.

Sharrock was the last to leave the room, shepherding everyone else out first. Quickly, he crossed the room to the wardrobe. He wanted to reassure himself that Seth was, indeed, hidden. He swung open the doors. In the gloom, there was nothing but clothes and boxes.

"We're going. Take care, Seth," he whispered.

As the guards came to the check the room, Sharrock was in the process of repositioning a large vase, before stepping back to admire his handiwork.

"Sir. Excuse us. We'll be needing to lock the door again. When you're ready!" said one of the guards.

Sharrock made to leave, replying, "Thank you. You're very thorough. No doubt the Prince will reward you for your duty."

Inside the wardrobe, Seth heard the departure of the guards, followed by the turning of the key in the lock. He was a prisoner, but safe for the moment. The closet was quite warm. A chimney lay at the back of it. The cloaks were soft and luxurious. Despite his best efforts, Seth found himself nodding off. Eventually, he did doze off into a slightly troubled and confined sleep.

It was the sound of the key in the lock that woke him. He jerked awake in an instant with that distinctive sound and then the mumble of voices. It was dark and the light fell into the room from the hallway outside.

"I'll light the candles before His Highness comes to bed," said a masculine voice.

"Do you want to have the room searched?" offered one of the guards.

"No. It's been locked, hasn't it?"

"Yes. All day. Except, of course, for when the flowers came!"

"The flowers?" asked the first voice, bewildered. The question was followed by the clack of shoes crossing to the doors. "Guard. When did the flowers come?"

"Late in the afternoon, My Lord. Quite a commotion!" the guard replied.

"Well. His Majesty will be delighted if he's still able to see as well as stand. It's probably best to warn you. If he tries to get up in the middle of the night to get more wine, you are not to let him go. You are to send for a steward," instructed the lead, masculine voice.

The two guards exchanged glances. One of them carefully ventured, "Pardon, sir. But how are we to stop His Highness from going when he wants to? We can hardly restrain him."

"Just tell him the night air is bad for complexion. Anything that slows him down. Then, send for one of us. He has mass to-morrow morning. Keep him from further drink and I'll see you both well-rewarded. Is that clear?"

"Oh. Yes, indeed. We'll keep him from doing himself harm. You have our word," vowed the other guard.

"Good. I'll leave the candles going and you can leave the door unlocked until His Majesty comes to bed."

The door closed. With the thin strips of light through the door gaps, Seth felt a trembling fear and excitement.

He had sunk back into the capes once more, when he heard voices outside the door again.

"I'll just be a moment. His Highness is sick of this cape and wants me to bring his big, dark blue one. It won't take a minute."

Seth knew the voice. He shrunk down as low as the space would allow him.

It was Tad.

Seth held his breath as the door swung open. From the gloom, Seth saw him place a parcel to one side of the wardrobe, and then search until he found the huge blue velvet cloak that the Prince was known for wearing.

Swiftly, the cloak was taken, followed by the door being closed. Seth heard him exit the room and joke with the guards on the way. For a moment, Seth waited before he felt his way towards the parcel that had been left. The hair on his neck rose as his hands encountered the hard object that was buried in the folds of the hip-length cloak.

It was a dagger.

From what Seth could tell, it was not as long as a sword, but larger than a mere knife. And there it lay, held in folds of the cloak. For an instant, Seth thought he might be wrong, perhaps it was simply one of the ceremonial swords that accompanied each outfit of clothes. Except, when he placed his hand on the hilt and felt—not the intricate web of filigree and embellishment—but a solid wooden handle, then he knew this was not one of the Prince's accompaniments. It a tool such as a labourer or butcher might use.

Now, he felt *scared.* Now, he knew for certain that Tad would try to kill the Prince. And that Seth was the only one who stood the best chance of saving his life. He considered taking it to the door and showing the guards, before he remembered how that would look—a boy in the Prince's room, with his own knife about his neck, handing over a second knife and talking about a plot to kill the Prince, and to guards of doubtful loyalty.

No. He would wait. He would not hide the dagger, but watch, and be ready when it was to be used.

He shivered. Seth held his oaken stick in his hands and waited for the nausea to pass.

Sometime later, he heard the Prince making his way to bed. There was a shouting and movement that made Seth worry the attack was beginning. However, as the sounds came closer, Seth could only hear laughter and singing.

The door exploded inwards, and Seth heard snippets of many conversations.

"No weapons allowed into the room. Sorry, My Lord. These are my orders. No one!" the guard insisted.

"What are they saying? What are they doing? Why are they taking your sword? It's outrageous! You. Give him his sword back. Go on, or I'll have you flogged."

But then, there was no time for the threat to be taken seriously, as suddenly, a crash followed and the cackle of raucous laughter.

"My Lord! Are you fine?"

"Fine. Fine. Just tripped on a…Well! My! Look at these flowers. I didn't order these. Guards, where did the flowers come from?"

"From the townsfolk, Your Majesty. From the townsfolk and the Duke's garden."

"How wonderful! Steward, I've told you! I have, haven't I? I said that people love me. My people. I always knew that they did. That they loved me and now look at this."

"You've always said it, My Lord!" offered the long-suffering chamberlain.

"Yes. But now I know it's true! What a grand day. Almost a shame to call a halt to it…"

There was more crashing and laughter.

"My Lord. You have the mass tomorrow morning. The early one!"

"The mass. Oh my God! Ha! Hear what I said. Steward. I said, 'the mass. Oh my God.' I find that so amusing. Don't you? It was! It was very clever of me!"

From where Seth sat, it was obvious that the Prince was very drunk, very unsteady and not willing to go to bed. Eventually, the noise and laughter stopped, and Seth heard the hushed voices.

"Thanks for that. He's passed out! Come. Help me to undress him and we'll roll him into bed," said the Prince's steward, who had done this all before.

"Is he often like this?" Seth knew Tad's voice this time.

"Often, unfortunately. He is the Prince, but he's an awful drinker. Just falls over while telling everyone how well he can hold his liquor. Thanks. Just roll him over and throw some covers over the royal person. Tad, you're to sleep in here with him tonight, along with his steward. Just make sure he doesn't roll out of bed or get up and want more wine. We'll lock you in. Call to the guards if you need to get out. I'll be here early in the morning to wash and dress him. Sleep well and look after our

Prince as best as you can," an exasperated and tired chamberlain advised before excusing himself.

Some candles were blown out. Seth heard the noise of people readying themselves for sleep and the creak of bodies being laid on bed. He heard the muttered 'goodnight' of the two who watched over the Prince, and then the sounds of gentle snoring begin.

Now, each sound and groan became important to his ears. Was it the sound of a man rising from his bed to slay a king-to-be? He waited and waited, his tension growing.

When his brain convinced him that he was waiting for something to happen which never would, he heard the telltale sound of someone moving in the room.

Blood pounding in his ears, Seth crouched as low as he could, and waited for the door to open. He heard the stocking feet pad across the floor and the muted light of the remaining candles flooded into the space. He saw the figure feel for the cape, finding the dagger to extract it from the pile, then turn back into the room.

There was no turning back.

Murderous treason was at hand. After hours of waiting, suddenly...*seconds* mattered.

21

To Save a Prince

Terrified that he might make a sound, Seth crept from his hiding place to crouch in the doorway of the wardrobe and peer into the room. His eyes took a moment to adjust to the dim candlelight, his heart threatened to leap from his chest.

As if he had seen it in a dream, as if he had always known it would be like this, Seth saw the figure of Tad, clad only in a shirt and breeches leaning over the inert body of the steward. Horrified, he watched him slowly peel back the blankets and raise the dagger in his hand. As Tad hesitated as if to choose the best spot, Seth stepped forward, swung his walking stick back as far as he could and brought it crashing down upon the would-be assassin's head.

At the sound of the blow, two things happened simultaneously. Tad slumped forward across his victim, the knife falling from his hand, and the steward sat bolt upright in bed. Seth had not thought this far ahead, and in his absolute confusion, he grabbed Garvin's knife from around his neck and placed it to the man's throat, whose eyes opened with terror.

"Please listen. The man I just hit was about to kill you. In a moment, armed men are meant to break in here and kill the Prince. Please. Please. I need your help to save him."

Seth saw incredulity and terror change to attentiveness and comparative calm.

"What? What would you have me do?" he ventured, even as his eyes still bulged in his head at the sight of the knife that Seth still held then lowered.

"Help me bar the door from the inside. I think they may have a key already. Then, I need to tie up the man I just hit," explained Seth.

With Seth's help, they raised the heavy crossbeam that served as an extra internal lock and set it gently in place. Then, they checked Tad.

"Not moving," noted the steward. "You must have hit him right at the base of the skull. Come. I'll help you bind his arms and legs. As I do, can you try to explain what you're doing in the Prince's room with a knife?"

"I found out they meant to kill him."

He shook his head. "I don't know what to believe. How was this one meant to harm the Prince?"

Seth rolled Tad over and exposed the knife beneath him. "With this. He smuggled it in before."

Before they could talk further, they heard the sounds of feet on the stairs, then the sound of voices outside.

Ears to the door, they heard the jangling of keys and the key being turned in the lock.

Then, weight was applied to the door and the resistance of the beam encountered.

"Tad, Tad! Open the door," hissed a voice from behind the door.

If the Prince's steward needed any further convincing, then this was it. He took the discarded knife and waited.

"Come on, Tad. Come on. Open up. You've done your bit. The rest is ours," the voice demanded.

Later, he would not be able to explain why he did it, but Seth crossed to the door, knelt by the keyhole and yelled as loudly as he could, "You'll not get in. Traitors. Traitors is what you are."

This was followed by a silence and then the sound of arms, footfalls and the sound of blades on blades.

"What is it?" asked the steward.

Seth replied, "It's John and his men. They've been hidden down the hallway—waiting for this."

"What if your friends don't win?"

"Then we stay here. But they will!" Seth said with confidence.

The cries of battle diminished as they waited against the door.

Then came a knocking and the sound of a familiar voice. "Seth. Seth. Are you in there?"

"Yes. I'm here. The Prince is safe."

"Open up. It's John. We need to come in. We've got one of the Riders alive."

They wrenched the beam out of its stays, hauled the door open and looked out onto a scene of devastation. Bodies lay slumped and twisted. In the midst of John's men, stooped and bleeding from a stomach wound, was the lieutenant, who had threatened tongues in a forest some years before. His face was pale and haggard.

"Let's get him in here. We can't have him die on us now. Rouse the Prince and have him call for his own guard. We've driven off the rest of the Riders, but whether they come back in force or flee we've yet to see," advised John.

The Prince was roused and his response was almost comical until John showed him the bodies. "My god. It's a dream, surely. Who are these?"

"Riders, Your Highness! Sent to kill you. You haven't got time to waste. Send for your guard at once," John said.

"I'll raise the Duke," the Prince remarked, shakily.

"I doubt that's a good idea, My Lord. We don't know who sent these killers."

The Prince's face registered disbelief, but at that moment, the dishevelled Prince came across the body of Tad trussed like a chicken and slowly returning to consciousness.

"Who is this?" the Prince asked, pointing at Tad.

John took the Prince by the arm and stared him full in the face. "My Lord. There is real danger here. Just for the moment, do as I say!"

His eyes opened wide with shock, then he blinked and said, "Tell me what you'd have me do!"

Following instructions, the Prince called for his cloak, sent the steward for his guard and began dressing. In a flurry of inactivity, he sat back in his bed again.

John checked the door again, spoke to his men. "If the Duke's men come, regardless of what they say, you're to treat them as if they're the enemy. You'll lock us in!"

The Prince noticed the room and Seth. "Boy, who are you?"

"I'm Seth. The man tied up was about to let the Riders in to kill you, but I hit him with my stick. He is a friend of the Captain."

The Prince crawled to the edge of his bed to look. "Heavens! You're right. This man is the Captain's right-hand man. He accompanied me to the jousts. Who is he?"

"His name is Tad. He's a killer that someone paid a lot of money to," Seth explained.

"To kill me?"

"No. Just to let the real killers in after he had killed your steward."

By now, the reality of the danger had actually settled onto the Prince. He raised Tad's head, who was struggling to return to consciousness.

The Prince demanded, "Who did this? Who paid you? I'll have your tongue—"

Who knows what other parts of his body he would have threatened to remove, had they not been interrupted by the sound of heavy feet in the corridor. Then, came a most unwelcome voice. One Seth knew only *too* well.

"Stand back. Stand away from the door. Let me through to the Prince!"

John's troops were hesitating when John peered through the doorway. He saw the Captain dressed as an officer in the Duke's garrison at the head of a considerable troop of men, some of whom may have been dressed in black just a few days before.

"Stop him," warned John. "Stand on guard. Do not let this man through." And with that, he pushed past his men to confront the Captain directly with his own body and sword.

"How dare you!" growled the Captain. "The Duke will have your head for this. Stand aside! We're here to protect the Prince."

Seth grabbed the Prince's hand. "He's the leader of the Riders. He's here to kill you."

Aghast, the Prince turned to Seth for counsel. "Tell them to withdraw."

Seth got the Prince into his blue cloak and half-helped; half-bundled him to the door. Suddenly, he was the Prince playing a role, not just a fearful and confused young man.

"Thank you, Captain! I am very safe with these men, and my own guard is on the way as we speak!" proclaimed the Prince.

For a moment, the fury and shock of his thwarted plans was apparent on the face of the Captain. By now, the Prince was in full flight.

"I must make myself clearer, it seems. Leave us. I am perfectly safe," reiterated the Prince.

The Captain's face drew into a grim smile. For an instant, it was uncertain whether he would risk leading his larger force up the hallway to attack.

At this moment, Seth stepped from behind the Prince's blue robe. The Captain saw him and pointed, "You—the boy who insists on poking his young nose where it shouldn't be!"

Suddenly, Seth was full of courage and scared of nothing. If he had held a sword, he could have run at him. As it was, he had only his words.

"Also, the boy on crutches that knows you and saw you wear black robes and kill people," Seth countered.

Right then, there was the locking of their eyes, and Seth swallowed in fear as that smile returned to the Captain's face.

"So, the very same! It will soon be of little use to you, boy!" The Captain raised his hand, signalling his men forward.

"Take him back into the room, Seth, and bar the door again," John ordered as he raised his sword.

But with mere feet between the two forces, there came the sound of armoured men moving at speed. A second later, the captain of the Prince's own guard led his men into the other end of the corridor. With him, was a breathless steward.

The Prince began, "Thank you. Your speed is appreciated. I think, perhaps now, you might surrender your weapons—whoever you are!"

The Captain smiled.

"I think we might still have a need for them," was all he said, as he turned and ordered his men back the way they had come.

The Prince's guard went to follow them, but John stopped them. "Let them go! Our first actions must be to guard the Prince."

"But surely with them fleeing, we've done that!" argued a guard.

"There's been a plot," stated John. "We don't know who is involved, but obviously the Captain and some of the Duke's men have been involved.

"The Duke!" gasped another guard. "You mean it could be…"

"Don't know. We just know that we need to stay tight about the Prince."

There was comparative calm until a soldier pushed through. "Sir, the drawbridge is down, and a troop of men are leaving the castle at speed."

"Will be the Captain and the Riders," affirmed John. "No doubt they'll be fleeing for their lives."

"The Duke is on the way," volunteered a guard.

Inside the Prince's room, the steward attempted to dress the Prince in his clothes from the night before, but he was having none of it.

"If I'm to be killed, I should at least be looking my best," declared the Prince.

Seth stood, open-mouthed.

"Boy, tell me how you met these Riders. Amuse me as I dress?" As he spoke, he twirled and pranced in front of the full-length mirror, trying on and discarding clothes with little snorts of disdain or approval.

"It doesn't matter what you wear," Seth said. "The people just want a real king."

This stopped the Prince in full twirl and a look of puzzlement crossed his face. "What do you mean, 'a real king'? The people love me. Look at these flowers!"

"A king has to rule, to interfere, to make things better. That's what a king has to do!" Seth exclaimed loudly. Far too loudly.

"Don't raise your voice to me. I'm the Prince. I won't be yelled at by a boy, particularly on a night when I could have been killed. What do you think of the blue?"

Seth found himself wondering what might happen to him if he hit him with his stick.

"You could be a good king, you're just too…" Seth realised that as he spoke, tears were pouring down his face. "I thought you were great! I thought you'd help."

For a moment, the Prince of the realm stood transfixed, his hands stopped at his throat like a hare caught in a sudden light as if he was unable to quite comprehend what had been said to him.

Sounds from the door interrupted them. The Duke with a gathering of nobles and advisors, some with robes hastily thrown over night gowns, were attempting to gain entrance.

"My Lord," the Duke began in surprise. "What is this I hear? Your life in danger and in my castle! How will you ever forgive me?"

The fully dressed Prince stared at the Duke a moment. "I fear that it is much worse than that, My Lord Duke. It seems that the plotters were a part of your own guard. We have prisoners who, no doubt, will be willing to confirm the details!"

"I'll have the truth flogged from them!" the Duke declared.

The chorus of disagreement was loud from John, Seth, and the captain of the Prince's guard. Seth saw the Duke's eyes narrow briefly with disappointment, but the Prince, interrupted.

"Thank you, but no." The Prince shook his head. "My own guard will care for these prisoners until such time as we are sure of their overall intentions. And of whom they served."

"My Lord Duke," began John. "A party of men led by the captain of your own guard just attempted to kill the Prince. We believe that he and his men have fled the castle. We also believe that this troop of men are the Riders, who have terrorised the countryside for the last years."

A moment before, he had tried bluster, but now the Duke feigned shock and amazement. He clutched his heart and had to be led to a bed, where he wheezed and panted.

Attended by the accompanying nobles, he protested his horror, dismay, and incredulity. "How? how could this happen in my own castle? My own men! I trusted the Captain with my very life. With your life, my Prince! Oh! My heart! My heart!"

If Seth hadn't known better, he would have been moved. But he knew better. He went to protest when John laid an arm on his arm.

"Where is my guard?" wheezed the Duke.

"In the hallway, My Lord. No one with weapons will be allowed near the Prince, except his own guard," said John.

"I want them followed. I want the men who fled, followed and killed."

"I would like them brought back alive," suggested John.

"Dead men will tell us nothing," the Duke proclaimed.

A messenger asked to be admitted. Breathless and hatless, he bowed to the Prince and the Duke. "My Lord. My Lord Duke. I have ridden to tell you that a large group of armed men has been seen approaching the castle. We are not sure of the numbers, but they are considerable."

At this stage, the Prince blanched and the Duke looked uncertain.

"You have no idea who they are?" the Prince enquired.

The messenger shook his head. "No, My Lord. We thought it imperative to send news as soon as we could."

"Close the gates. Pull up the bridge and prepare the men on the walls and towers." It was John who spoke.

The others glanced at the Prince who followed his promptings and spoke directly to the Duke, "Your Lordship. As of now, you will place the command of your men in my hands. You, what's your name?

"John!"

"John. You will take charge of the Duke's men. Sir, you will take a dozen men and escort the Duke to his quarters."

The Duke protested, "But, My Lord—"

The Prince ignored him, pressing on. "If you are innocent of any crime, you will receive my apology. But until we know the depth of your men's duplicity, we will take no chances. Do as I say! Now!"

Men hurried. A protesting Duke was hurried away and the Duke's own guard placed themselves, somewhat reluctantly at John's command.

"Shall I send men after the Riders, sir?" asked a guard.

"No. Hold all men here until we see what threat this is. Your Highness, I think it best if you come to the main hall where we will leave a guard. If this is some threat, we will have a party ready to take you out via the rear gates. Seth, do inform some friends of ours what has happened. They will be worried," instructed John.

Seth made his way down the stairs to collide with Sharrock coming the other way.

"Oh. My goodness, Seth! Quick. Come. The ladies are worried and waiting."

They dodged soldiers running down steps and came to the Lady Eloise's door. Sharrock rapped three times with his staff. The door was flung open.

Seth was shocked and delighted to be hugged in a fierce embrace by Bella.

"It's fine! Honestly. The Prince is safe and John is in charge of the garrison. The Duke is held in his quarters, but there's a large troop of men coming this way!" he blurted it out as quickly as he could.

"Slower!" said his teacher. "Slowly! Begin at the start."

He tried not to fill in too much detail, but details were required; particularly about, 'how hard he had hit the spy,' 'the role of the Captain,' 'the battle outside the door,' and the 'stupidity of the Prince.'

"Who are the soldiers that are coming? Does anyone know who they are?" asked Sharrock.

"No. It could be allies of the Duke," Seth answered.

Lady Eloise noticed that he was shivering and sent for a cloak for him.

Gently, she said, "It's not cold. You're suffering from exhaustion and a little too much excitement. I had the devil's own task keeping Bella here away from the Prince's door."

"It's not fair that I wasn't there," Bella said with some feeling.

"What of the Duke? Tell me again. Is he attempting to bluff his way through this as if he knew nothing? Is that his plan?" interjected Sharrock.

"He just pretended to be horrified that it could happen under his roof and with his troops. I think it depends on capturing the Captain. Otherwise, the Duke may escape," Seth informed them.

There was a thumping at the door. A steward's voice called, "My Lady. I have news!"

Sharrock carefully opened the door to admit the steward.

"My Lady. We have reason to believe that the large troop of horsemen arriving presently is the Lord Gloucester with your husband in attendance. John begs your attendance and says to pardon the lateness of the hour."

"How do you know, for sure?" enquired Lady Eloise.

"We don't. But a messenger reported that he had seen pennants carried by the troop which seemed to confirm that they were as we have reported," said the steward.

There was relief and joy at the news.

"Let us not get our hopes too high," Sharrock sagely advised. "But if it is them, they have made excellent time. Come. Let us take ourselves down to meet them. Lady Bella, I assume that you will wish to accompany us?"

Her smile showed her agreement.

Lady Eloise turned to the steward. "Tell John that we will join him as soon as we can dress and make our way downstairs."

For the second time in a few short hours, Seth found him rustled out of the room to allow the ladies to dress.

2 2

The Mill Revisited

As their party made their way down the dark stairs, servants ran in front of them with burning torches to light the way.

Once they gained the courtyard, they could see the battlements were lined with rows of archers and troops moving into defensive positions. Torch light leapt and flashed off armour and weapons. All was movement and noise—so much noise!

They were hailed from the keep tower. "If you would join us, we would be grateful!"

And so, with the ladies holding their skirts high, they made their way up the stone steps to join John. Nearby, were John's group of officers, who in full armour were peering into the gloom beyond the castle walls. The wait was not a long one.

From a distance, they could hear the rumble of many hooves and men calling to one another. Seth prayed that they turned out to be friends and not foes.

"We shall know soon enough. I can see a rider approaching."

Sure enough, a solitary rider disengaged from the gloom and came to rest before the castle keep where torches lit up the area.

"Ho! The castle! Why are your walls defended and your gates closed to friends?"

"Ho! Yourself! We have had some trouble deciding who is friend and who is foe tonight. Who are you? Identify yourself, sir," ordered John.

"I am Lord Gloucester's man. He is now approaching with a group of knights and with Lord Alfred. We have come because we feared for the safety of the Prince, whom we are told presently resides within these walls. We are friends of the Prince and come as such."

"You will pardon our suspicions, but some whose duty it was to defend the Prince betrayed that trust tonight. You will please convey our message to your Lord and request that he present himself with Lord Alfred before our castle," John instructed.

"That is most uncommon and even impolite!" huffed the rider.

"Again. I don't ask this gladly or for my own sake. The life of the Prince is my immediate concern. I ask you to convey my request as courteously as possible!"

"I shall," he called before he turned his horse and cantered away, back the way he had come.

John turned the leader of the Prince's guard. "Captain, call your men to the ready. We wait on their reply."

A party of men approached the castle but stayed beyond arrow's range.

A huge man, clad in black armour and mounted on a massive charger, rode on a few paces with a smaller figure alongside him.

"Ho! The castle! What is the meaning of this?" the voice boomed.

Seth was enthralled. Either side of him as far as he could see, soldiers stood to attention, weapons ready, the light of lit torches stretched along the length of the castle wall picking up the burnish of their weapons and armour. Seth was surprised to see how terribly beautiful the scene was, and how calm he felt in the midst of the dreadful expectancy.

"My Lord Gloucester, excuse our welcome," John greeted. "Already tonight we have seen treachery and betrayal. As such, we were cautious at your approach."

"Is the Prince safe?" the taller man enquired.

"He is, My Lord. May we talk to Lord Alfred?"

The smaller figure rode forward.

"My Lady," beckoned John.

Lady Eloise stepped forward and spoke down to the figure.

"Alfred, is that you?" Her tone was almost one of admonition, as if he had been too long in the forest hunting. It was a small, but clear voice in the anxious silence.

Several hundred men heard her tone and chuckles broke out amongst them.

"My dear! It is I, with Lord Gloucester, who is a true and loyal retainer of the Prince," Lord Alfred replied.

"That's all I need to know," suggested John, but Lady Eloise checked him.

"Alfred," she began. "Any insistence by us will be pardoned, and so I must ask you—are you here freely and without any threat to yourself or other persons?"

"It is as it looks, my dear!"

The order was given, the clash of boots and metal signalled the standing down of the defending troops.

John hollered, "In that case—open the gates. Lower the drawbridge and stand easy. Prepare to greet them!"

A small party of horsemen entered the castle courtyard.

Seth noticed among them was the familiar figure of Hewitt. Some knights needed help to dismount; Gloucester needed no such assistance.

"Who are you? Where's the Duke?" Lord Gloucester questioned, impatiently.

"My Lord, I am, or was, Lord Alfred's man. I have been placed in temporary command of the castle by the Prince. My Lord Duke has been confined to his quarters," John informed, calmly.

"Confined to his quarters? What do you mean? On whose orders?" he bellowed.

In that silence, a voice broke through.

"On my order, dear Gloucester!"

The Prince emerged onto the steps surrounded by guards and young stewards bearing torches. He was dressed in a suit of peacock blue. Both Lords and their party fell to one knee at his entry.

Bella whispered to Seth, "Great clothes!"

"He needs them!" answered Seth from the corner of his mouth. "He's an idiot!" he whispered to himself.

"Your arrival is both timely and one for which we are grateful," the Prince said, eloquently. "The Duke is being detained because a group of his trusted men attempted earlier to have me killed. He may be as innocent as newly born lamb, but it was the wise opinion of the young man here that we should take no chances with the royal person."

"For which, he will be well-rewarded, my Lord!" Gloucester barked in agreement.

"Indeed, he will. Between him and a crippled boy, I have much to be grateful for," the Prince remarked, thoughtfully. "But tell me. My Lord, what brings you here? I hardly think this is the right time of year to be at manoeuvres with such troops?"

"My Lord. We heard of a plot to kill you and usurp the crown. As such we came as fast as we dared!" explained Gloucester.

The Prince sighed, "I must ponder, why half my kingdom knows of plots to kill me, while I am left to remain ignorant of them. Perhaps you will enlighten me further on this when we have escaped this night cold."

Seth felt unease in his stomach, which warned him that he was going to risk speaking aloud to his betters.

"Sir Prince. My Lord Gloucester," he began.

Gloucester looked at him as if he would a worm or perhaps a frog. "You. Boy. What do you think you're doing speaking out of turn? I don't speak with boys." He turned to walk up into the main entrance.

"Wait!" began the Prince. "This is the impudent young boy who saved my life, and then had the temerity to question my rule of this realm. You have given good advice before, and so in deference to that, we will allow you to speak."

"I think I know where the Riders have gone!" Seth blurted.

"The Riders?" enquired Gloucester.

"They were at the heart of the attempt upon my life," the Prince quickly explained. "Where do you think they are, boy?"

"The old mill. I feel sure that they will rest there!"

"How can you be sure, boy?" the Prince wondered.

"They did before, and it is the best place for men and horses," Seth answered.

Hewitt added his voice to it, "My Lords. I know the place. I think he is right. The group that fled the castle is only small. No more than thirty men. Fifty fresh men on fresh horses could be there in a few hours and catch them by surprise"

"You have it planned. Horses will be made ready. But I will take no chances here. You will take another twenty of my own guard with you. If they are there, we will allow no escape. Hewitt, you will take charge of the pursuit. My Lord Prince, we will get you and I out of the cold where we may talk with the Duke. Lady Eloise and Lord Alfred, as is befitting your roles in this defence of the Prince, you will join us. Make haste or the morning will be here before we get near a bed," Lord Gloucester directed with ease.

The castle came alive. It was an ordered pandemonium as troops were moved, tired horses stabled, and the pursuit force mustered. Gloucester's men diplomatically, yet energetically, took charge of the castle. In the pandemonium, there were still many patches of darkness where it was possible for two smaller figures to drop back into and plot.

"If you're going, then so am I," whispered Bella.

"You'll have to dress up like a boy. Like when I had to pretend to be a girl," Seth pointed out.

She grimaced. "I'm not doing that."

"Well. Don't. Just don't blame me when you get caught and sent back."

There was a long pause.

"Seth, you're really annoying."

"Only when I'm right." He grinned at her.

There was a longer pause, Seth was just wondering about the wisdom of standing so close to her. He was definitely within hitting range.

"Promise you'll wait for me. Promise!" Bella insisted.

Seth automatically went to spit on his hand, but she was already gone. It took time to assemble the pursuing force. Behind the armoured men, came the bowman in lighter armour, followed by the support party of stewards, squires, and armourers. No one noticed the two hooded figures who dropped into the pace of the main force.

After a while, Bella dropped her mount alongside Seth. He looked over and saw the huge smile of exhilaration on her face.

He was pleased to have her there and couldn't even think about what trouble they'd be in when they returned. What if they were not there? What if they had been too smart by half?

It was a long ride, and there was little effort to rest either the horses or the men.

Just minutes from the mill, Hewitt called them all to a halt.

"If they're there, there will be guards," warned Hewitt. "The Captain is too good a soldier to not watch for pursuit. Take four of your men and sweep behind the mill to come up behind whoever is watching. We will not move until we hear your word."

Seth moved to accompany them; however, Hewitt recognised him and would not allow it.

"Stay with us," he said. "I don't know how you came to be here, but your help might be more valuable as we move forward. Go with an advance party to the turn off from the main road and check it. Be careful!"

The scouting party with Seth and Bella also attached to it, moved down the road to the spot where the path moved off down to the mill.

Seth warned the commander of their little troop, "If they're in hiding to watch, it will be most likely in this undergrowth."

Quietly on foot, with Bella skulking alongside him, they approached the bush that covered the track. As they did, they could see the slight movement within the brushes.

"Be ready!" warned the commander. "They must not get back to the mill to warn them!"

They pretended to move past the brushes as if they had seen nothing, before two of them plunged back into the bush. There was a brief flurry of activity, and then…quiet.

The two men emerged carrying the sagging body of another between them. They moved forward slowly, until they could see the scouting party emerge from the back of the mill.

"You two. Go tell Hewitt that it's safe to approach," the commander directed.

Bella and Seth scurried back to the troop of men, mounted their horses, and led the others to vantage points about the mill.

"Shall we try to attack them while it's dark?" enquired one of the men.

"No. Take the horses back to the road and keep them quiet. We'll wait 'til dawn. In the dark, there are too many chances that one or more might escape. Settle the men and have them ready as soon as light shows," Hewitt said.

There was not long to wait. Still, it was cold as the men waited in the gloom. Seth looked over and saw the line of men—the archers from Gloucester's troop resting with their unstrung bows over their shoulders.

The waiting seemed to take forever.

Eventually, the birds began to twitter and move in the forest.

"Not long now," muttered Hewitt. "Bring up one party of horsemen just in case. Quietly."

The mist had come down, shrouding the scene in wisps of vapour. It was freezing. The first movement was a sleepy soldier from the mill. He stepped outside and peed on the steaming grass while he yawned and stretched. Seth didn't dare turn to see if Bella had been watching. The soldier buttoned up his trousers, and then called out across the clearing to where he thought there was a dutiful sentry.

"Hey! You still awake there!" he called.

Hewitt knew there was nothing to be gained by not replying. He did an imitation of a rough and ready voice. "Still here. It's cold, but nothing to report!"

The man grunted and was about to return inside, when he stopped and swung around.

"Hold on. That's not Morgan. That's not you!" Hastily, he ducked inside the building, calling as he went.

"Ready, archers!" called Hewitt.

The row of men rose as one to notch arrows in their strings while wringing their hands against the cold.

As the men broke cover and ran from the mill, Hewitt commanded, "Release!"

The air was filled with humming of the arrows. A moment later, the running men were struck down, shrieking and crying in agony as they were hit. The ground was covered with writhing shapes. The rest fled to the safety of the mill. Then, there was a pause.

Hewitt stepped forward.

"There's no point in more bloodshed. The mill is surrounded!" he proclaimed. "Come out without your weapons, and we will negotiate with the Prince for your lives. Stay there—you die!"

There was the sound of disagreement from inside the mill. Soon, a row of men emerged from the mill, their hands now empty, held in the air.

"Watch for the back of the mill. The Captain will never surrender. He knows that only death awaits his capture," Hewitt calculated. "Come. Have horseman mounted and ready in case a small party tries to escape." And then he was running, sword in hand, between the surrendering soldiers to see who remained in the mill. A party of men, including a limping Seth, accompanied him.

It was gloomy in the mill. It seemed that everyone had left the shelter, but it still felt dangerous and risky.

"Has anyone come out the back?" called Hewitt.

"No one!" came the cry.

"Then he's still here," he muttered. "Be careful. He is still capable of causing mischief. Watch every dark corner!"

They crept through the mill, past the horses, waiting at each moment for a rush of feet or the sound of weapons.

When they found him, there was no need of defence.

"Over here!" called a soldier.

Hewitt, Bella, and Seth raced to a small room, converted into a sleeping bay where the Captain lay on his back, his hand clutched about the bloody wound that gaped above his belt. Despite his pain and the pallor of his face, there was still no fear—just the same defining defiance.

"We meet again," spat the Captain. "You will excuse me if I don't rise to formally greet you. It seems one of my men lacked the loyalty I felt I deserved!" He saw Seth. "Well, well. Come to gloat, but I fear you're a little late!"

"No!" said Hewitt. "We'll save your life long enough to see you hanged. Staunch the blood flow, somehow. We'll take you back to see the Duke, we need you alive!"

Hoisted onto a make-shift stretcher, the Captain was raised above the throng of surrendering troops and swung between two horses.

"Will he live?" asked Bella carefully, mindful of her disguise.

"Hopefully long enough to implicate the Duke," replied Hewitt.

Seth had his doubts. As they walked through the throng of men, their spirits fell. Around them, they saw wounded men patched up to ride back. Or in other cases, sword thrusts ending the lives of grievously wounded men. Corpses lay dotted across the grass like discarded bundles of clothing, the sound of groans, cries, and curses filled their ears. All their daring and excitement evaporated. Seth looked and saw tears in Bella's eyes.

"It's so horrible!" she whispered to Seth, who could only nod his agreement.

They stepped around a dying soldier, who was not much more than a boy. A Rider tried to complain about the tightness of his bonds but was smashed by a sword hilt to his knees. To Seth's right, a Rider impaled by an arrow was carried to a horse knowing that his choices were to have the arrow removed, his death likely there and then. Or an agonising ride to the castle where the result could be the same. Further on, bodies were being strapped to horses—going home to wives and children who would mourn and face poverty.

"I wish the Prince was here right now," said Seth.

"Why? Why would you want that?" Bella wondered.

"Perhaps he'd rule a little better. Are you all right?"

She brushed back tears. Seth went to put an arm around her, but she stopped him.

"Don't! I'm a boy, remember!" With her head down, she walked to her horse and mounted for the trip back.

Seth spent most of the return journey riding alongside the litter on which the Captain lay. At times, he was conscious and at other times, mercifully, he had lapsed into a coma. At one stage, he woke and looking up, saw Seth riding alongside him. He looked up at Seth. "It was a long time ago that we met in a forest. As I remember, you were a mouse at the time."

A memory stirred in Seth. He shuddered.

They were met by a second party from the castle, who came with fresh horses and food. Prisoners were taken in tow and exhausted soldiers stood about, resting their horses and themselves.

"Do you want to rest here or come on with us?" asked Hewitt.

"I'll come!" requested Seth.

It took forever to get to the castle, and Seth was swaying in the saddle by the time the turrets came into sight. It was at that moment that he remembered that Lady Eloise would be awaiting their return.

Inside the courtyard, all was a buzz. Willing hands took horses to feed and rest, while helping others off saddles. He was happy to be home and to see the tired, satisfied smile of Bella as she dismounted.

They had no time for relief. A steward awaited them: "You are both expected in the antechamber. Now. At once!"

Exhausted and now anxious, the two trailed their way behind the steward who took them to a door, knocked once and stood aside to usher them in. It was as Seth expected—a room full of silent adults with worry lines etched in their faces.

Lady Eloise made no move to welcome either of them. "Well. You return. What do either of you have to say?"

Seth tried to apologise, but he was too tired to do it properly. "I'm sorry. I asked her to come to look after—"

Bella interrupted. "That's a lie. I made him take me. I wanted to see what happened. Seth had nothing to do with it. It was all my doing. I wanted so badly to go, and now I hardly wish that I had." Her grief and fatigue were obvious.

Seth saw Lady Eloise relent.

"Ah. You silly, strong headed one!" Lady Eloise hugged her. "We thought you might come to harm!"

"I'm sorry, but you must know by now that I'll come to no danger with Seth around," she assured.

Lady Eloise looked over at him as she cradled her ward. "I should have had more faith in you, young man. But the world can be cruel. We had planned to punish you both, but that seems to be most inappropriate. I will take you off to the punishment of a bath and sleep. I leave Seth to your wise words, my Lords."

Sharrock smiled at him. However, Lord Alfred looked old, tired, and concerned.

"What are we to do with this one, Sharrock? You have for years favoured the carrot over the stick and generally with good results. What do you advise?"

"I think that, on balance, his positives outweigh the acts of spontaneous stupidity," answered the wise sage.

There was a silence as Lord Alfred considered. Finally, he sighed and reached out with his hand to tug at his right hand. From it he plucked a large, plain ring whose central feature was a dark blue stone, and then he crossed to Seth.

"This was given to me by my father," began Lord Alfred. "I have come to value people more than baubles, but it is still a bauble that may aid you at some stage. You seem a quite remarkable young boy, and Bella seems to think highly of you. I have little experience of boys. Here. It will be too big. For now, we will place it upon the largest of your fingers."

Seth, unsure of what was being said or offered, looked to Sharrock for advice.

Sharrock nodded. Seth reached out his hand and saw with shock and dismay, that tears rolled down Lord Alfred's cheeks as he did.

"I have no real advice to give anyone; except, perhaps to say, whatever you do, do the opposite of what I advise, and you will probably be happy and successful." With a sigh, he placed the ring on Seth's finger and then withdrew from the room.

Seth sat flabbergasted and twirled the ring on his finger, hardly daring to look up at Sharrock.

"Don't worry about His Lordship, Seth. His despair will ease, but at the moment his cares weigh heavily. It was a great honour he has bestowed upon you, no matter the style in which it was done. Value the ring, Seth."

Seth remembered a ring on a dead finger just a few short days and a lifetime ago. Eventually, he knew he would have to ask.

"Sharrock. If you have promised something to someone, even if it is an evil person, should you do it?"

"Do you want to tell me more?"

Seth shook his head. "I'm sorry. I can't. Just—should you keep your word to someone who might not even value such a thing? Should you?"

Sharrock considered for some time. "Your word to yourself is very important. If you would lie to yourself, then who could you trust in the future? Your word is your word…does that help?"

Seth nodded, but not very happily.

Sharrock added, "But you must not do things that would help evil prevail. And now if you wish, I will make you up a bed here in this room. I doubt a bath has much appeal for you. I will look in, in the morning."

Seth collapsed onto the eiderdown and wished that he was at Hestor's, with the fire going and Tiny moaning in his sleep, his belly pointed to the coals, and life so much simpler.

23

A Promise Kept

Bella burst into the room the next morning as if the castle were under attack. "Wake up! Wake up! Quickly! They're going to question the Captain!"

Seth blinked awake. "How do you know? Isn't he too sick?"

"One of the guards told the cook as they were taking food over to them. He said that there are close to twenty men on guard and that Gloucester and Hewitt are coming in a moment."

"They'll want to know if the Duke is involved!"

Bella bristled with indignation. "But we know he is. He is. We know that!"

Seth swung his legs out of bed. "Come on. He'll just keep blaming the Riders and pretend he's never known about it."

"Will they hang them all?" Bella asked as they raced down a hallway.

"Probably. It's treason to be plotting to kill the Prince," Seth remarked.

"You can get a really good look at the gateway to the dungeon from the French classroom."

The room was unlocked. As Bella had said, they could look down on the guards who stood at the steps down to the underground prison. They didn't have to wait long. They heard the

263

voices long before they reached them as Gloucester, Hewitt, and John swept from the dungeons.

Gloucester's voice could be heard booming above the rest. "I tell you again, I do not believe him! He's lying. Some time on the rack might persuade him to tell the truth."

"He's badly wounded," pronounced Hewitt.

Seth and Bella saw the Lord Gloucester turn on him and rebuke him in a voice that most of the castle heard. "And killing Kings and Princes isn't? What do you make of that?" Then, he strode across the yard.

"Quick!" Seth said, abruptly.

"What?" enquired Bella.

"Down the stairs. Maybe Hewitt will tell us!" Seth explained, hurriedly.

As fast as they could, and narrowly missing an assistant chef carrying a plate, they wound their way down the steps to burst into the courtyard just as Hewitt was about to enter the main hall.

"Hewitt!" Seth panted.

He waited for them.

"What's happening? What's he said?"

"He won't budge. He insists that it was he, alone, who led the Riders and that he did it without the knowledge of the Duke. That he did it all himself!" Hewitt gruffed, clearly frustrated.

"But why?" Bella demanded. "Why won't he tell that the Duke was behind it?"

Hewitt shook his head, frowning. "I don't know. It's either loyalty or stubbornness or both. But no one is saying a word to implicate the Duke, and no one wants to make a public enemy of him. So, unless something changes, then he'll get off scot-free."

"But that's awful!" she gasped.

"It's not what we wanted, but what else can we do. The Duke is one of the most powerful men in the kingdom. There's never been a hint of treachery from him before, so people are believing him," explained Hewitt, his voice sounded defeated.

"But what about all that—last Saxon King? Isn't there someone who can tell?" Seth probed.

"I can't say anything without implicating a lot of guilty, but naive men. I won't have their deaths on my conscience," affirmed the soldier.

"What does the Prince think?" asked Seth.

Hewitt looked about before he answered. "Does not care one way or the other. No one is saying anything else to him, except that he's safe and that it must be the will of God that saved him."

"Seth had more to do with it than God," whispered Bella.

"That well may be. A day is a long time for His Majesty to remember, unless it was the fitting of a new suit. But Seth, he has said that he wishes to see you once this is all over. Despite what he has said, he'll reward you in some way, I'm sure," Hewitt assured.

"When I see him, can I bring Tess—I mean, Bella?"

"You ask his steward," he directed. "I think, despite your efforts to upset him, that he would listen sympathetically. I have to go. Gloucester is having the Duke brought to see him in the presence of the Prince."

"One last thing," requested Seth. "Will they hang the Captain?"

"If he's lucky! There's a troop of nobles wanting to prove their loyalty and valour by having him drawn and quartered. But yes. He'll die. It's just a question of how and when. I'll try to see you after this is all over," Hewitt bid before he departed from them.

As they walked back for breakfast, Bella pounced. "You're still thinking about that silly promise you made to him in the forest, aren't you? That's why you're asking."

Seth was so angry that she could see through him. He tried to grit his teeth and say nothing, but she was not going to let up.

"Admit it! Come on! The lion and the mouse! You're still working out if you have to let him go. You are, aren't you?"

"What if I was?" he flared at her.

Before she was half-guessing; except once certain, she was amazed and furious. "That's really stupid, Seth. That's not noble. That's really, *really* stupid. He led the Riders. He killed scores of innocent, unarmed people. He tried to kill the Prince *and* you—you're actually thinking of trying to free him. He's an evil, cruel man, Seth. Even if you could—you're just letting him free to do it again. You're so stupid, sometimes!"

Again, Seth had no words.

That afternoon, Seth sat in the ease of Jeb's hunt and talked with his friend.

"So, you're worried about this promise, you made to him. Is that it?" the blacksmith clarified.

"Yes. I did promise him. He let Bella and I go because I told him about the mouse and the lion. Otherwise, we would both have been dead."

"He's a bad man, lad!" intoned Jeb.

"That's what Bella told me."

"But it doesn't help you, does it? You're thinking that a promise is a promise."

Seth nodded sadly.

"I want it to be simple, Jeb," he stated.

There were many rumours rife with proclamations that were made before the castle the following day. They were short and to the point. There had been a plot hatched by a few to kill the Prince and destroy the authority of law and order. This plot led by a foreign soldier had sought to destabilise the country. The Riders were the means, by which this process was to have taken place.

But there was nothing to fear. The Prince was safe, and with the help of the Earl of Gloucester, had smashed the ring and arrested the leaders. Who have since confessed their parts in it, would be hanged as soon as possible. The bulk of the Riders, having been misled in their roles, would be spared and broken as a force, sent to outer parts of the realm. God save the Prince!

No mention was made of the Duke.

***

A day later, Seth was summoned to see the Prince. True to his word, Seth asked if Bella might also attend and his request was granted. Dressed in most unfamiliar clothes, Seth and Bella were announced and ushered into the Prince's presence. Dressed in a suit of pale blue, the Prince was surrounded by nobles and his younger friends.

Seth was terrified.

Bella curtsied while Seth bowed.

"Come. We will not stand on ceremony. Seth! You are the young man who saved my life and, as such, I have summoned you here to thank you and to invite you to name your reward. You may not have my kingdom"—the Prince paused for the laughter, which inevitably followed and then waited until it subsided before continuing—"but you will find me most generous. Ask!" Full of royal magnanimity, he sat and picked imaginary fluff from his tunic arms and waited.

Seth had known this would happen. He had been warned and had been counselled to ask for a place of study, or a job as a page to a noble family. Although, while nodding at these, he had already made up his mind.

"My Lord," he began in a voice not much above a whisper. "For my friend who helped me, I ask that when she is of age that she might be admitted to the Royal Court!"

The room of nobles examined Bella who under her red hair still managed to blush, then curtsey.

"That is a pleasure. We will welcome her with the blessings of her guardians," the Prince granted. "But, now for you?"

"I want you to spare the Captain! Just that!" Seth said in a rush.

There was a shock of surprise through the room. Shouts of disapproval come from many.

The Prince quieted, then asked, "Surely not. This is the man who tried to kill me and then turn my kingdom into a nest of outlaws. Why would you want me to pardon him? I'm happy to hand you a castle, young man. Why this?"

"I owe it to him, My Lord. It was a promise I made a long time ago!"

Gloucester heaved his weight from the bench and began, "This is nonsense, my Lord Prince, you cannot pardon him. Just think what message that would send to every plotter and mischief maker in the kingdom. Give the boy something else and let him be grateful!"

Seth bravely spoke again even though he was scared. "I don't want anything else. Just that." He thought they would hear the sounds of his knees knocking.

Again, there was an uproar and Seth felt Bella give his hand a squeeze. He took it as being one of begrudging support. Others implored the Prince not to agree, but Seth could see the Prince considering.

He held up his hand and when there was silence, he began again, a little ponderously. "I have given my word and that is what you have chosen. I think your choice is poorly considered when you could have something of substance or value, but this is your choice. I will not pardon the Captain. Instead, I will banish him on pain of death if he returns. Beyond that, I will not do. But a Prince must honour his pledge, particularly to one so young who risked his life for mine." With a twirl of his cape and a straightening of his sleeve, he sat.

Gloucester sat again in a silent rage.

The Prince added, "As soon as the Captain can be moved, he will be sent under guard to the coast where he will be shipped from our realm. That is my wish. Seth, does that satisfy you?"

Seth nodded and bowed deeply.

"He should be hanged. Make an example of him," blustered Gloucester.

"Dear, loyal Earl. Again, your concern for my safety is both clear and touching, but we must keep our royal word!" the Prince said.

Gloucester snorted. There were expressions of approval and praise from around the room. Then, Seth and Bella were shown out.

Once outside, Bella began, "How could you! You asked for something wonderful for me and asked for that evil man's life with your only wish. Don't you realise? You could have set yourself up for life; but no, you have to ask for that!"

Seth had been waiting for it. "Bella. It's the thing I most want or else he'll die and I'll be left owing it to him for…forever."

Bella huffed and puffed, but Seth thought she understood and even approved in a grudging sort of way. Others were not so understanding or pleased.

That afternoon, Seth was once again in his plain clothes, and sat in the kitchen being chided by the huge cook as he ate her pies.

"What a chance! What an opportunity and that's what you do with it. It's a disgrace. What a waste! Should have offered it to someone else, not to an ungrateful boy like yourself!"

While she raved, Seth ate. The pies were very good, almost worth the price of the lectures and he knew there was no sense in trying to argue.

He was saved by the entry of a guard. "You. Boy! Are you Seth?"

"Yes. I am!"

"The prisoner—the Captain. He wants to talk to you. I said I'd come and ask you. Only if you want to…"

Seth grabbed the last of his pie and followed the guard.

As they left, the insistent cook continued to nag, "Ask him to grant you…"

The guard opened a door with a key.

"You can go in. I'll lock it after you. Yell when you're ready. He can't harm you," he told Seth.

There was very little light in the cell. A barred window high above a man's reach allowed a pale greyness to permeate the small stone room. It was so cold, it made Seth shiver.

The Captain lay on a wooden pallet, his face ashen. The brightest colour in the room was the faded crimson of his bandages. Seth approached slowly, still not quite believing that it wasn't all a sham.

He waited until the Captain spoke just one word: "Why?"

"Why, what?" replied Seth.

"Obstinate boy! You know what I mean. Why did you throw away your one real chance of money or position to ask for my life?" the man growled.

This was not what Seth had expected. He'd been hoping for gratitude.

"The lion and the mouse. That night in the forest," he answered, simply.

The sick man's neck swivelled as he turned to face Seth. Even that caused him pain.

"And the mouse came and gnawed the ropes of the net to free the lion," he recalled. "That's right, isn't it? And you really are that boy—the one that reared up from the forest floor?"

Seth shuffled a little before he owned up. "Yes. That was me."

The Captain smiled and shook his head. "All this just to keep your word when you could have had riches and wealth? What an odd boy you are."

Seth said nothing.

"So, I am to be spared—to be banished. Seth, you must promise me something. Boys can still believe anything. You must promise me that you won't start believing that this act of yours will change me—turn me into a knight of the realm or a holy monk," declared the Captain.

"'Good begats good.' That's what Hestor says," Seth quoted.

"Well, this Hestor must live in a different world to me. Where I live, Seth, good is seen as weakness and only allows powerful evil to flourish."

Seth felt lost for words, but he tried anyway. "This way I don't owe you."

"I could also be free to be so much worse. I could bring Norseman to invade. Oh, deeply trusting one!" The tone was still mocking, except strangely gentle.

By now, Seth was totally bewildered.

He heard the Captain chuckle, then grimace at the pain the chuckle caused him.

"Seth, I'm teasing you. Here—take this!" He held out his hand.

Seth reached out to shake it, but this only brought further chortling, grimacing and clutching at his wound.

"No. I'm not shaking hands. Take the big ring off my finger."

"Why?" asked Seth.

"Because I want you to take it. It's valuable. One day, you might need it to buy some land, pay a dowry and raise small, fierce boys who keep their word. Go on. Take it," he insisted.

"I don't think I can..." Seth said, uncertain.

"If you don't, the jailers will. I'd rather it was with you. Take it, Seth," the Captain offered.

So, he did; reluctantly, but he did. He stood in the silence turning the big, green ring in his hands. Two rings in two days. How strange the world was.

"Goodbye, little mouse. Your debt is now repaid in full. And remember—the world is not all light and well-being. Power lies at its core. Remember," he bade, his voice heavy with final wisdom.

Seth moved to reply, then checked himself. He turned and called out to the guard who unlocked the cell and let him out.

Seth wished that he felt happier about what he'd done. He wished that he felt somehow strong and good and proud, but he didn't. He felt confused and sad; and suddenly, very, *very* tired. Seth thought he would have felt worthy and brave after what he had done, but he felt doubting and foolish.

Perhaps the Captain was right, and he knew nothing about the real world—nothing at all.

24

Normality

Life settled for Seth. Bella informed him what was happening at the castle and the courtly gossip. The Prince was about to return to his home in the city. Bella's guardians were to return to their home in the north. The Duke was not prosecuted because no evidence could link him to the Riders; but as Bella explained, Gloucester took no chances.

The Duke might not be able to be charged but some of the mud had stuck. His private guard was reduced to a skeleton force and his protests were dismissed. He knew that his life could have been taken from him and his lands distributed to others, if the Prince had taken at all seriously the charges laid against him. Some nobles retired to their far-flung estates to prune roses, breed cattle, and keep very low profiles—others to still brood and plot.

A force of soldiers was to remain in the region, they were under the direct command of one of Gloucester's men. Tad and the lieutenant were publicly hanged, Seth felt no need to attend.

In the cells, the Captain recovered, plans were made for his removal and journey to the coast. Seth saw no more of him. He kept the green ring with the one Lord Alfred had given him, but he still pined for the delicate one he had placed on the finger of a dead man.

Jeb kept poking Seth and telling him to buck up, now that all the fun was over. "Come on, lad. Anyone would think that we'd lost and it was you heading for the gallows. You've been moping around for a week."

Seth knew Jeb was right, but it didn't help. His life felt in limbo. Hewitt had accepted a position, that meant he had no need to care for horses anymore. John had joined the Prince's own guard. Bella would return to the north. Jeb would continue to blacksmith. Everyone had his or her place, yet nowhere felt right for him. He wished he could return to Hestor and be happy, but he doubted if he could.

Then two things happened which stirred his world. Firstly, Sharrock called to see him, his presence causing consternation amongst their neighbours.

"Seth. I hadn't meant to disturb you. I just wished to let you know that I leave in a few days. If you are to accept my offer, then you will need to be ready to accompany me when I go."

Jeb was delighted. "He'll be going. Don't you worry, sir. We'll have him all ready. He can't miss out on a chance like this. Can you, Seth?"

Sharrock looked Seth in the eye. "But Seth, you don't have to. You know, I don't want you to come if you have other wishes."

Seth nodded dumbly as Sharrock left.

He felt worse than ever. He knew he should go, even though he didn't really want to; and what was worse, he didn't know why he felt like he did.

It was in the middle of this blue funk that the second event occurred. Seth was summoned to see the Prince. When the courier came, Jeb attempted to throw his best cloak about him but there was no time.

"He wishes to see you now!" urged the courier.

As Seth was hoisted onto the horse, Jeb could only shake his head in wonderment. "…To see the Prince? What next?"

Seth was hustled from the horse to a waiting steward who ushered him along corridors to the main hall. During the bustle, Seth caught a glimpse of Bella before he was announced into a smaller room. The Prince sat at a desk while around him scribes and secretaries worked.

He welcomed him. "Ah, Seth! Thank you for coming. Please. Be seated. The Captain is on his way to the coast, as no doubt you know. I do keep my word."

Seth thanked him.

"That is not why I have summoned you," said the Prince. "Stewards, take everyone with you while I talk."

Seth's throat was dry. *What could he want of him?*

The room cleared and the Prince lent forward in his chair to stare at Seth. "I have been thinking about what you said the night you saved my life…"

Seth's heart sank. Perhaps he was to be punished.

"You said something to the effect of…that I should learn to be a good king."

Seth attempted to interrupt, but he was overruled.

"No! No! I do not wish to be reassured. I wish to know if what you were saying was the truth?" the Prince enquired.

Seth cursed his loose tongue.

"I will not punish you—that you need to know. I am a man of my word, even to the point of pardoning traitors who try to kill me. So, go ahead!" He gestured for Seth to speak.

Seth closed his eyes for a moment in bewilderment. He was surprised, but not shocked, to see Hestor's face in his mind's eye and he was reminded of the time he had foreseen this scene and this moment.

"This is the chance you said you wanted!" she seemed to say. It was then, Seth had an idea.

"Your Majesty. It doesn't matter what I tell you, but it might if I could *show* you. Would you be willing to dress up, and come with Lady Bella and I on an adventure?"

He wasn't sure if it was his insistence or 'dress-up' that carried the day, but twenty minutes later he was outside the main hall and looking for Bella. The formulation of his plan had Seth knowing that, on the following day, he would be showing the Prince over his kingdom, except in a very different guise to how he normally went forth. By the time he found Bella, she had to sit him down and have him take deep breaths before he could tell her what he had done.

Bella was waiting at the castle keep for him the following morning. She had borrowed a maid's dress and had tucked her hair into a cap that hid its colour from view.

All the way up the hill, Seth had been fighting with the demons in his head that danced and capered and mocked him, *This is really, really dumb! What do you think you're doing? What do you think the vain, selfish Prince will learn from your inspired tour of his realm; except a wish to go home, have you thrashed, and then flee back to the capital?*

The worry was etched on his face as he approached Bella.

"Stop worrying!" she hissed at him.

"I think I've really made a mess this time. What will I do with him?" Seth fretted, uncertain.

"Just take him about," she assured. "Remember, he's your elder cousin twice-removed who has just moved from Cornwall."

The Prince arrived and stopped their argument. He was unrecognisable, wearing a stained, torn cloak, plain breeches, and doublet without a trace of adornment. He was not happy as he was arguing with a steward who was trying to talk with him, while pretending he wasn't the Prince at all.

"I will be fine! I will be safe. Who would want to attack me wearing this hideous garb? They'd have to take pity on me, surely!" the Prince insisted, pointing to his humble clothing.

The steward wished to accompany them. "If you won't go with a troop of soldiers, then at least let me accompany you, armed and ready!" he pleaded.

The Prince would have none of it. He dismissed him and turned to the young people. "Will this do? It better! I'm not going to roll in the dust."

They looked him up and down. Without the splendid clothes, he looked like a steward out of luck, or perhaps a travelling musician who had fallen on hard times. Even the rings had gone from his fingers. They assured him that he was fine, and then together, they strolled down from the castle into the town. The Prince's education was in their hands.

For poor Jeb, it was almost too much. Caught between pretending that this thin youth was a visiting cousin; meanwhile aware of his true identity, reduced the huge man to a stuttering, trembling wreck. He kept almost touching his hand to his head, then remembering, halting his hand in mid-motion, and then not knowing to do with the rest of what he had started. The Prince's attempts to engage him in conversation led to naught, as Jeb refused to make eye contact and shuffled out of sight to bang and chatter about with tools.

After this most unsatisfactory beginning, Seth and Bella took the Prince out into the market place where they wandered in a desultory fashion.

"This isn't working!" whispered Seth to Bella quite fiercely.

"What do you expect?" she retorted.

Seth watched the Prince examine his twelfth leather belt and exclaim, "How charming!"

Seth realised that he must not let this chance go begging. He appeared at the Prince's elbow and began talking to the stallholder. This was a large man who worked hard and had not had the benefit of polite education.

"What do you think about events at the castle? We've heard the Prince is about to leave," Seth ventured.

As if on cue, the store holder snorted and began, "Running home. What else can you expect? Probably got a tailor coming from France!" He laughed and others joined in.

He saw the Prince's face drop at this offering. He stuttered and then questioned the man, "What do you mean? Running home? What's that?"

The owner looked him up and down as if he was perhaps an imbecile, or at least an idiot. "What do you mean 'what do I mean!' He's the Prince, isn't he? Everyone knows that's he's a useless prat. Apparently well-meaning, but lacking a backbone—only able to give orders to tailors and cobblers. Maybe it's a shame that bloke they hanged didn't do him in. Might have done us all a favour."

The laughter this brought had an effect upon the Prince. He went purple and Seth thought he might have an apoplectic fit of some sort.

"Now, see here! How dare you blacken the name of the Prince when you have no idea who he is! By golly, I've a mind to have you whipped or even drawn and quartered," he seethed.

The store owner was not a small man. He was not used to discussing issues at length nor of being threatened by thin, young men who were of no standing. He lent across the stall and picked up the Prince by the neck of his robe and smiled nastily into his face. The Prince almost gagged at the strength of breath—fish, ale, and eggs.

"Just who do you think you are threatening, you weasel looking piece of shrimp. I've a mind to throw you back into the fish stall yonder," the larger man growled.

Seth was now terrified the Prince would either burst a blood vessel, be physically hurt, or claim to be the Prince and call for a non-existent guard. Luckily, Jeb intervened. He rushed from the forge with pain etched on his face and appealed to the better nature of the store owner, while at the same time, threatening violence if the former tactic failed.

"Now there, Clem! He's just a newcomer. He knows nothing of the Prince, comes from Cornwall. Maybe he's heard different things. Come on. Let him be!" shouted Jeb.

Clem looked at the Prince at the end of his arm and over to the size of Jeb, then decided that vengeance was probably not worth the cost.

"Aye. Oh well. We'll give this weasel the benefit of the doubt—the benefit of his ignorance!" he grunted.

As the store owner said the word 'ignorance,' he hauled His Royal Highness across the table towards him. Seth saw Jeb move to intervene, but there was no need. Clem let him go. The Prince fell back clutching his throat and making very disturbing choking noises.

Among them could be heard, "You. Blacksmith. Pound him. Kill him! Maim him! Reduce him to crushed bone and I'll promise you wealth beyond your dreams. Just punish him!"

Seth saw horror cross Jeb's face before something like calmness settle on it.

"Indeed, I can't do that. He's just a simple man who doesn't know who you are and is expressing his opinion, rude and insulting though it may be!" explained Jeb.

The Prince cleared the air, looked around for allies and saw none. But he was not done yet. He hauled himself to his feet, clambered onto a trestle table and shouted to the assembled crowd:

"This man. This—this stallholder has dared to insult the name of your Prince, a man of great nobility and worth. I call on you all to defend his good name."

Blank faces stared at him.

A vast silence settled on the scene. Seth moved to extricate the Prince, but he was not finished yet. He pushed Seth away, announcing, "Stout yeoman, good people! I call on you to defend the good name of the Prince, as you are required to do! Rise up against this stain on his honest reputation—he who loves you and suffers on your behalf."

And there he stood, clad in his ragged garments, arms aloft, stupidly defiant; but clearly looking different to that in his own mind's eye. You could see it in his face. The Prince thought he was being heroic.

It was a pear that hit him first. Luckily, it was not a firm *Williams Bon,* but a very soft *Beurre-bosc.* It splattered against his cloak, which was then followed by a veritable fruit salad of spoilt wares. In an almost leisurely manner, stallholders reached for their softer wares and hurled them at him.

For Seth, had he hadn't been so fearful of the consequences, then it may have been worthwhile. A teachable moment for the Prince, whose gaping mouth and face aghast registered the soft *kerplop* of spoilt fruit against his august person.

"Watch for potatoes, nuts, and other solids!" was all Jeb warned in a monotone before he moved to resolutely shield the Prince, carefully moving him out of the square as missiles still thudded about them.

"You. You. How dare you!" The disguised Prince gesticulated towards Seth. "I will be back in no time and have you all hanging from trees before the night is out!"

With finality, the Prince ran towards the castle, hose awry, shirt crumpled, hat barely holding, and without a backwards glance.

The full horror of what had happened settled upon them.

"Quick. We need to get the people packed up and out of the square as soon as we can!" Jeb said, desperately.

"No. Don't worry. John is in charge of the guard. He'd not harm innocent people," advised Bella.

They made ready. As expected, within a half an hour a troop of horse guards arrived in the square. Hewitt was among them. Seth went to speak to him, but there was no need.

John drew up his men and addressed the crowd. "There have been rumours of loyal folk speaking ill of His Royal Highness, the Prince. Is this so?"

There was much shaking of heads and negation of such an idea.

"Well, then. Let's hear three cheers for the Prince! Hip-hip!"

The first chorus lacked enthusiasm. However, at the sight of guardsmen fingering sword, the next chorus filled the air and would have made its way to the castle ears.

"Very well, then. We'll hear no more of it." John lent from the saddle to Seth, murmuring, "Give the castle a day. Let him have a day to recover his pride. I'm going to tell him that the stall owner has fled. It just may be some time before His Majesty can face fruit again."

Bella made her way back to the castle. Poor Jeb kept checking the door for soldiers who might drag him off to a damp and uncomfortable cell, or at least break his door off its hinges one more time.

He kept shaking his head, saying, "To think I met the Prince. The one time in my life, and I had to go and make an enemy of him!" Jeb muttered on until sleep put a stop to his anxious ramblings.

***

It was several days before Seth returned to the castle, and this was only because Bella came to ask him to accompany her there.

"We have to see the Prince. Both of us!" she told him.

"Is it safe?" enquired Seth.

"I don't know. His steward came to Lady Eloise and requested both our attendance, so I think it must be."

"What do you think he wants?" he asked her.

Bella shrugged. "I don't know. I suppose he's going to yell at us for the other day."

The rest of the journey they travelled in anxious silence.

They were shown to his door. A steward admitted them. It was a pensive Prince who awaited them. He was sitting in the frame of a window, eating an apple and made no attempt to greet them as they entered.

They stood and waited for him. Eventually he spoke, "You may wonder why I have called you after the fiasco of the other day. But I have realised that it was not your doing. You were just showing me the truth; unpalatable as it was. I have never been so humiliated in my entire life, but it has given me food for thought. Seth, why did you wish to show me that? Why did you wish that upon me?"

Seth began quite slowly, "I didn't want that to happen. I just wanted you to know what ordinary people thought and said, so that…"

"So that I might see it and become a decent and useful king? Isn't that so?" he concluded.

"Yes."

The Prince stepped down from the window seat, sighed, and made his way across the room.

"I may still not be a decent king, but I have decided that I must try to make the effort, at very least. The reason I have asked you two here, is because anyone else I ask will either lie, praise me, or yell at me like Gloucester does. Neither is any help. So, I have enlisted your aid. This time, I will not accompany you on any adventures, but I will listen to you both. What should I do to be a good king?"

Bella and Seth were flabbergasted. They were tongue-tied.

"Come. What must I do?" the Prince reiterated.

Bella tried to answer, "Your Majesty, how could we tell you what to do?"

The Prince looked at her. "You're still being polite. But you, Seth, you weren't polite when last we talked. So now you have your chance. What would you do? But be careful. You may get what you wish."

Seth thought before he answered, "My Lord. I think you should find out about your kingdom first hand. Travel over the land and see how people live."

"And what would sleeping in tents or strange beds do for me or my people? Tell me!" His Majesty demanded.

"If they thought that you cared about their lives and listened to them, they would love you. They just need to you to see them, and they would see you."

"The nobles wouldn't like it. They'd think I was interfering!"

"It's your job to interfere!" Seth said it again.

The Prince sat up and looked at him. "That's the phrase you used. That's what you said to me that night they tried to kill me. You said it was my job to interfere!"

"And it is," Seth insisted. "If you don't, then who else can, or will?"

"You could travel with your friends. You could take your court with you," Bella ventured.

He paced, then sighed, "What else? What else should I do?"

"Sire. I'd take Sharrock with me," Seth replied.

The Prince started in surprise. "Sharrock! That old teacher?"

"Yes. He's very wise. And he'd help you to see what needed to be seen."

"So, I could take my wardrobe with me and excellent food. I could take my cook and my stewards?" the Prince said, thoughtfully.

"Absolutely! Think of it as a holiday, except that you're finding out about your own kingdom," Seth suggested.

"And who would look after business of the kingdom?"

"Gloucester and Albany," Seth answered immediately.

Now there was a spring in the Prince's step. "I could, you know. I could do it. And it would be wonderful! I would see the country and my people would see me."

"And not throw fruit?" ventured Seth.

For a moment, he thought he had been too insolent, but the Prince's face burst into a reluctant grin. "I thought they would rise up and support my good name. You know, I really thought they would. Instead, if hadn't been for your large blacksmith friend, I may have ended up amongst the fish."

They were amazed to see him still smiling.

"I don't want it to happen again. However, I did find the whole thing quite—well—*invigorating*. Humiliating, as well. But it felt very real. Perhaps that is what this tour might do. Perhaps I could rough it a bit. And as you say, my people might be happy to see how utterly human I really am."

The fact that he said it without a trace of self-mockery made the children too afraid to even glance at each other.

"One last thing to you both. As a Prince, I am able to do things for people—to even interfere. There may be people that you would want me to help. I will summon my scribe in a moment and then you will tell him what you might like done. No. Don't argue. Just tell me. I don't think you want castles or riches, so just think of ways in which you might help your friends."

Leaving Seth and Bella to deliberate, the Prince went to the door and shouted for his scribe. When the flushed individual had seated himself, the Prince drew his legs up and commanded them to begin.

"You. Lady Bella. Begin!"

The two conferred amongst themselves, and then Bella began, "I would like to come to court when I am of age, though really, I ask for my guardians. I don't know the full story of it, but it seems that they have fallen on hard times and that their lands haven fallen into disrepair."

"You'd like me to repair things?"

Bella shook her head. "No. Not really. I think that Lord Alfred just needs someone to help him put things in place again. I also know he is very proud and I don't wish to humiliate him. So, I can only ask you what he might do?"

"Even I can do that." The Prince stated, "As part of my gratitude for his role in saving my life and kingdom, I will make him a grant of monies that will be administered by a very trustworthy and diplomatic advisor. Scribe, we do have some of those, don't we?"

"Indubitably, Your Majesty," the scribe replied.

"Done! Anything else, while I am in this generous, expansive mood?"

"That's all, My Lord!" said Bella.

The Prince nodded, then declared, "When you are of age, you will make a journey to see the royal dressmaker and she will make a dress or two for you. I think, blue for you. Your colour!" He turned to the boy. "Now, Seth. Ask."

"Hestor," came his immediately reply. "She lives in the forest, and I think she would really like some firewood."

"Firewood. Just firewood? No clothes or titles or…? Very well. Write this down, scribe!"

"Jeb. He's the blacksmith. If the castle could keep having their horses shod there would help, and I think that…" Seth's voice faltered.

"What is it? Come on!"

"Sire. Would you mind riding there—to the forge and publicly thanking him? Just—he's been such a good friend and he tried so hard to help!"

"Perhaps we might invest him with some title. Perhaps we might invite him to be the royal blacksmith and grant him a small annual salary. How would that be?" the Prince suggested. He chuckled, adding, "After all, he did save me from the fish stalls."

"Would you ride there with your royal party and grant it to him personally? You know, with all the speeches and everything?" requested Seth.

Seth had a picture in his mind of the royal party arriving at the forge and Jeb being overcome with embarrassment and pride of it all.

The Prince agreed and then enquired of Seth, "This is all easy. I'm feeling better and better as I do this. But…what would you wish for each other? What do you say, scribe?"

The scribe swallowed and nodded half-heartedly.

"You first, Seth. What do you think the Lady Bella would like, but perhaps isn't asking for?"

Seth glanced at Bella before beginning. "Sire. I think as well as French classes, she would also like to know how to ride, shoot a bow, and use a sword."

The Prince looked amazed. He checked with Bella. "Is this true? Don't you wish to be a Lady and marry some handsome young noble?"

Seth had the satisfaction of seeing Bella colour as she stumbled over her words. "Eventually, Your Highness. But it is true that Seth had guessed what I would like to know other things."

"We may need to talk to Lady Eloise. In the absence of a male heir, we could argue that you need to know how to run all aspects of your land and even use weapons. Yes. That can be done," he said, nodding to himself. "And now, what do you wish for our young Seth here?"

Seth could feel anxiety and some fear in his stomach as Bella scrutinised his face. "I think…I think that Seth doesn't want to leave where he is. But that he really needs to, because he can't stay here forever—not and be happy. Maybe he needs to go with you and Sharrock and learn to be really wise and not so…"

It came out with a rush. Bella looked at Seth as if she hoped that he would understand what she had said.

"Stupid?" volunteered an unwilling Seth.

"Is that true, Seth?" the Prince asked.

Seth didn't know what to say. He felt that what she had said was right; he was just cross that she knew before he did.

The Prince stared at him for a moment, then began, "Seth. For six months of the year, you will travel with Sharrock, wherever he goes. But for the second half of each year, you will return to the square. When you are sixteen and approaching manhood, then you will come to court to serve me in whatever way is appropriate. In the meantime, my gift to you will be a pony that my steward will have you choose from my own stable. How is that?"

Seth could only mumble his thanks. He was not used to gifts from anyone.

"Very well. We are done," stated the Prince. "Until I see you both again, good luck to you both, and go with my heartfelt thanks."

The Prince rose to bend over Bella's hand and then to offer his ring adorned hand to Seth. He gave them a smile of such radiance and generosity that they both floated from the room, barely able to believe what had happened to them.

"Do you think he means it all?" asked Seth, as they walked down the hall.

"Yes, I think he does. And what's more, I think he actually intends to be a good king," Bella whispered.

"Do you think he could be?" replied Seth.

"Perhaps. He'll need a lot of help! He's just so—"

"Don't say it," suggested Seth.

25

Farewells

"**I** leave in a few days," explained Seth.

He was sitting in Hestor's cottage. One external wall of it was almost dwarfed by the supply of split, dry wood that had preceded him. Hestor was busy making some concoction on the stove. By the fire, Tiny snoozed and dreamt with legs occasionally kicking in dog dreamland.

"And how do you feel about all this, young Seth?" enquired Hestor.

"I don't really want to go. I'd like to stay here with you."

Hestor sighed. "Ah! But you can't. You've moved on. Your life is calling you, Seth. To not follow would just lead to misery."

"Why can't I stay?" he asked in a small voice.

"Oh! You can. But it'd be no good. You'd be happy here for a few months. You'd dig in the garden. You'd play with Tiny, but your mind would be elsewhere, and you know what it'd be thinking?"

He shook his head.

"It'd be thinking, 'I wonder what the Prince is doing? I wonder how Hewitt is doing? Perhaps the Duke is plotting some more? Is Jeb alright? I wonder how Lady Bella is managing with her lessons up north?' Yes? Of course you would? Once you've taken the cork out of the bottle, you can't put it back."

"Can I stay with you until I have to go?" Seth requested.

She smiled at him fondly. "You're welcome here whenever you want. You know that. And I'd be always wanting to know what's happening!"

"Will you be all right here, on your own?" he asked a little tentatively.

"All right up until now."

"But what will you do?"

"What I've always done. Life gets different when you're older, Seth. Some things don't matter as much and other things matter a lot more. It's not your time to be settling down with an old lady. You need to be off slaying dragons and rescuing maidens."

Seth looked puzzled at her words.

"No. Silly!" she laughed. "I don't mean that you *actually* do that. I mean, that this is the time you need to be out exploring and learning. There'll be lots of time for sitting about talking when you're older and your dragons are slain. Just remember, that this is your home whenever you want it to be."

She hesitated a moment. "At one stage, I thought you'd be the one that I'd teach, but that's not to be…"

"I'm sorry. I never thought that you would want to—"

Hestor cut him off. "No. Don't apologise. I think it needs to be a girl that I teach this to. No offence, young'un. But that's what I need to do."

"So, how? How will you find someone?"

Hestor looked at him as if he was daft. "What? What did you say? Haven't I taught you anything? How do you think I'll find someone?"

Seth reddened and dropped his head.

"She'd find you? You'd just ask—she'd turn up?" he asked hopefully.

"You have to believe it, Seth. Then it works. Don't forget. If you do forget, then you keep thinking that you have to do it all on your own. Then it gets a bit much. Now go and see what I've done with your garden. Off you go! Take Tiny; he needs the exercise."

He hesitated at the door. "Hestor…the Captain told me that at the centre of it all was power. All of it just power. What do you think?"

"Well! A type of power, Seth."

"What sort? What do you mean?"

"I'm old enough to know that I know little, but I do know that's it's not your Captain's type. Power isn't the centre. *Love is!* Just sometimes it gets pretty hidden and mucky. When you don't believe in love, then you turn to power and that's when it gets really mucky," she explained, eyes glittering. "You'll see."

Seth squatted on his haunches while Tiny tried to bury his head in his lap, like dogs will. Seth saw the order in the vegetables and the heavy mulch over the fallowed ground and felt that sad gnawing in his stomach as he sensed the changes that were rapidly approaching. He knew that beneath it, he was also excited and apprehensive about it all.

At that moment, he wished that he had never left Hestor's and followed the Riders. He wanted to dig the garden, hunt for rabbits, savor tea with Hestor. He yearned to look forward to climbing into a familiar bed while a few paces away, Hestor sat quietly knitting or spinning by the light of the dying fire. That's what he really wanted, but he knew it was his past.

Seth didn't want to cry, but the tears were there, bubbling beneath his thoughts.

"If I'm meant to go, then let me know!" he whispered to himself.

The breeze stirred the trees. The water ran in the stream and Tiny made another foray into Seth's lap.

Nothing.

Nothing happened.

Seth scoffed and rose to walk away back to the house. As he did, the birds exploded into a cacophony of sound just above his head, jerking him to look up—his heart skipped a beat. Soaring low over the small clearing, while tormented by a squadron of smaller birds who squeaked and cried, the black shape of the eagle cast a shadow over his face as it swept down, then up and away. It came close enough for him to see its sharp eyes and the curve of its beak.

Seth looked to the cottage and saw Hestor standing and watching him with a knowing smile, "Get your answer, did you? An eagle. My! That's impressive."

"What does that mean?" enquired Seth.

"It's a shame that garden is in such good shape." She shook her head in mock dismay.

"Hestor!" he yelled after her. "Hestor. Come back! What was that about? Where did the eagle come from?"

Hestor's voice floated out. "Why ask me? It wasn't my eagle!"

"Sometimes she's no help," Seth confided to Tiny.

***

A week later when Seth was at the castle, it was impossible to believe what had happened there a few short weeks before. Normality had returned. The Prince had left, taking with him all his household staff. The Duke had bitterly taken himself and his family to spend time in their estates to the north.

"Fresh north air. Good for the lungs. Clear the head!" was what the Duke exhorted to any listeners.

Privately, all knew that north was where the last of the old Lords and sympathisers lived, occupying a strange, shadowy world of spies, intrigue and half-formed plots. There was no doubt that the Duke would sit long into the night with such folk planning further treachery.

Gloucester's answer to such going-on was blunt and predictable: "Follow him up there, catch him with a few of those old fools and hang the lot of them. There! Done!"

So, a compromise was reached. The Duke was allowed to go north, but now among his faithful retainers there was a well-paid court advisor—a small thin bespectacled man who did sums and accounts, said little and sniffed for any scent of treachery.

Seth watched them depart. A subdued, yet defiant Reece watched him from his saddle as he went. He showed no sign of recognition. He rode past with his eyes fixed upon some distant object.

It was a bare and almost deserted castle that now housed Hewitt and a military force, though not much else. Seth stayed with Jeb, who by now, had recovered from his ordeal. The Prince had kept his word before he departed. Knowing Seth was there, the Prince had swept down from the castle surrounded by his young nobles in full court attire, and with due pomp and ceremony, had publicly thanked Jeb for his loyalty.

In front of a silent and almost disbelieving crowd, the Prince had handed him a scroll of parchment upon which was written a royal statement of gratitude, an honoured title of 'Blacksmith to the Prince,' and a guaranteed annual pension for as long as he lived.

Seth could only watch his friend's face as it was swept by a myriad of emotions—gratitude, pride, embarrassment, awe, and confusion. In the short ceremony, Jeb said nothing intelligible to anyone.

As quickly as he arrived, the Prince was gone. This time for good. In the centre of an amused and amazed group of townsfolk, Jeb stood holding his scroll of parchment, blinking in confusion and wondering where the whirlwind had just come from.

At length he found his voice. "Go on, then. Get going! What are you all gawking at? Haven't you seen the Prince before, and a good one at that. Go on. Get about your business and let me get back to my forge!"

A few wags in the dispersing crowd called:

"At once. Sire! At once."

"Your Royalness!"

"All hail, Sir Jeb!"

The myriad of jests were careful to do it while sneaking for cover in the crowd.

Seth saw Jeb search him out. The first look was angry and reproachful, but it didn't last. He swooped over to him and as of old, picked him up.

"Your doing! It had to be, didn't it?" he affirmed.

Seth protested but was no match for Jeb. "I just asked him to thank you!"

"Thank me?" Jeb frowned. "Made a laughingstock out of me, more likely. I'll have men dropping curtsies to me for the next few years. I'm just not used to royal people sweeping into my home and talking with me. Honest. I didn't know where to look!"

"No. But you did when you told him you wouldn't whip Clem the store owner who was about to hurl him among the fish!" implored Seth.

"That was different. He wasn't the Prince then. He was just your nincompoop cousin from far away. Tell you the truth, I liked him best like that." His stern expression melted into a smile.

They laughed.

"You'll have to read what this says," he told Seth. "That's one thing I haven't learnt, and I doubt that I will. I like the thanks, but I really wanted to know what all that bit was about 'annuity in perpetuo' or something like that?"

They unrolled the scroll.

Seth read aloud, "It says that each year, on Easter Monday, you'll be paid a sum of twenty guineas. That this will be paid to you each year as long as you're alive."

"Well, well. That's wonderful. That's as much as I make from the forge each year, I'd guess. I'll be a rich man, Seth. I might even be able to have a house, a proper one. Who knows, I might even marry again. Who knows? What a turn-up for the books, eh? Who'd have guessed it? I might have a big cottage with even a room for guests—for when you come to stay. Even when you're grown up and have become a royal advisor—steward to the king."

"The Prince is gone now. Sharrock will leave in a day or two and I'll have to go with him!" Seth said sadly.

"Aye! But it's not for good," Jeb assured. "You get to tramp about a bit, and then you're back home here to spend time with Hestor, John, and me. It's a good mix. You'll be back home in no time and who wouldn't give their right arm to travel with a teacher who is going to advise the King-to-Be?"

"Garvin wouldn't!" said Seth and then threw a hand across his mouth, horrified by what he had just said.

They both pictured the one-armed man and laughed until they couldn't stand. They sat on the edge of the stone wall that surrounded the forge, and barely prevented the royal scroll from falling into the still glowing embers.

Finally, Jeb spoke through hiccups of laughter. "So, how was it? You know what I mean? How'd you go taking your leave of the young Lady Bella? How was that?"

Seth remembered a few days ago when the party has been readying itself to depart the castle and go north. Lady Eloise kissed him on both cheeks. Lord Alfred clapped him on the shoulder. Then, there was Tess, transformed into Lady Bella, dressed for the journey in front of him.

Suddenly, Seth had no idea how he was to farewell his friend in front of her family and half the castle garrison. So, he stood gawking, unsure and conscious of what a figure he cut as he stood there. He had always known she could be beautiful. In her heavy green cloak, with the jewels in her hair and at her throat, the flush of cold air on her cheeks, Seth felt both his admiration and his misery at her departure.

Luckily, Bella saw his confusion. In a very formal manner, she approached him and following Lady Eloise's lead, she took him by the shoulders and kissed him on both cheeks. She stepped back.

"We—that is, Lady Eloise, Lord Alfred and myself—we look forward to hearing from you and hope that you may come and stay with us some time, when your duty allows of course."

"That'd be good," he somehow muttered.

"I will try to learn all the lessons that have been arranged for me when I get home!" she said with a knowing smile.

Then, they gave a little bow to each other, and the party was astride horses, ensconced in litters and on their way amidst the barking of dogs and squawking of runaway chickens.

Seth stood and watched them until John touched him on the arm. "Don't gawk! Undignified for a future royal advisor. Here! I have something for you! From the Lady Bella! To be given once she was gone."

His heart gave a leap as the soldier handed him a tiny leather pouch. Inside, he found the small, carved figure of a man with deer antlers protruding from his head like the shaman figures of the old gods. He held it in his hand and showed it to John.

"What do you think it means?" Seth asked.

"Old gods, Seth. A nice present! I'd keep it close."

"What did she say when she gave it to you?"

"Ah!" said John with a smile, playing with the anticipation he saw in Seth. "She said she'd never talk to you again until you won the royal jousting dressed as a chicken!"

Blinking out of his memories, Seth reached inside his doublet and showed the little figurine to Jeb. "She left me this!"

"Ah! The Foundling. The Deer Man."

"You know it?" Seth asked.

"Only what others know. He's the god of the woods. An old god."

"So, why did she give it to me?"

Jeb leant over and rubbed the frown marks from his young friend's face. "Far too serious! Don't try to know it all, Seth. It's a present and I reckon it's a reminder of how you two first met. You remember. You rising up out of the ground covered in leaves and sticks and spooking the mighty Riders as they held her captive. It's a thank you! That's what I reckon…and a reminder of other ways. If you get my meaning."

"Is that a good thing, Jeb?" asked Seth.

"Could have been a carving of a pig or of the famous chicken boy?" smiled Jeb.

"You're right," Seth admitted.

"Who knows what the future holds?" advised Jeb.

Both looked at each other, then answered at once: "Hestor!"

They shook their heads.

***

Two weeks later, Seth clung to the sides of his wet, blowing, stamping pony as he struggled to keep it on the muddy quagmire that had been a path a few days before the heavy storm had fallen on them. Up ahead, Seth could barely make out the hooded, bent figure of Sharrock, urging his steaming mount up the rise and to the bank of the small stream that had grown to be swiftly flowing.

With their hair plastered to their faces and the grooms struggling with the unhappy pack of mules, Sharrock shouted through the rain to Seth, "Let's hope His Majesty has found shelter in a nearby castle or else he may not be overjoyed to see the architect of exploratory journeying at close hand."

Seth ducked his head and smiled. He also hoped that the Prince was warm and dry before they caught up with him. He doubted that good intentions might outlast the reality of wet horses, muddy roads, and water damaged silken outfits.

With the rain running down his face, Seth couldn't stop the image of the ranting Prince from forming in his mind, bringing a smile to his face.

Following Sharrock's urging, he coaxed his pony to the banks of the stream. Together, they rested before moving slowly into the currents of the mud brown water. He heard the sounds of small birds still delighting in the moisture and his hand instinctively went to touch the small figurine of the horned one that hung from his neck.

Then, Seth coaxed the pony deeper into the stream while spraying water over a complaining Sharrock.

The forest on the other side of the stream steamed and beckoned.

It had begun.

About the Author

ROBERT LEWERS

At 74 years-old, Robert boasts a rich career journey. From farming to teaching at Swinburne Community School, navigating Ashrams in India to counselling in Ballarat, his experiences shaped his YA debut. An avid writer, loving teacher and parent, Robert's life echoes in *Seth,* his first fiction work, following a trail of diverse adventures.

EXPLORE NEW HORIZONS WITH US AS WE SAIL
ONTO SHORES OF LATEST PRODUCTS, EVENTS,
GREAT TITLES, AND BEYOND.

VISIT US:
WWW.OCEANIACOM.COM

OCEANIACOM PRESS